THE WOLF DECEPTION

by

Olivia Claire High

Fireside Publications

A Romantic Suspense Novel

Fireside Publications II
5144 Harbour Drive
Oxford, Florida 34484
www.firesidepubs.com

Printed in the United States of America

ISBN: 978-1935517-28-3

For additional copies of this book, please visit:
http://kadinbooks.com or
www.Amazon.com

Or, contact the author at:
joeclaire2424@comcast.net

Dedication

To the very special man in my life;
My husband,
Joe.

Acknowledgements

To Jan Corey;
The lady who loves wolves.

ONE

Pippa Scott didn't like the dark. Having to change a flat tire at any time was difficult. Being forced to do it in the middle of a forest with trees crowding out the last bit of daylight gave her the jitters. This place felt like an alien planet for a city girl used to tall buildings and streams of traffic.

Rain dripped off overhead branches sending chilly water sliding beneath her coat collar. She shivered, cursed the wet weather along with her bad luck for getting lost, when the sudden sensation that something besides trees stood nearby made her glance over her shoulder. Her insides turned colder than the freezing water dribbling down her neck at the sight of the large black wolf standing there. Ears held high, rigid legs, and tail straight up, the animal looked ready to leap toward her.

"Jesus, Mary, and Joseph!" she yelped before quickly scrambling into her car.

The animal stared at her with amber eyes for a moment longer before he loped away, melting into the darkness as silently as he had appeared. Had she really seen a wolf, or were her tired eyes playing tricks? It'd been a long day. Pippa looked at the narrow road before her and how it cut a path through the woods. It reminded her of a strip of black plastic made shiny from the recent rain.

Hopefully whatever awaited her at the end would be more welcoming than this gloomy spot, including the canine reception committee. She'd come here to start a new a job. Getting lost wasn't part of the plan. Now thanks to her flat tire, she'd lost more precious time and a chance to make a good first impression on her new employer.

Her future boss, Mrs. Lila Avalon advertised for someone with a good imagination and a love of children's literature to help write an anthology of short stories. Pippa applied, and much to her delight she got the job, including room, board, and a modest stipend.

No one had bothered to mention that she'd be sharing the neighborhood with wolves, however.

Pippa knew life was full of unexpected twists and turns, just like the road in front of her. Some too good not to miss; some so bad they were best forgotten. Getting lost had given her a tour of this part of northern California, which was nothing like where she lived in the southern part of the state. Being in a place where trees outnumbered people was definitely a novelty.

But such charm had begun to fade along with her flagging energy, as she started driving again. Pippa hunched over the steering wheel, squinting into the darkness. The rain picked up, falling in fat drops straining the windshield wipers. A burst of lightning flashed in a jagged streak across the night sky, followed by a crack of thunder that made her body jerk.

"I sure hope there's a cup of something hot with my name etched on it if I ever get to where I'm going," she murmured.

Pippa assumed the Avalon house would be a huge log cabin, as the first Avalon to settle in the area was a lumber tycoon according to what she'd read on the family. She could never understand why people called them cabins when they often ended up being luxurious multistoried homes.

Just when she thought she'd never come to the end of the road, a massive two storied stone mansion suddenly stood silhouetted against the sky, reminiscent of a medieval castle. She drove between two stone pillars, gawking at each one topped with its statue of a crouching wolf. They made menacing looking guardians with their flanks gleaming and teeth flashing in the rain.

Rows of tall pine trees lined the driveway, whipping their prickly branches back and forth in the wind like angry Titans. Disneyland, this was not. The house looked cold and uninviting. Her vivid imagination easily conceived of an assortment of demons lurking behind the stone facade.

Pippa stopped her car at the foot of wide stone stairs leading to a set of enormous wooden doors. Her pulse hitched up a few notches at the images of wolves and the word WOLFHAVEN carved into the huge panels. The Avalons obviously had a serious thing going on with wolves. But then who wouldn't when you had the beasts running around in your backyard?

She sucked in a deep breath, got out of the car, and dashed up the stairs just as the houselights went out, leaving her surroundings as dark as a coal pit. Her heart pounded as she groped for the heavy door knocker, only to yank her hand back when one of the huge doors eased open.

A man, short and round with frizzy gray hair stood there holding a flashlight. The small circle of light gave his features a distorted look making Pippa instinctively step back.

"Forgive me, I didn't mean to frighten you. The storm's knocked out our power. I was on my way to start the generators when I saw your car lights. You must be Ms. Scott."

"Yes I am," Pippa replied, letting out a relieved breath at the sound of his friendly voice.

He opened the door wider and gestured for her to enter.

"Please, come in out of the storm. I'll get whatever you need from your car if you'll just give me the keys."

"It's not locked. I only have one small suitcase and a backpack. They're in the backseat. I'll get them myself since I'm already wet," she offered, but he shook his head.

"No need for that." He turned when a tall somber looking woman entered the foyer holding her own flashlight. "This is my wife, Enid. My name is Ross. We're the Hendersons," he made the introductions before jamming a hat onto his head. "This is Ms. Scott, Enid. I'm going for her bags."

"All right. Mind the wet steps."

She turned to Pippa.

"Please follow me. I'll show you to your room if you're ready." Polite words spoken with a hint of frost around the edges.

"Oh, but shouldn't I wait to meet Mrs. Avalon first?"

"Mrs. Avalon has retired for the evening. You were expected several hours ago." More frost. "She will see you at breakfast tomorrow, nine o'clock sharp in the morning room."

"I'm sorry I'm late. This is my first time up this way. I got lost and then I had a flat tire."

No reply. No empathy.

Pippa followed her up the steps of a wide intricately carved wooden staircase that curved in a graceful arc to the second floor. Mr. Avalon may not have used wood to build the outside of his house, but he'd made up for it inside.

Enid stopped in front of a door and swung it open before stepping back, motioning for Pippa to enter. Flames crackled in a stone fireplace casting flickering shadows around the room. Heavy pieces of antique furniture, including a huge four poster bed filled most of the area. She shivered in her wet clothes making her gravitate toward the fire, unable to resist the tempting warmth.

"Mrs. Avalon chose this room for you. Your bathroom is through there," Enid pointed.

"It's a terrific room. I sure appreciate the fire. It's a pretty wild night out there."

"We often have storms like this here. Are you afraid of thunder and lightning?"

"No, but I don't particularly like driving in weather like this. Who does?"

Ross puffed his way into the room with Pippa's bags. He set them on a low bench at the foot of the bed. "Here you are. I'm going to go see to those generators now."

Pippa watched him leave with real regret, when his wife turned her aloof gaze on her again.

"May I get you something to eat or drink?"

The words sounded more like a dare than an invitation, banishing all thoughts of the hot drink Pippa had envisioned.

"Thank you, but I'm fine," she lied, not wanting to risk more disapproval.

"Use the house phone by the bed should you require anything."

She breathed a sigh of relief as soon as Enid left. She may work here to serve others, but late arriving guests obviously did not bode well with the woman. Pippa looked around the room taking in more details. Everything looked old, but well cared for. The air held an interesting potpourri of lemon furniture polish, lavender, and a woodsy scent from the fire.

Drawn by the room's two large windows, she eased back the edge of a heavy ruby velvet drape. Darkness hid the view while rain lashed against the glass like a relentless whip. The house had an eerie feel about it. Thinking of the housekeeper made her wonder if that skinny popsicle would ever thaw toward her. She hoped Mrs. Avalon would turn out to be more the fairy godmother type and not some kind of wicked forest witch.

Pippa trembled from the unpleasant thought as much as from her wet garments. She walked to the bench and dug pajamas out of her suitcase. She would worry about the morning's meeting with Mrs. Avalon later. Right now the priority had to be a hot shower and a good night's sleep. She couldn't wait to crawl into the big inviting bed that beckoned like a mother's warm embrace.

Pippa woke to pale sunlight pushing weakly through the narrow opening she'd left between the drapes. She rubbed her cheek against the lavender scented pillow before sitting up to finger comb her tangled long red curls. The night's fire had burned to a pile of ashes in the grate leaving the room chilled. Still, it didn't stop her from going to the windows to check out her view.

The scene below gave Pippa a pleasant surprise. An eclectic assortment of flowers filled the area in profusion, scattered in splashes of colors that reminded her of an artist's palette. The house greeted her last night in a dark sinister way. The cheery hues of this garden filled the morning with an unexpected beauty making her feel much better. Her eyes caught signs of movement below.

A man, well over six feet with broad shoulders and ink black hair emerged carrying a handful of flowers. The gardener, she guessed, out to collect an early morning bouquet. She watched his long fingers flick raindrops off the petals with a surprisingly gentle touch a moment before he looked up at her window as if by some invisible signal.

She saw sharp, sculptured features, a straight nose, and a firm unsmiling mouth. His gaze riveted her to the spot. She couldn't remember ever having the sensation of being pulled into a pair of eyes. A tiny quiver ran up her spine. Pippa had no idea how long she would have stood there if he hadn't broken the odd hypnotic spell by simply walking out of her range of vision.

She scurried back across the room on shaky legs to flop down onto the bed. She wasn't sure what just happened. She did know she'd never experienced a look so powerful that it felt as intimate as a physical touch. A frown pinched her forehead while her teeth gnawed her lip.

"What have I gotten myself into? I'm stuck with a housekeeper who has all the warmth of an iceberg and a gardener who looked like he wanted to take a bite out of me. Well, at least Ross seemed friendly. Please, God, let Mrs. Avalon be a sweet old lady without any nasty quirks."

A glance at the bedside clock made Pippa realize she'd better get moving. She didn't want to meet her new employer in her pajamas. Mrs. Henderson said she'd be seeing Mrs. Avalon in the morning room. Morning room – now there was a term you didn't hear every day. Then she'd never been inside a private home that looked big enough to be a small hotel, either.

She washed and plaited her hair into a single thick braid. Pippa had no idea how she was expected to dress. Not that she had much choice. Everything she owned, with the exception of her underwear, came from secondhand stores and yard sales. She chose a rust colored tunic with a fringed hem and tie belt, black leggings, and a pair of low heeled slightly worn black half boots.

She wrinkled her nose at herself in the mirror. "I look like an elf."

She opened the door and collided with the man from the garden. Strong hands grabbed her shoulders to ease her away from his hard chest. Startled by the unexpected closeness, Pippa blurted out the first words that came into her head.

"Are you supposed to be in here? Shouldn't you be outside weeding or something?"

Two dark brows slowly winged up.

"The mistress is a very tolerant woman."

Eyes raked over her outfit.

7

"Even to the point of allowing scruffy late arrivals to wander the halls."

His voice had a rich, smoky sound that made an involuntary quiver flutter in Pippa's belly; not to mention that she was still tingling from his touch. She forced such feelings away and mimicked him by letting her eyes travel slowly over his faded paint splattered jeans and sweatshirt.

"Look who's talking. When's the last time you checked with your tailor? As for me, I'd change, but I'm afraid I left my silk gown and tiara at home."

His unexpected grin showed even white teeth.

"You've an Irish temper to match your hair."

"Just because I have red hair doesn't mean I'm Irish," Pippa said, fighting for composure.

"I'm well aware of that. I merely used the common stereotype as a comparison." He looked at his watch. "As much as I'd like to continue this scintillating conversation I know you have a morning appointment. Last night has been forgiven. Today is a new day. Try not to spoil it for her."

Pippa heard the reprimand in his tone. It made her feel self-conscious to realize even the gardener knew about her late arrival. Didn't the staff have anything else to gossip about? What made this guy so haughty? She would have protested the way he lectured her on how she was supposed to act if he hadn't turned and walked away leaving her standing there glaring at his back.

"Who the heck does he think he is telling me what to do?" she grumbled. "What a jerk."

Ross greeted her at the foot of the stairs. "Good morning, miss. I hope you slept well."

"Thank you, I did. The bed is very comfortable."

"Mrs. Avalon will be pleased to hear that. She's waiting for you to take breakfast with her."

The thought of food made Pippa's mouth water. She entered a room with several windows, walls paneled in wood, and a high beamed ceiling. A fire burned in the stone fireplace. Two large leather sofas stood near a trio of chairs covered in rich brocade.

Flowers, skillfully arranged in a tall crystal vase sat on a table. Pippa felt sure they were the same ones the gardener had carried. He may be rude, but she couldn't deny that he kept a beautiful garden. Her eyes strayed to where an elderly woman sat in a wheelchair.

"Come in. At last we meet," she said in a reedy sounding voice.

Pippa smiled, and walked forward taking in as much about the woman's appearance as quickly as she could without appearing to stare. White hair swept back into a neat chignon framed a narrow face. The lavender sweater she wore gave her pale cheeks much needed color. The woman looked frail enough to break, but her smile was warm and inviting.

"We'll have our breakfast now," she said, nodding to Ross.

"I'll bring it right away, Mrs. Avalon," he bowed and left the room.

"Please sit down," she said, waving Pippa to a chair near her. "I'm Lila Avalon and you of course are Pippa Scott. I hope you found your room to your liking. I apologize for not greeting you last night, but at my age and with this arthritis, I usually take to my bed rather early."

"My room is lovely. Thank you. I'm the one who owes you an apology for arriving so late. I'm usually a punctual person. I'm afraid I got lost and then I had a flat tire."

"Yes, my grandson told me. How awful for you. I've asked him to join us for breakfast."

Just when Pippa wondered if there was anyone in the household who didn't know about her mishaps, Mrs. Avalon nodded toward the door and smiled.

"Ah, here he is now. Come in and meet Ms. Scott, dear."

"We've already met, actually," he said in his familiar smoky voice.

Pippa's heart plunged to her toes.

Hello handsome.

Goodbye job.

TWO

"No need to show me the way out. I'll just get my things and leave now," she mumbled.

He leaned so close his breath fanned her cheek while the scent of his aftershave teased her nostrils making her body tingle. "Sit down, Ms. Scott. Breakfast will be here any moment."

"Why didn't you tell me you were her grandson?" Pippa hissed under her breath

"Let that be a lesson to you not to be so quick to label people," he chastised in return.

Lila looked from one to the other and frowned.

"Is everything all right?"

"Everything is fine, Gram." He pointed to her chair. "Ms. Scott?"

Pippa sat down, watching him with wary eyes while he occupied a chair next to his grandmother. He'd changed into a pair of black jeans and black turtleneck sweater. The outfit emphasized every muscle in his long, powerful looking body. Her eyes glazed over for a moment, thinking about what that physique must look like underneath those clothes.

Lila smiled at her.

"I'm so happy you and Shade had a chance to meet."

Shade? Pippa wondered if she'd heard correctly. What kind of a name was that? Were they talking about a person or an umbrella?

"We, um, bumped into each other earlier."

Ross arrived with the food. Fluffy cheese omelets, thin slices of smoked ham, and delicious miniature

11

blueberry muffins couldn't keep Pippa's mind off the fact that she was being thoroughly scrutinized by Shade Avalon. Was he conducting some kind of personal evaluation? The thought made her stiffen with indignation. You'd think she was here to donate a kidney, for heaven's sake.

She did her best to respond to Lila's gentle flow of conversation while wishing their table companion would eat and leave them alone. The man made her feel twitchier by the minute. Pippa knew she probably would end up being sent away if he told his grandmother how rude she'd been to him. She could only hope he wasn't the run-and-tell-granny type.

Shade didn't leave when he finished eating, as she'd hoped. But he did take his coffee over to stand at the windows. Pippa knew he had to be hearing the conversation with his grandmother. She made herself concentrate as Lila set about devising a rough work schedule for them.

"There, now I have that settled I want Shade to take you around the house and gardens. I think it might help my stories to include your impression of our home."

He walked back to the table and set his cup down. Pippa had a feeling he wasn't thrilled about Lila's request, even though his expression gave nothing away.

"Thank you for the delicious breakfast, Mrs. Avalon. I'm looking forward to starting on your book."

"So am I, Pippa. I love your name. It's so whimsical. May I call you Pippa?"

"I'd like that."

"And you must call me Lila. I'll send for you when I'm ready." She gestured to Shade. "You two run along now and enjoy yourselves."

Pippa followed him from the room, and stopped as soon as he closed the door behind them. "Thank you for not telling your grandmother about our little chat earlier."

"I can see that she likes you and as long as she does, I won't jeopardize your presence here. But if you do anything to upset her, you'll be gone before you can collect gas money."

"Well, so much for us enjoying ourselves; weren't you taught to play nice with the other kids, or are you always such a bully?"

"You don't want to find out. Take my word for it."

She let out a nervous little laugh.

"Thanks for the warning."

The house turned out to be even bigger than she thought with servants' quarters, guest rooms, a couple of salons, gym with indoor pool, kitchen, dining room, and private family areas.

Pippa pointed to a wing Shade seemed to be avoiding.

"What's down there?"

"My suite of rooms."

"Which I assume are off limits on this tour and probably any other time as well."

"That would be correct."

"This house is enormous. I could get lost and wander there by mistake."

"See that you don't."

Pippa tilted her head back to look up at him.

"You know, you're not being very friendly. It's obvious you have a great deal of influence over your grandmother. If you dislike having me here so much, why did you give her your approval to hire me?"

"You're here to help with her stories, not to be my friend."

He led her outside to the gardens. Besides the one she'd seen from her window, another one complete with a couple of hothouses that sheltered a myriad of herbs, vegetables, and miniature fruit trees stood nearby.

Shade gave the distinct impression that he was impatient to complete his duty as tour guide. He reminded

13

Pippa of a restless animal straining at the confines of what was expected of him. He led her back to her room a few minutes later.

"Thanks for the tour. I still think I'm going to need a map to find my way around, though."

"You'll get used to it – if you end up being here long enough."

"I take it that won't happen if you have your way."

He shrugged.

"That'll be up to you. Just try to stay out of trouble. Good day, Ms. Scott."

Pippa watched as his long legs took him rapidly out of her sight.

"Not exactly the friendliest branch on the family tree."

She stepped into her room to finish her unpacking only to discover it had already been done for her. Her meager wardrobe hung in the closet with other pieces folded neatly in the dresser drawers. Even the wet outfit from last night had been laundered, dried, and ironed.

Clean bed linen and fresh towels sent off the familiar scent of lavender. Pippa stood in the bathroom and couldn't help noticing how pathetic her scanty collection of personal toiletries looked lined up on the counter next to the luxurious shampoos, conditioners, soaps, and body lotions her hostess had provided.

She assumed Mrs. Henderson had taken care of everything, although with a house this size there must be other people to help. The Hendersons' quarters were mentioned during the tour. They obviously lived in the house, which accounted for the fact they greeted her last night.

The phone by the bed rang with a call summoning her to meet with Lila.

"What do you think of the house?" she asked from behind a dainty Hepplewhite desk.

14

"It's beautiful, and fascinating, too. I feel like I've stepped back in time."

"I suppose all my antiques make it a bit outdated. I prefer things that way. It's my world and I'm too old to change. I hope the surroundings will put you in the mood for my stories."

"No worries there. How many stories did you plan to put in your anthology?"

"I haven't decided, but I do want to feature several of our local woodland animals."

"The one about wolves ought to be very popular," Pippa said, smiling at Lila's eagerness.

"Wolves? Oh, you mean because of the name of the house. My late father-in-law was quite enthralled with them. I can't say that I blame him, as they really are such impressive creatures. It's a shame there aren't any left in the forest around here now."

Pippa's forehead scrunched into a deep frown.

"Oh, but there are. I wouldn't presume to tell you about your own property, except that I saw a large black wolf last night when I was changing my tire. It scared me half to death."

"I hope it wasn't a mountain lion or a bear. You must always take care when going out on your own, especially at night."

"I wouldn't want to run into one," Pippa said with a shudder. "The wolf was bad enough."

"I'm afraid that's not possible. There haven't been any wolves here in years. I'm not saying you didn't see something. Perhaps it was a stray dog."

Lila shuffled some papers.

"I'd like to start with a story about the family of squirrels I see from my bedroom window. I've made a few notes for you to look over."

It took Pippa a moment for her brain to switch from wolves and mountain lions to squirrels. Had she mistaken

15

a stray dog for a wolf? Possibly – the rain, darkness, and her fatigue could have combined to play a trick on her weary brain.

But none of her excuses could explain away the sound that woke Pippa that night. She bolted upright in bed listening to the unmistakable howl of a wolf. She tossed back the blankets and ran to the window. With no storm to hinder her view, the garden shimmered beneath the moon's pearly light. And there among the flowers stood a black wolf just like the one from the night before.

The beast lifted his muzzle, testing the air before bounding around the corner of the house. Pippa stood mesmerized as a man appeared a few seconds later. She knuckled the sleep out of her eyes. Her breath caught in her throat when she recognized Shade. She shoved open the window.

"Come inside. Hurry! I just saw a huge wolf in the garden."

He scowled up at her.

"You must have been dreaming."

"I wasn't. I really think you should come inside. Now."

"Stop yelling, and go back to bed," he ordered and walked away.

She stood there gripping the windowsill dreading that any moment she would hear sounds of him coming upon the wolf. What might happen? Would the animal run away or attack Shade? Seconds slowly ticked by. An eternity of silence followed. Perhaps man and beast had gone their separate ways, each escaping the other – this time.

Pippa got up early to shower and dress. She sat on the edge of the bed going over last night's scene inside her head. Nothing could persuade her that the animal in the garden had been anything but a wolf, despite the Avalons' denial about there not being any here. How did the beast manage to get inside the walled grounds? Maybe a gate had been left open.

She got up to pace the room waiting for the call to breakfast.

The summons finally came.

She felt so anxious to talk to Shade she barely managed to swallow her food. Luckily for her, Lila's attention was diverted by a phone call. Pippa motioned for him to join her in a far corner.

"What?" he asked, as soon as they were a safe distance away.

"Do you have a dog?" she asked without preamble.

He arched a dark brow at her.

"I beg your pardon?"

"A dog? Is there one living here on the premises?"

"Not unless you smuggled one in."

"Very funny. I yelled at you because I saw a big black one in the garden just before I spotted you. Only I don't think it was a dog."

"You're making about as much sense as you did last night."

"Okay, try this then. What I saw was definitely a wolf, and before you tell me there haven't been any sightings in this area for years, I'm telling you this is the second time I've seen one."

"Is that so? How interesting; you've spent a couple nights in my house, and I've lived here all my life; yet you insist I have a wolf roaming the grounds. There are no wolves. As for seeing a dog, it's not possible. The compound is surrounded by walls too high for an animal to get inside."

"Well, this one did." She frowned. "What were you doing outside at that time of night?"

"Not that it's any of your business, but I often enjoy a nighttime stroll in the gardens. I'm telling you right now I'm not going to appreciate you spying on me when I do."

"I wasn't spying on you. I heard a wolf howling, and I went to the window to investigate."

"A wolf howling? I don't think so. You should save your imagination for your stories."

"It wasn't my imagination, darn it. I know what I heard, and I know what I saw."

"Then I suggest you have your hearing checked; and your eyes examined, while you're at it."

Lila called them back to the table at that moment, leaving Pippa so frustrated she felt like kicking something, mainly Shade's very fine looking butt, snug in his black jeans.

Pleased with the progress on their first story, Lila gave Pippa an advance on her salary, which meant Pippa could go clothes shopping. She seldom indulged herself because she'd never had much money for such extravagance. But the Avalons dressed for dinner, and her scanty hand-me-down wardrobe looked pretty pitiful next to their elegance.

The closest store sold general merchandise. Their line of female clothing looked more conducive to a Miss Lumberjack contest than evening dinner wear, so Pippa knew she'd have to drive a little further if she was going to have any luck finding something more appropriate.

She went to Enid for advice, as much as she was loathed to ask, but the woman was surprisingly helpful. Pippa supposed her unsuitable attire had offended the older woman every time she walked into the dining room to help Ross serve.

She'd just stuffed the money into her purse and headed for the front door, when Shade strolled into the entryway. She looked up and gave him a tentative smile, as he approached her.

"Going out?"

"Yes. Your grandmother said it was all right because she needed to rest. I'll only be gone for a couple of hours. I need to do some shopping. She gave me an advance on my salary."

"Which you obviously can't wait to spend, like some poor little waif who has suddenly won the lottery."

Pippa's body tensed at his criticism. Being wealthy, he obviously had no idea what it was to do without anything, or be forced to count pennies. She'd had enough of his belittling attitude.

"So what? It may not be the lottery, but at least I earn my way."

"I sense a hidden meaning in your comment," Shade said, folding his arms over his chest.

"How astute of you! But then you're a pretty clever guy, aren't you? It's not every man that can get away with sponging off his elderly grandparent with a clear conscience just by picking her a few flowers, and pushing her wheelchair around, and thinks that makes it okay."

Too late Pippa realized she'd let pride overcome her common sense.

Shade's arms slid down to his sides.

"Are you trying to get yourself fired?" he snapped, before whirling around to walk away.

"Wait, please!" she begged and hurried after him, her pride gone like a puff in the wind.

THREE

"I'm sorry, Mr. Avalon. I didn't mean what I said."

He glared at her with an undisguised iciness.

"I am not now, nor have I ever been a parasite."

"I'm sure you're not. I'm thankful to be here. Really."

"You certainly have a strange way of expressing it."

"It's difficult to show my gratitude when you criticize me. I have feelings, you know."

"And you think I don't?" he countered before turning away from her again.

Pippa let him go this time worrying if her hasty words had indeed cost her the job. She sagged against the door, shaking. Small wonder that he thought she didn't care if she worked here considering her late arrival the first day, and insulting him, not once, but twice. If she were the boss she'd have kicked herself out long before this latest fiasco.

It wasn't in her nature to be deliberately cruel. She rarely could think of anything to say to defend herself when someone sent a nasty barb her way. Being the aggressor had her acting out of character. Pippa didn't think she liked the new role.

Maybe the fact that she'd never met anyone quite like Shade before had her acting so peculiar. He'd made it pretty obvious he didn't want her here. But that didn't stop the strong physical pull she felt every time he came near her.

Pippa supposed she dealt out her insults because it was the only way she could shield herself from giving him the slightest inkling that she found him attractive. She had a feeling he'd probably be insulted if he knew.

She'd lost her enthusiasm for shopping just as she probably lost her job. But sitting around the house waiting to get the ax wasn't going to do her morale any good. Shade wasn't the only Avalon she needed to please. Lila had sounded sincere asking Pippa to show her what she bought.

She may not have tomorrow, but she was here today. And sometimes today was all a person could hope for. She opened the door and marched determinedly out to her car.

Pippa knew how to shop on a tight budget. She planned to squeeze out every penny from Lila's advance. Next to buying used clothing, markdown sales racks could be a girl's best friend. Her prize was a long sleeved forest green jersey dress with a scarf shimmering in fall colors, followed by a black crepe skirt, an ivory satin blouse, and a pale blue pullover sweater.

A pair of black leather heels and silk stockings almost wiped out her cash. She had just enough left to get a simple brooch for Enid and a box of delicately embroidered handkerchiefs for Lila.

Ross came hurrying to meet her, as Pippa drove up the driveway.

"Mrs. Avalon will be most anxious to see what you have. It's not every day she has the opportunity to take part in such a female ritual. She's waiting for you in the small salon. You go right in. I'll put your car away."

"Thank you, Ross." He'd told her he didn't mind if she wanted to call him by his first name. Enid, however, was still Mrs. Henderson.

"Would you please give this to your wife?" she said, thrusting the small gift wrapped box into his hands. "It's just a little thank you gift for her help in telling me where I could shop."

He blinked in surprise.

21

"Why thank you. She'll be very pleased that you thought of her."

Pippa liked the idea of sharing her purchases. Partly because she rarely got to buy new clothes, but mostly because no one ever paid attention to what she wore. Shade wasn't mentioned and Lila seemed to expect her at dinner. Was she fired or not?

"I don't think your grandson likes me very much."

"I'm sure that isn't true. I know he can be abrupt at times. You must make allowances for him. Shade's life isn't easy. He has a great deal on his mind."

Which no doubt included getting rid of mouthy employees.

Pippa decided to wear her new dress that evening. She took special care with her makeup and hair. Hopefully this would give her the extra courage she'd need to accept his decision with some dignity, especially if Shade planned on making her dismissal announcement at dinner.

Her eyes anxiously scanned the dining room looking for Shade before Lila explained he left that morning and didn't expect to be back for several days. Pippa wondered if her insults had caused his sudden departure. Not likely. No mention of her job. If this was a reprieve she'd take it.

"Does he usually go off on such short notice?"

"He tries to stay home with me as much as possible and take care of business from here. Unfortunately it sometimes becomes necessary for him to handle situations onsite."

A tiny niggle of misgiving stirred inside Pippa.

"What business is he in?"

Pippa recognized the name as soon as Lila said the title. She'd accused Shade of leeching off his grandmother when he was in fact the CEO of a well known international corporation.

22

"The Avalon family has a great many interests throughout the world. Shade has competent managers, but he sometimes must sort things out when there's a serious problem. Apparently there's something amiss in the New York office."

"Now I see why he doesn't want to be disturbed in his rooms. He'd need to have quite a bit of time alone with so much responsibility."

"True. He also has a very good other reason that requires privacy."

Pippa forced herself not to ask, despite wondering what that reason might be blaring inside her head like a car alarm gone amok.

Pippa spent most of the night rehearsing the apology speech she intended to deliver to Shade as soon as he returned. He may not want to hear it, but she had to try for her own peace of mind. He'd gone away thinking she didn't care about her job. Worse yet, she'd called him a mooch. She had a feeling he let her stay to keep Lila company. That would probably end as soon as he returned. The only thing left for her would be to enjoy the time she had left.

They were into the middle of the second week since Shade's departure. Pippa dressed for her nightly dinners with Lila, but found herself losing her desire to try and impress anyone with her new clothes, now that he was obviously in no hurry to come home.

Why did it matter so much to make an impression on him and not his grandmother? Could it be because Shade had called her clothes scruffy that first day? Or that he thought she didn't know how to dress properly? Whatever the reason, Pippa hated the idea of him thinking of her as the poor little waif he'd left behind.

23

She passed the time helping Lila with her stories, walking in the gardens, and becoming better acquainted with the Hendersons. Their routine remained simple and uneventful until Enid came down with a bad cold. She took to her bed fretting about who would help Ross. Pippa offered to do the cooking, when he was unable to get the woman who usually helped out in emergencies.

Lila didn't seem to mind what Pippa wore to dinner even after Enid felt well enough to return to her kitchen duties. So she put on her old multi colored long skirt and bright top, flat sandals, and skipped makeup. It may have helped Pippa's self-esteem, if she realized her youth and innocence gave her a softness and natural beauty that didn't need cosmetics to enhance.

The fact that she actually missed Shade enough to feel depressed at his continued absence disturbed her. Pining for him meant that he had somehow started to be important to her without even trying. The realization came as a very unsettling thought.

He had her hormones in an uproar from the very first moment she spotted him in the garden. Now every encounter with him since had only created more chaos throughout her body. It didn't matter that they didn't get along. All Pippa had to do was be in the same room with Shade and he made her pulse gallop. Just thinking about him right now made her heart begin to flutter.

She checked the bedside clock. She wasn't hungry, but Lila looked forward to dining with her. Pippa grimaced at herself in the mirror. The waif had returned. She sighed and made her way downstairs reminding herself to put on a cheerful face for Lila.

But Lila wasn't alone. Shade had returned. And he'd brought company.

A woman stood next to him. They made a striking couple. Her tall slender figure and expertly styled blond hair framed a flawlessly made up face. She looked chic in a simple black dress. Pippa had a feeling the garment cost more money than she could earn in months.

She felt like an ill kept charwoman in comparison. It had to be her bad luck that she decided not to dress for dinner tonight of all nights. She thought about turning around to flee back to her room to change when Lila saw her hovering in the doorway and motioned her forward.

"There you are, Pippa. We've been waiting for you. Look who surprised me with his unexpected return, and if that wasn't enough he brought his Vanessa with him."

The 'his' registered loud and clear. So this was Shade's woman? Pippa knew she shouldn't be surprised that he would have someone. No wonder he'd stayed away for so long. Apparently his trip to New York hadn't been all work.

"This is Pippa Scott. Pippa, I'd like you to meet Vanessa Allan, a dear family friend."

Lila made the introductions while Shade stood silently watching. Pippa made a concerted effort not to look at him, as she nodded to Vanessa and crossed the room to stand by Lila.

"How do you do, Ms. Allan?"

"So you're the little storyteller." Appraising eyes skimmed over her. "You remind me of a child playing dress up in a carnival gypsy's cast off clothing. You're almost as short as a child."

"That doesn't sound very complimentary, Vanessa," Lila said coming to Pippa's rescue.

"Oh dear," she said treating Lila to a pretty pout. "I didn't mean to offend. I'm sure her outfit has something to do with your stories. I hope you'll forgive me, Piper."

"It's Pippa, not Piper. I know I'm short. It puts me on a level with a lot of kids. I like to write stories and read to them. As for my outfit, children tend to like funny looking getups."

25

"Is that so? Well, the last time I looked there weren't any children here."

Shade finally spoke.

Pippa wondered if he did it to save her from more embarrassment or because he'd grown bored with the conversation. Probably the latter, she decided. After all, why should he come to her defense?

"I know you don't drink alcohol, but would you like something else before dinner, Pippa?"

"No thank you," she mumbled, barely sparing him a quick glance from beneath her lashes.

"Shade was telling me about his trip. We missed him didn't we, Pippa?" Lila said.

Vanessa raised carefully sculptured eyebrows at Shade, as she laid a proprietary hand on the sleeve of his suit coat.

"Why would she miss you? Surely you haven't been socializing with the hired help, darling. It's a good thing I came back with you if you were that desperate for company."

Lila frowned at her.

Shade held up his hand.

"That's enough, Vanessa."

"Oh don't look so serious, you two. I'm only teasing."

"Try the dip," Lila urged. "It's Pippa's recipe. She prepared our meals when Enid took ill."

"I appreciate your willingness to help out," Shade said." I understand the woman we usually call when we need an extra hand in the kitchen was away on vacation."

He leaned down and took a sampling of the creamy mixture.

"Very tasty."

Pippa felt a little glow of pleasure at his praise. It didn't take long for Vanessa to spoil it.

She scooped a dab onto a tiny cracker and barely touched it to her lips before wrinkling her nose.

"Too salty for my taste."

Her condescending attitude began to feel like a fist kneading Pippa in the stomach. But she dare not say anything to make her position any more precarious with Shade. Appreciating her help in the kitchen and liking her dip didn't guarantee he wouldn't still fire her.

Dinner turned out to be a dismal affair for her with Vanessa dominating the conversation about things she and Shade had done or planned to do together. Pippa pushed the food around her plate. She ate little, finally managing to escape to her room by pleading a headache.

Leaving here wouldn't be such a bad idea if she was going to have to put up with Vanessa. Since she clearly believed the hired help shouldn't mingle socially with their elite employers, she seemed to enjoy taking every opportunity to remind Pippa of their different stations in life.

Her thoughts strayed to Shade. He looked so handsome in his dark suit. But he was the kind of man who would look good in a loincloth. Now that was an image to stir the blood. Remembering how Vanessa had monopolized him all evening convinced Pippa that they were a couple and even now sharing his bed. The vision of them entwined in a sweaty clench depressed her so much she swallowed a couple aspirins, undressed, and got into her lonely bed.

It took a long time to fall asleep, so she wasn't too happy when something woke her. Pippa lay there trying to pinpoint what had disturbed her slumber when she heard the spine-tingling howl of a wolf. She realized she hadn't heard any howling while Shade was away. In fact, she hadn't even thought about wolves. She pulled the pillow up to cover her ears trying to block out the sound.

"Sometimes having a good imagination can be a bad thing," she muttered into the darkness.

She didn't go to the window even though she knew in her heart the sound was real.

Pippa awoke longing for a cup of coffee. She decided to take the chance that Enid would take pity on her despite it being too early for regular breakfast time. She knew the housekeeper got up early to do her daily baking. Hopefully she'd be in the kitchen mixing her batter.

She pulled on a pair of jeans, slipped a sweatshirt over her head, and headed downstairs in her bare feet without bothering to comb her hair. Much to her surprise she found Shade and not Enid standing by the coffeemaker measuring out the dark granules. She was about to back away when he glanced over his shoulder.

"Looking for this," he said pointing to the coffee.

"Yes. I was, um, hoping Mrs. Henderson would be here."

"She will be shortly I imagine. Come and wait with me. We'll have our first cup together."

Who was she to deny the boss? She wondered why he was being so nice to her considering the way they'd parted before he went away. But this could be a good opportunity to deliver her apology speech. She just needed to be sure of one thing first.

"I'd rather not be here if Ms. Allan will be joining you."

"No chance of that happening. She's not a morning person."

God forbid if he should think she was jealous.

"I didn't want to intrude."

More importantly, Pippa didn't want to spoil this unexpected camaraderie with Shade as long as he seemed to be in such an amiable mood.

He pointed to a stool by the counter once he had the coffee brewing.

"Have a seat."

Pippa sat down while he came over, hooked his foot around another stool, and sat next to her. His nearness, plus his steady stare almost made her forget what she wanted to say. She managed to relax when she noticed they were both barefoot until she remembered her hair. She began to try and smooth out the tousled tresses with her fingers.

He reached over and gently pulled her hands away. "Don't do that."

"I look a mess."

"Not to me. You have lovely hair. It's nice to see it out of that braid you always wear."

Pippa blinked in amazement at his unexpected comment wondering if her heart could beat any faster. She decided she'd better say something while she could still form a coherent thought.

"Well, I am a mess." She looked down at herself. "Besides my untidy hair, I'm dressed like I'm getting ready to go out berry picking. It's probably a good thing Ms. Allan isn't here because I'm sure my clothes would offend her fashion sensibilities even more than they did last night."

"Is that why you left early? You mustn't mind Vanessa. She's a clotheshorse."

"Which I definitely am not, as you well know." She cleared her throat, squirmed, and made herself hold his gaze. "I'm glad we have this time alone because I need to talk to you."

A brow winged up in that way that Pippa found so intriguing to watch.

"About?"

"I think you know. It concerns our conversation before you left. I really am sorry for the awful things I said, especially the sponging off your grandmother crack. I know you love her and would never deliberately do anything to hurt her. I'm not normally so rude."

29

Pippa looked down and began to twist her fingers in her lap. Her voice had dropped to almost a whisper, making Shade lean closer to hear her.

"It's just that I know you'd prefer I wasn't here. The wrong words jump out of my mouth because I'm so nervous. I also didn't appreciate you thinking I'm a compulsive shopper. Nothing could be further from the truth. You've seen my clothes. I've never been a vain person. But I felt I should buy more appropriate attire for the evenings, so I'd fit in better here."

She raised her head and gave him a pleading look.

"I stand corrected. I'll accept your apology on one condition."

"Whew! I'm glad that's over. Wait a minute, what do you mean 'on one condition?'"

"That you have dinner with me."

"I had dinner with you every night before you left."

"I'm not talking about here. I want to take you out to a restaurant."

"Really? Why would you want to do that? You don't even like me."

Shade folded his arms over his chest.

"Have I ever said such a thing?"

"Well, no, but you can't deny that we haven't exactly hit it off. What about Ms. Allan?"

"What about her?"

"You're obviously an item. I don't want to cause any trouble between you two."

"Thank you for the advice, little Miss Manners. But I've asked you out to dinner, not to sleep with me, and for your information my relationship with Vanessa is strictly business."

"Does she know that?" Pippa slapped herself on the head. "Ignore that. I'm running off at the mouth again. I didn't mean to imply you were setting me up for a grand seduction."

Amusement danced in Shade's eyes. "So you'll accept my invitation, then?"

"It's tempting, but I shouldn't because I'm not your type."

"Is that so? I'd be interested in knowing what you think my type is."

"It would have to be someone like Ms. Allan with her polished manners who knows the right thing to say for every occasion."

"You don't seem to have a problem with speaking your mind."

"See, that is my problem. I say the wrong thing. You know the old saying, if you put both feet in your mouth, you won't have a leg to stand on. That would be me. I'm sure Ms. Allan is used to rubbing elbows with blue-chip people. I'm more comfortable around blue collar folks."

"I happen to like blue collar folks." Shade stretched his legs out, and leaned his elbows against the counter.

"If you won't take me up on my invitation, then I don't accept your apology."

"That's blackmail."

He shrugged. "I prefer to call it a form of persuasion. Also, you didn't seem to be enjoying your meal last night. I'd like to take you out to make up for it."

"You don't have to do that, but I'll go since it's the only way you'll accept my apology. I should tell you not to worry about my clothes. I bought a nice dress when I went shopping."

"I look forward to seeing you in it." His tone suggested he'd rather see her out of it.

Pippa blushed to the roots of her hair. Her rampaging pulse made her hop off the stool and scurry over to where the coffee pot sat.

"The coffee's probably ready."

"Saved by Folgers," Shade murmured with a deep, throaty chuckle.

31

FOUR

Giddy little bubbles of happiness rippled through Pippa as she practically floated up the stairs to her room. Shade wanted to take her out to dinner. Who would have thought such a thing was possible after their past caustic conversations? She hadn't expected such a pleasant twist in their relationship. But she had every intention of enjoying their peace pact for as long as it lasted.

He hadn't given her a day or time for their dinner. Pippa supposed they'd have to wait until Vanessa left the house. She wondered what the woman would say if she ever discovered that Shade had asked the hired help out. A tiny imp inside her imagined what fun it would be to approach the older woman and ask her advice on what to wear for her date.

Four days into Vanessa's visit had Pippa's patience stretched to the limit, along with everyone else in the household who were expected to cater to the woman's slightest whim. When she wasn't running them all ragged with her constant demands, she spent the rest of each day closeted with Shade in his room. Pippa wasn't sure which behavior bothered her the most.

She didn't have the opportunity to see Shade again, except during meals. He treated her with polite reserve making her wonder if that was for Vanessa's benefit. Or maybe he regretted his dinner invitation issued in a moment when he'd let his guard down.

She couldn't help wondering how the Avalons put up with Vanessa's behavior. Lila had called her a dear family friend. As far as Pippa could see there wasn't anything dear about her. Vain and snobbish, the spoiled woman expected everyone to be accommodating, while she gave nothing of herself in return.

Mealtimes became a nightmare for Pippa. She endured them knowing she couldn't plead a headache every night. She also didn't want to hurt Lila who enjoyed having her there when Shade asked about their writing. Vanessa made it clear she wasn't interested when they talked about the stories, glaring at Pippa until she could shift the conversation back to herself.

Finally, after a full week of tolerating the woman's unpleasant company, Pippa ran into Ross struggling to carry two large suitcases down the stairs. She recalled how difficult it had been for him to carry her meager belongings and could see these cases were much heavier. Enid followed behind him with her arms full of a garment bag and smaller suitcase. Pippa rushed forward to help her.

"Here, let me take one of those for you, Enid. I'm sorry, I mean, Mrs. Henderson."

"Thank you; and you may call me Enid."

Pippa noticed a gradual thawing toward her since she'd helped out during Enid's illness. Maybe she had compared her to Vanessa and decided she was a far easier person to tend to because Pippa never made any demands for special treatment. She supposed that alone might have endeared her to the housekeeper. She also felt sure that being so protective of Lila, Enid had been reserving judgment until she could assess how her relationship would go with the frail mistress of the house.

"Do I take this to mean Ms. Allan is leaving?"

"Yes." There was no mistaking the relief in Enid's expression.

Pippa had the urge to dance a jig. They reached the bottom of the stairs as Shade came in the front door. He immediately lifted both bags from Ross with very little effort.

"I'll handle these while you grab the other two from the ladies."

"We, that is my wife and I don't mind taking the bags, Mister Shade. It's our job."

"You two have done enough for Ms. Allan during her stay." He looked at Pippa. "I see you've recruited some extra help."

"They didn't recruit me. I volunteered," she replied, anxious to defend the Hendersons. "Everyone can always use a helping hand now and then."

He hefted the bags in his strong hands. "What in the world does she have in here, a couple of dead bodies?"

Pippa barely managed to stifle a giggle while Ross and Enid schooled their faces into polite expressions at their employer's humor. Vanessa came out of her room at that moment and stared at them in her usual arrogant manner.

"For God's sake Vanessa, must you always bring so much luggage?" Shade grumbled.

"I only do it so I'll look my very best for you, darling. You know I'm not the kind of woman who is so careless about her appearance that I'll wear the same things over and over."

Pippa had little doubt she referred to her meager wardrobe. She'd tried to make do with a couple of skirts and a few tops while saving her new dress as a surprise when Shade took her to dinner. Even if she had worn the dress, her meager wardrobe could never compete with the amount of clothes Vanessa brought.

She motioned to Pippa to come upstairs. "I have something I'd like to give you before I go."

Shade and the Hendersons gave her surprised looks, but Pippa felt certain they couldn't be any more flabbergasted than she was at the offer. She climbed the stairs and followed Vanessa into the opulent room. Pippa raised a questioning brow when Vanessa stood there with her familiar scowl.

"You said you wanted to give me something."

"Advice. I have to leave now because of other obligations. I'm warning you to stay away from Shade while I'm gone. There's something about him you don't know. I'm not at liberty to go into it, but keep your distance if you know what's good for you."

"I have no intention of going after him."

"See that you don't. As long as you're here you can take my cosmetic case down."

"Gee, thanks." Pippa would have refused if she didn't want Ross or Enid having to do it.

Vanessa swept out the front door leaving a cloud of heavy floral perfume behind, along with some very relieved household staff.

Pippa lay in bed that evening trying to fall asleep when she heard Shade's car come up the driveway. She knew this would be the only indication he had returned unless she actually opened her bedroom door to see him walk by. He moved around the house so quietly she never knew where he'd show up. He processed a fluid grace that one wouldn't expect in such a tall man.

Pippa wondered if Shade would mention their dinner now that Vanessa left. She'd meant it about not going after him, but surely it would be all right to have this one date with him since it had already been set up. She thought of her green dress hanging in the closet. It may not be the fanciest garment in town, but she might turn a few heads. She smiled in anticipation and closed her eyes.

Wispy curls of sleep drifted through her brain like fog on a dark night. Cool air blew in through the open window bringing with it sounds of the nocturnal forest pulsing to life. Unique wildlife music flowed like a soothing melody lulling Pippa deeper into slumber until a new sound suddenly broke through, disturbing the soft harmony.

She stirred, dragged her eyelids open, and looked around the room. What had made her wake from a perfectly good sleep? A huge yawn escaped, making her press her head back into the warmth of the pillow. She closed her eyes ready to doze off again, only to have them snap open, as a distinctive wail penetrated her grogginess.

She sat up to stare at the window. Had she heard her wolf? She claimed him in her mind because no one would admit the animal existed. Alert now, Pippa kicked back the blankets and ran to look. The outside lights helped her spot him. Her eyes followed, as he made his way slowly down the rows of flowers stopping every now and then to lift his head and issue another howl.

It began to rain. She watched as the water beaded atop his black hair adorning the coat with tiny silver coins. Pippa felt certain he must be the alpha male if a pack still existed in the woods. He carried the look of dominance well. She continued to study him enjoying the magnificent animal until he turned a corner and disappeared from her view.

She felt excited and even a little fearful remembering what it had been like to be so closely examined by the beast that first night. How did the animal get over the wall? Why did he come here to walk in the garden and why was it that no one else in the house ever saw or heard him? Or if they did, why wouldn't they just say so when she talked about hearing a wolf howling?

No one would probably admit it, but maybe she wasn't the only one wide awake at this hour. Curious, Pippa tiptoed to her door and opened it a slit. Someone walked by. She eased the opening to a wider crack and peered down the hallway hoping to identify the person. What she saw made the breath back up in her lungs.

Shade. Naked. Water dripped down his back, as he headed toward his rooms. Mesmerized by the sight, she continued to watch when he stopped and shook his head, scattering those all too familiar silver coins of rain from his heavy black mane of hair.

Pippa closed the door as quietly as her shaking hands would allow, and stood there wide eyed. Why wasn't Shade wearing any clothes? How did he get so wet? Surely he wouldn't be walking in the garden in a pouring rain. She walked back to bed and laid thinking.

She fell into a troubled sleep just before dawn, with visions of herself being chased by the Avalon household, as she fled through the woods on the back of her mysterious wolf.

Pippa moved slowly down the stairs the next morning feeling tired from her restless night. She stopped at the sound of voices. One belonged to Ross and the other to a woman she didn't recognize. Ross spoke in his usual calm way while the woman's voice rose in anger.

"Are you sure you want to fire me? It'll be my word against yours. I could cause trouble."

"I wouldn't advise it. Be thankful I'm willing to keep this between us, Nona."

"You haven't heard the last of me," she shouted.

"I hope I have, for your sake. The consequences could be very bad for you if you talked."

Pippa stood there frozen, as she heard them walk away. Who was Nona, she wondered, and what had the woman done to be fired? Whatever it was Ross apparently decided to keep it a secret.

She found Lila sitting alone at the breakfast table. Pippa greeted her and slid onto a chair. Why wasn't Shade here? Curiosity made it almost impossible to concentrate on her food.

"Are you not feeling well, Pippa? Have I been working you too hard?"

"Oh no, not at all. I didn't sleep very well last night. It's not your fault."

"Whether it is or not, I've only just realized that I haven't given you a full day off since you've been here. You'll begin to think I'm trying to keep you a prisoner."

Pippa shook her head.

"I love working with you and helping to create your stories."

"Be that as it may, a tired mind loses its creativity. You shall have today off. I know Shade wants to take you out to dinner. I will inform him that tonight is the perfect time, if you agree."

A slight flush pinked her cheeks.

"I didn't think he'd mentioned our dinner to anyone."

"Yes he did; and he's quite looking forward to it. He would have taken you out sooner, but Vanessa came. They have to take advantage of each other's time when their schedules allow."

Pippa wondered yet again what that availability entailed.

"I thought he might not be feeling well since he hasn't joined us for breakfast."

"He's fine. I know you're curious about my grandson. His life is complicated. He has to wear many hats. He's often involved late into the night and takes his rest in the morning."

Her words reminded Pippa about Shade saying he sometimes walked in the gardens at night and didn't want her spying on him. Why did he care whether or not she saw him? If he was so paranoid about his privacy they should have given her a room on the other side of the house.

An idea suddenly hit her. Maybe it wasn't Shade she wasn't supposed to see. Could it be the wolf he wanted to keep from prying eyes? Everyone certainly did their best to insist she was seeing and hearing things every time she brought up the subject of the animal. What could be so important that they wanted to keep the animal's existence a secret? Were there other wolves here?

Another, more disturbing thought came to mind.

The Avalon's corporation had extensive interests in various areas, including cosmetics and pharmaceuticals. Were they raising these animals to be used for some invasive biomedical research? Maybe they preferred wolves to rats and chimpanzees. Had she discovered the truth for the reason behind their mystery? Could this be what Vanessa had been alluding to?

Had other CEOs of the Avalon family taken part and condoned such a terrible thing? Did Shade know and continued to carry on with the cruel practice? Pippa didn't know how they could have the gall to call this place Wolfhaven. Haven? This wouldn't be much of a refuge for those unfortunate animals if she was right.

She gave herself a mental shake knowing she had to be careful where she allowed her lively imagination to take her. Whims of the mind helped in fantasy, not in reality. The animal testing idea made her feel sick inside, especially when she thought about the stories Lila loved writing.

Could it be the poor old soul really didn't know what was going on? Pippa bet everyone else did. A wolf howling wasn't exactly something you could keep under wraps. Did she want to go out with Shade if he turned out to be coldhearted enough to abuse animals?

Doubts continued to build inside her head. What would Shade do if she told him she suspected his dirty secret? Big companies could make a whistleblower's life a living nightmare. Had other employees before her discovered the hush-hush activities here? Was that why the woman Nona had been fired? Ross sent her away with a warning to keep her mouth shut.

What happened to anyone who dared to expose what they discovered? How safe would they be from retaliation? Shade might go to drastic means to silence them. Her fork slipped from her fingers clattering to her plate. Lila spoke, drawing Pippa's attention.

"You've gone very pale. Are you certain you're not coming down with some illness? Perhaps you should go back to your room and lie down. Do you need me to call my doctor?"

"I'm just a little tired. Maybe I'll take your advice and try to get some rest."

"I wish you would, and please don't hesitate to ask for medical help if you need it."

"Thank you. I'm sure I'll be fine after a nap."

Pippa hurried to her room anxious to be alone now. She warned herself she must concentrate on being rational. But the more she thought about Shade, the harder her heart pounded. The anticipation of having dinner with him fled along with a sudden aversion. Her only protection would be not letting on she may know about his secret.

She gnawed on her lip. She'd already mentioned seeing and hearing a wolf. But as long as they believed they had her fooled she would probably be safe. Pippa realized that could change if she let on she assumed something illegal was happening right under her nose.

Lila said she didn't want her to feel like a prisoner. She doubted if Shade would hesitate to do whatever it took to keep prying eyes out of his business. The frightening prospect of being kept here against her will filled Pippa with dread. Wolfhaven could easily become a prison considering its isolated location.

Better not wait to find out what Shade had in store for her. This may be her only chance to protect herself. She also felt obligated to report her suspicions to the authorities. But not here. The locals relied too much on Avalon money to keep their economy going. They wouldn't want to do anything to jeopardize that cash flow by helping an outsider like herself.

Knowing how inept she was at hiding her feelings, Pippa realized it would only be a matter of time before someone figured out she knew too much. If she'd stumbled onto something against the law she had to get out of here before anyone decided she might be a danger.

She rushed over to the closet for her suitcase and backpack with the thought of escape uppermost in her mind. Pippa jerked open drawers and began emptying them. She hurried back to the closet and reached for the things she'd bought with the money from Lila. Her hand hesitated. Did she want anything bought with money that may be at the expense of some poor animal?

Definitely not.

She ran to the bathroom and grabbed her own toiletries before returning to the bedroom for one last look around. She had everything. Now all she had to do was find a way to get out of the house without anyone seeing her. Pippa began to pace the floor while she went over in her mind various ways to achieve her getaway.

She plopped back down on the bed after rejecting several ideas. If she tried to leave via any of the outside doors she would surely be seen. The excuse that she was going for a walk in the garden would hardly be accepted when she carried her suitcase and backpack.

She'd just about decided to chance sneaking out a door when an idea popped into her head.

Who said she had to leave in the conventional way? Her eyes strayed to the two large windows. They were plenty big enough for her to fit through. She just had to figure out a way to get from the second story to the ground below.

She looked around the room again hoping for inspiration while her fingers clutched the bedding. Pippa stopped when she realized how strong the sheets were. Nothing but the best for the Avalons. Thanks to their expensive taste she'd found the answer to her dilemma.

She'd tie the sheets into a rope, secure that to a bedpost, and lower herself out the window. She cautioned herself to wait until everyone had gone to bed. Capitalizing on the fact that Lila thought she wasn't feeling well, Pippa decided to ask to have a dinner tray sent up to her room tonight. She'd need all the rest she could get if she was going to pull off her daring exit. She flopped back onto the bed and closed her eyes, willing herself to relax.

With her imagination operating in tiptop form it became impossible to control more outlandish ideas as they materialized. Her eyes flew open. What if the animal testing wasn't to benefit the company, but more to help an individual? Could the Avalon secret turn out to be something so bizarre and disturbing that no one outside of Wolfhaven could know?

Pippa leaped off the bed. All sense of reasoning completely abandoning her now. Was it the atmosphere here, or hearing the wolf howling that had suddenly made her feel a little crazy? She pressed her hands to her temples. Her head buzzed and her pulse leaped with this latest most disturbing thought, making her wonder if she really had gone insane.

Lila said her grandson's life was complicated. Vanessa told her there were things she didn't know about him. Why did he walk in the gardens at night? How could the wolf get over the walls?

God forbid, but what if Shade and the wolf were one and the same being?

FIVE

It became impossible to sit still with so much turmoil going on inside her. Pippa paced back and forth stealing glances out the window. She didn't stop until she could see the sun beginning to move down behind the trees. She knew her imagination could sometimes get out of hand. But the people here were too closed mouth to make her want to stay, even if she was wrong about Shade.

The house phone rang making her jump. Enid inquired if Pippa felt well enough to have her dinner. Pippa knew she had to keep up her charade of being sick and asked for something light. Ross brought the food. The concern on his face made her feel guilty for lying about being ill, until she reminded herself they'd all been keeping the truth about the wolf from her.

"My wife sent a light soup, a pot of tea and a bit of Jello-O. I hope you'll be able to eat."

"I'm sure I will. I'm feeling a little better. Thank you, Ross, and please thank Enid for me."

The aroma from the soup didn't tempt Pippa. Nerves had robbed her of any appetite despite not eating for hours. She knew she had to get busy preparing for her grand exit now that she had full darkness. She yanked the sheets off the bed. Lucky for her the big mattress required large size bedding. She'd need plenty given the height of her room from the ground.

Pippa spent the next half hour knotting the sheets into a rope for herself. The bedspread would do for her belongings. She looked out the window making sure the garden was empty of wolf or man before she lowered her suitcase and backpack down.

She secured her sheet rope as tightly as she could to one of the bedposts and gave it a few good tugs to be certain it would hold. Perspiration trickled down her back despite the cool night air. Pippa gripped the sheet with both hands, lifted her legs one by one over the windowsill, and propelled by sheer nervous energy, began to slowly lower herself out of the house to freedom.

Her descent started as she had hoped it would, even though it was turning out to be a lot more difficult than she had expected. It always looked a lot easier when she'd watched people do this kind of thing in the movies. She gritted her teeth and persevered. She almost reached her goal when the tie job on the bedpost came loose causing her to tumble. Thankfully she didn't have far to fall. She landed on her rump in the soft dirt.

She got to her feet and bent down to pick up her things when the hairs on the back of her neck stood up in a familiar warning. Pippa whirled around, her worst fears realized, when she found herself facing the wolf. Her knees grew weak, her body swayed, and she did something she'd never done before in her life. She fainted.

Shade was kneeling over her when her eyes flicked opened.

"Are you all right? What happened?" He looked up at the window. "Did you fall?"

Pippa scrambled to her feet. "Get away from me, you, you . . . whatever you are!"

He stood up and frowned at her.

"What the devil are you yelling about?"

"Don't you dare come near me," she insisted, as he started toward her. "I'm leaving here."

"Obviously. But wouldn't the door have been more convenient?"

"I didn't want anyone to know."

"Well, now that I do, would you mind explaining why you found it necessary to mess up a perfectly good set of sheets?"

Pippa's legs trembled, as she continued to back away from him. "I . . . I can't tell you."

"I see. Maybe I should check to be sure you haven't helped yourself to the family silver."

"I like your grandmother too much to steal from her."

"I noticed you omitted my name in your declaration," he said, reaching for her backpack.

She snatched it out of his hands. "Give me that! You have no right to search my stuff."

"I damn well do when I see you climbing out of a window in my house this time of night. Are you going to tell me what this is all about or is it going to be your little secret?"

"Look who's talking about secrets. If anyone has something to hide, it certainly isn't me."

"You're usually challenging me in some way or another during our conversations, but this one is boarding on the bizarre. What label are you trying to slap on me now, I wonder?" He eyed her closely. "I was under the impression that you weren't feeling well. Don't you think it would be best for you to get out of the night air?"

"That's what I'm trying to do. I plan to go to a hotel."

"There aren't any in the immediate area."

"Then I'll drive until I find one because I'm not staying another night under your roof."

"Bizarre," he muttered. "Your absence at dinner caused my grandmother a great deal of concern. She thinks you're upstairs in your bedroom lying in a sickbed. If you don't show up at breakfast she's going to be very upset. I think you know that wouldn't be good for her."

"I don't want to worry her. You're the one who makes me uneasy."

"I'm beginning to get that."

"Lila told me all about you." Pippa saw him stiffen. "You know, being the CEO of . . ."

"Ah, yes. I assumed that particular hurdle had been cleared. It still doesn't tell me why you want to leave here. What do you have against people in management?"

"Nothing."

"I thought we were beginning to be friends when you accepted my dinner invitation. I apologize for letting you down, by the way. The invitation is open if you're still interested."

"No thanks. I've decided to pass on that."

"All right, let's try this, then. Will you stay if I promise to keep out of your way except at mealtimes? I'm not asking for myself, Pippa. Hell, if it was up to me I'd let you go, especially after this stunt. But I haven't seen my grandmother in such good spirits in years. It's the stories you two are working on. It's given her a new lease on life. Even her doctor has noticed the positive change."

"Really? I knew she enjoyed them, but I didn't realize the stories meant so much to her."

"Now that you do, will you stay?"

Pippa did feel obligated to Lila. Shade presented the problem. She wondered if he really would stick to his bargain. Thinking of bargains made her remember one of her foster mother's when she'd tried to wheedle a favor from the woman. The words came to her now, 'Don't try to bargain with God, and don't try to bargain with me. You can't win either way.'

"I guess I could for Lila's sake if you meant it about making yourself scarce."

"Scout's honor."

"Will you let me leave when I decide I have to go?" she asked suspiciously.

"Of course. But I hope it won't be until my grandmother is ready."

"I guess that'll have to do."

46

Shade picked up her suitcase and slung her backpack over one shoulder.

"Do you mind if we use the door? I'm a little old to be climbing second story windows."

"How old are you?" Pippa asked, gathering up the pile of bedding.

"Thirty-three."

"I wonder how old that is in dog years," she muttered under her breath.

"I beg your pardon?"

"Nothing." They entered the foyer. "Oh, and would you mind not prowling in the garden?"

"Prowling?" He lifted a brow. "Since when is a walk in the garden considered prowling?"

"You know what I mean."

"Actually, no I don't. Has it ever occurred to you that you could stop looking?"

"Of course it has, but I happen to like the view. When you're not there, that is."

"How will I ever survive such a blow to my ego?"

"It's not like you don't have a whole forest to roam around in. Do we have a deal?"

"Yes, for my grandmother's wellbeing. Do you need to pinky swear?"

"Aren't you the funny one? I will hold you to your promise. Otherwise, I'm out of here."

Shade nodded, and followed Pippa upstairs where she dumped the linens on her bed.

"Do you want help with this mess?"

"No thanks. I made it. I'll clean it up."

She collapsed on the bed as soon as he left. Her body began shaking so hard her teeth rattled. She'd faced the wolf and came away without a scratch, even after demanding how he should behave in his own house.

Shade stood outside Pippa's room for several seconds, his brow furrowed in deep thought.

Pippa woke the next morning wondering if she'd dreamed everything that happened the night before. Now, safe in her room her heart raced remembering how the wolf had been so close she could have touched him. Not that she would have even if she hadn't fainted. Coming to and finding Shade leaning over her wasn't that big of a surprise since she'd convinced herself he switched back and forth between man and beast.

Now that she'd calmed down, she knew very well such a thing was impossible. She'd blocked out every sensible thought, worked herself into a frenzy, and came up with some pretty ridiculous conclusions. An overactive imagination could be a great asset in writing stories, as long as she didn't make herself part of the tale.

But she knew the wolf existed, and would keep an eye out for any signs of animal testing.

True to his word, Shade stayed out of her way except at meals. Pippa felt relieved that he kept his part of their bargain, until feelings of guilt began to make her wish she hadn't been so adamant. She stuck to her end of their agreement by continuing to help his grandmother with her stories. Pippa worked on the shawl she was crocheting for her, and did some of her own writing, or read one of the books she'd borrowed from the library here when Lila had her rest periods.

She walked in the garden during the daylight hours, using every opportunity to examine the walls trying to see a spot where an animal might be able to get inside the grounds. She located gates leading in and out of the garden. She opened each one noting how they all had paths leading into the forest. Would one of them take her to the testing site? She chose one that looked well used.

Cool air brushed her skin while scented earth and pine filled her nostrils. Golden sunlight decorated the path with strips of abstract shapes slicing through the shadows at the whim of the breeze. The forest surrounded her with a soft peacefulness. She could see why Shade loved it here.

Pippa stopped when the path took a sharp curve to the left. She looked over her shoulder toward the house and saw the roof barely visible through the thick canopy of trees. She turned to go back to her walking a second before hard fingers gripped her shoulder from behind. She gasped out a breath, her body jerking backwards as the pressure of the hand fell away.

A burly man dressed in jeans, sweatshirt, and wearing heavy rubber boots blocked the path. His face had the ruddy look of someone who spent a lot of time outdoors.

"Were you looking for something, miss?"

The man's sudden appearance startled her making it difficult to swallow. She tried to smile, but her facial muscles didn't seem to be working properly. She glanced back toward the house.

"Uh, no. I'm staying with the Avalons. I came out for a walk and some fresh air."

"Not a good idea this far from the house. Wild animals, you know. Let me escort you back."

Pippa nodded realizing he wasn't going to give her a choice when he continued to block the path. She hurried to the gate she'd used. He waited until she stepped inside and slammed it shut himself after advising her not to go into the woods again.

Or had it been a warning?

Did he work for the Avalons? Something bothered her about the man besides having him scare her. Something he'd been carrying. It looked like a leather leash sturdy enough to be used for a large dog.

An elderly woman friend of Lila's arrived in a chauffeur driven car for a visit just as Pippa walked back into the house. She decided to take advantage of her free afternoon with a drive.

"Hello," Shade said, surprising her as she went to the front door.

The sound of his voice flowed through Pippa like warm honey. It made her want to taste the mouth that uttered them. One minute she was running from him and the next moment she wanted him to kiss her. The man had certainly messed with her mind.

"Hi." She swallowed. "I thought I'd take a drive. Your grandmother has company."

"Yes, I know. I'd be happy to give you directions if you're going anywhere in particular."

"I don't have any destination in mind. It's such a lovely day I just felt like getting out."

"I feel like taking a drive myself. Would you be willing to call a truce for a couple hours? I'd like to take you to lunch as a way of making up for the missed dinner invitation."

She looked at her simple cotton blouse and jeans.

"I'm not dressed for anything too fancy."

"Neither am I," he said pointing to his jeans and denim shirt. "The place I have in mind doesn't have a dress code. Just lunch. Scout's honor," he said when she hesitated.

"Well, you said that before and kept your word, so I guess I can trust you."

They walked out to his car together.

"Were you ever really a boy scout, by the way?"

"No, but I always wanted to be. You know, learn knot tying, camp out."

"I wanted to be a Brownie and sell cookies. Have you lived at Wolfhaven all your life?"

"Yes, except when I went away to school."

"This is a very beautiful area."

"I think so. I never tire of it. I find a peace here that I can't seem to find anywhere else."

"I suppose besides the serenity you find, it's the one place where you can truly be yourself."

"That's very perceptive of you."

"Your grandmother said you do a lot of work from home, so you can be with her. I bet there's a lot you can't do with a computer, like overseeing lab testing and stuff like that. It'd probably be handy to have things like that right on the premises."

"One can do quite a bit with a computer and a cell phone these days."

Frustrated at his evasion, she searched for something else to say to keep him talking.

"What happened to the rest of your family? Lila never mentions them."

"That's because it's too painful for her."

Pippa watched his hands tighten on the steering wheel and had a terrible feeling.

"They're dead, aren't they?" she whispered in a quiet little voice.

"Yes, in a private plane crash – my grandfather, my parents, and my younger sister. All gone. They were going to a baseball game. Lila stayed home with me because I had the chicken pox. I was ten. Now we'll talk about something else."

The idea of trying to get Shade's admission to fronting a lab doing animal testing fled.

"Before we do let me say how very sorry I am for your loss. I'm glad you had a family for a few years, and you still have your grandmother who loves you very much."

"I am grateful for her every day. You know I'm protective of her, so I hope you won't take this the wrong way. I had a background check done on you before I let my grandmother hire you."

"I don't mind at all. I did one on your family, too, although I didn't find out much in the way of personal information. I get the impression that despite being responsible for heading the family company, you don't seem to enjoy your prestigious position."

"I run the company because it's expected of me. I didn't discover a lot about your personal life, either, except that you were literally raised in foster care. It must have been lonely for you."

"Sometimes. No roots. Never feeling like I belonged. But I grabbed every fleeing moment of happiness I could. I also used my imagination to keep me company, so things weren't that bad."

She had no idea how much her voice revealed a bleak vulnerability.

"What brought you into the system and kept you there so long? You said no roots. What about your family?"

"What family? A cook found me right after I was born in the dumpster behind the restaurant where he worked. The umbilical cord was still attached to me."

He pulled in a breath.

"Now it's my turn to be sorry. How did you get your name?"

"The story I was told is that the restaurant manager called the police. A couple of officers with a lady from Child Protective Services came. They interviewed the cook. He told them when he found me I was covered in garbage, including strips of green pepper. The social worker took pepper and turned it into Pippa. Her name was Elizabeth. She saw a package of Scott napkins on the counter in the kitchen, so that's how I became Pippa Elizabeth Scott."

"Pippa is unusual. I like it."

"Thank you. If you want to talk about someone having an unusual name, I'd have to say you would take the grand prize. Why Shade?"

His impressive shoulders lifted in a shrug.

"It is what it is."

Pippa had hoped for a small piece of a clue. Shade hadn't even given her a crumb.

He pulled onto a side road a few minutes later, following it through the woods, until they came to the end where a large Victorian Mansion stood, tucked in among the trees.

Pippa stared in surprise. "I thought your house was the only big one around here."

"There are a few others in the area built by old lumber barons. This one is a bed and breakfast with a dining room open to the public, except in the winter when they're snowed in."

"How do they stay in business being so out of the way like this?"

"Word gets around if you give good service and provide excellent food, which they do."

Shade got out and came around to open the door for Pippa, before taking her by the elbow.

He guided her up several long wooden steps. After a friendly greeting from the owner, they were led to a table outside on a large wooden deck facing a stream.

"What do you recommend?" Pippa asked after studying the menu.

He nodded toward the gurgling water.

"The trout is very good. It's fresh."

"I'll pass. I had trout once and there were so many bones I couldn't enjoy it. Sorry."

"That's all right. They also do some very nice sandwiches and salads for lunch."

"I think I'll try the chicken, red grape, and pine nut salad on field greens with dill bread."

"They make all their own breads," he said choosing a ham sandwich for himself.

"I can't believe I'm sitting in the middle of a forest eating lunch. I grab a yogurt at home."

"I'm happy I've given you a chance to experience something different."

Shade stood up, and held his hand out to her as soon as they finished eating.

"I'd like to show you something."

He led her over a narrow wooden bridge, across the flowing silver water, and through a grove of trees set amid a carpet of pine needles until they came to a little meadow. It sparkled like a bright green gem in the sunlight, with wild flowers sprinkled over the ground like colorful jewels.

"How lovely. It's like a tiny slice of Eden. Thank you for bringing me."

"I had a feeling you'd like it."

He suddenly cupped her face making her shiver despite the warmth of his hands.

"You're trembling. Am I frightening you?"

"I thought you said this was just going to be lunch."

"Does the fact that I want to kiss you make you afraid?"

"Yes, but I think I'm more afraid that you'll change your mind," she whispered, surprising herself.

SIX

Pippa expected the kiss to be as full of power as the man himself, but Shade's lips touched her mouth with a gentleness that somehow felt even more electrifying. Nothing had prepared her for how he made her feel. Drawn by his magnetism, she couldn't help clinging to him.

She put her arms around his neck straining on her tiptoes to kiss him back with a surge of passion that obviously surprised him, if his sudden intake of breath was any indication. He lifted her off her feet. She wrapped her legs around his waist giving them better access to each other's lips.

Pippa plunged her fingers in his hair filling her hands with the thick, dark waves. He deepened the kiss, stealing the air from her lungs, scorching her with his hot mouth. She had never wanted a man so quickly or so much, and right now she knew Shade wanted her, too.

The knowledge thrilled her until she reminded herself he could be hiding some dark secrets behind his suave façade. Desire quickly evaporated at the thought. She untangled her legs to stand back on the ground again, as she slowly pushed herself away from him.

"We shouldn't be doing this."

"It was just a kiss, Pippa. I'm not going to apologize and neither should you for kissing me back."

He ran a fingertip down the side of her cheek.

"You're an intriguing little minx. Perhaps I kissed you because I'd like to get to know you better."

She shook her head.

"No, you can't."

"And why not, may I ask?"

"Because you're my employer's grandson. You come from high class. I come from trash; literally. You know as well as I do the two don't belong together."

"I wasn't offering you a proposal of marriage," he said in a dry tone.

"I know that. But what would have happened if I let you continue kissing me?"

"We'll never know now, will we?" Shade turned away. "It's time we headed back."

Lila, tired from her visitor ate dinner in her room that night. Shade's kiss had stirred up feelings making Pippa not want to face him across the dinner table alone. She opted to eat in her own room, although she barely touched the food. Sleep turned out to be as elusive as her appetite. It'd been a mistake to think she could avoid Shade as long as she stayed here. Perhaps leaving Wolfhaven would be best for both of them.

Let him keep his secrets. Let them all keep their secrets – whatever they may be.

It turned out Pippa had fretted needlessly about seeing Shade. Lila informed her at breakfast that he'd been called away on business again. His absence made it easier to work without having to worry she'd run into him. The fact that she couldn't stop thinking about their kiss was something still plaguing her, however. She hadn't kidded herself into believing he would develop any deep feelings for her and his crack about not proposing marriage did hurt her feelings. She had her own dreams, like a lot of young women of being swept off her feet by a Prince Charming.

She couldn't expect anything from Shade. Not when he had Vanessa in his life. Pippa wondered if Vanessa's warning had anything to do with the wolves. Would it make any difference in her feelings for him if she did? Probably not. Money was more important. If it involved doing testing on some poor animals to keep the cash rolling in that's all she'd care about.

The only way Pippa could keep thoughts of Shade out of her head was to stay busy. Since her time with Lila was limited because of the woman's fragile stamina, she asked permission to use the gym and indoor swimming pool. Enid found a bathing suit for her.

Pippa fought against her body's restless yearning to be in Shade's arms again, as she divided her time going between the treadmill and the pool, exercising every evening until she exhausted herself enough to fall sleep.

Two weeks dragged on, and although Pippa knew Shade kept in daily contact with his grandmother, Lila never let on when he might be coming home. Pippa wondered how she would manage not to feel uncomfortable when he did. The only solution would be to leave Wolfhaven.

She knew she would miss the place. She'd grown accustomed to going to bed to the sound of crickets, wind softly singing through the trees, and the scent of the garden flowing through her room. Waking to the musical twittering of birds welcoming a new day was a definite improvement over the noise of traffic or garbage trucks banging trash cans around.

She couldn't forget about Lila and the Hendersons. They treated her as an equal and showed genuine concern for her wellbeing. Pippa knew she would feel awful if she did walk out on Lila when she knew the woman still had so many stories she wanted to write.

Each one took a great deal of time because Lila refused to let Pippa use a computer while she dictated her ideas. This meant that Pippa wrote out everything in long hand in notebooks before going to the computer to transfer each day's work onto a disc for safekeeping.

Shade finally returned three weeks to the day of his departure with Vanessa in tow once again. The amount of luggage she'd brought looked like the household was in for a long siege.

Pippa would have packed up and left that very same day if it hadn't been for Lila's heartfelt declaration of fondness for her.

Never ever having known a grandmother of her own, Pippa couldn't help being moved by such words. But that affection couldn't erase her discomfort around Vanessa. Lila must have understood when she accepted her plea to be allowed to not dine with them during Vanessa's stay. The Hendersons solved the worry of her dining alone by inviting Pippa to join them for meals.

She managed to avoid Shade and Vanessa four full days after their return, until she had the bad luck to run into Vanessa sitting by herself in the small salon one evening.

"I came for a notebook I left here by mistake this afternoon."

Pippa grabbed the book and hurried to the door, anxious to get away.

"How much longer do you expect to be here?" Vanessa asked in her usual petulant tone.

"As long as Mrs. Avalon needs me."

"This book of hers is such a silly idea. I can't understand why she's so obsessed with it. If I didn't know better I'd say she and Shade's mother had been related by blood instead of marriage."

The mention of Shade's mother made Pippa take her hand off the doorknob. She turned around to face Vanessa. Despite her earlier desire to get away as quickly as possible she couldn't resist the temptation to learn something more about his personal life.

"You knew his mother?"

"Cara? Of course. My parents were friends with his parents. Although I never understood what my mother and father saw in them. Even as a child, I remember Shade's mother being an odd woman. She lived in a world of her own most of the time. She preferred to spend hours here at Wolfhaven planting flowers. When she wasn't doing that she was painting pictures of them."

Pippa felt a pang of regret remembering how she insisted Shade not walk in the garden. She realized now that he probably went there because it made him feel close to his mother.

"I didn't know she was an artist."

"Not a very good one, but Peter, Shade's father, thought everything she did was wonderful."

"He must have loved her very much. It's such a tragedy the way they died. Knowing the Avalon's would only have the most competent pilot I'm sure the accident was unavoidable."

"The business necessitates they employ accomplished pilots, but all the Avalon men are capable of flying solo if need be, including Shade. In fact, Peter piloted the plane the day they went down. There's still speculation as to whether or not it was an accident."

"Are you saying he deliberately crashed the plane? You must be mistaken. How could anyone do such a terrible thing knowing their family was onboard, especially a young child?"

"Yes, it was a shame about poor little Sheldon."

"Sheldon?"

Vanessa wrinkled her nose. "A man's name, I know. It just goes to show what I meant about Cara being strange."

"Maybe it was a family name."

"No. Just another one of her absurd whims. As to why Peter would want to commit suicide and take his family with him, he was even odder than his wife. Instead of taking his position as he should with Shade's grandfather, Warren, in their corporation, Peter would rather be involved with animal conservation. They fought constantly over it, so it's assumed Peter found a way to end what he undoubtedly considered personal torment."

"Why are you telling me all this?"

"It's time you understood how deeply linked I am to the family, and how far back our history goes. I see the way you look at Shade. You obviously haven't taken my advice to stay away from him."

"I don't know what you're talking about."

"A woman knows when another one is trying to encroach on her man, so I'm telling you that you're wasting your time. We haven't made it public yet, but Shade and I are engaged."

Pippa squeezed the notebook in her hands. Engaged! She supposed she should have expected it would happen given how long they'd known each other. The big shock was how deeply hurt she felt knowing any chance that Shade would want to be with her had just been lost forever.

Fate could sometimes be a cruel taskmaster. This time it kicked her in the teeth.

"I wouldn't think of trying to infringe on your relationship. That's why I've excused myself from dining with the family."

"That's not enough. You're an embarrassment to Shade, the way you've tried to ingratiate yourself into his private life. He assumed you'd be long gone by now."

Pippa's cheeks flamed to match her hair.

"I'm here because Mrs. Avalon wants me to stay. She still has several more stories to write."

"Lila is a lonely old woman stuck in the middle of nowhere in this mausoleum of a house. She would encourage anyone to hang around as long as they were willing to listen to her babbling on about her ridiculous tales."

"They aren't ridiculous to her. Are you suggesting I leave without finishing her book?"

"I'm not suggesting it, I'm telling you. You should go before things get more awkward."

"Does Shade know that you're saying these things to me?"

"That's Mr. Avalon to you, and yes he knows. Whose idea do you think it was that I speak to you? I would have done it sooner, but you kept hiding like a scared little rabbit."

"I don't believe you. He told me himself that I've been a big help to his grandmother."

"That's changed. He wants you to leave because you're causing Lila to use up what little strength she has. If she continues on like this she's going to make herself really ill."

"I never push Mrs. Avalon beyond what she wants to do. She sets her own pace."

"That's not the way Shade sees it."

"Then shouldn't he be talking to me himself about his concerns?"

"Why would you think that? He's a very busy man. He doesn't have time to waste on dismissing servants."

Pippa sucked in a breath.

"I'm not a servant."

Vanessa shrugged.

"As good as one."

The class distinction thing again, like she was a mongrel that had wandered into a showroom full of purebreds. Pippa took a moment, digging for pride to cover the insult.

"Well, that's your opinion."

"Not just mine, as it happens. The fact is you've worn out your welcome here. You can leave now, unless you prefer the humiliation of being fired by Shade personally." She reached for the house phone. "Shall I call him? Is that what you want?"

Triumph sifted through the mocking question. Defeat all but consumed Pippa while she fought to hold Vanessa's spiteful gaze.

"No. I would never stay where I'm not wanted. Congratulations on your engagement, Ms. Allan. I'm sure you and Mr. Avalon will be very happy together since you're so much alike," she snapped, putting heavy emphasis on the mister.

If she'd needed an inducement to leave Wolfhaven, Pippa knew she certainly had one now.

She ran to her room, feeling broken inside from Vanessa's callous words.

SEVEN

Pippa tossed the notebook on the bed and sank down fighting back tears. While it was true she'd made the personal decision to avoid Shade, it still rankled to know that he had actually started to dislike her so much he wanted her to leave. Apparently his aversion to seeing her was so great he couldn't even bring himself to kick her out himself.

He had asked her to stay for Lila's sake. When had he changed his mind about the positive influence she was supposedly having on his grandmother's health? Now Pippa had to wonder if Lila was tiring of her, too. The thought cut a cruel slash into her fragile confidence.

She tried to think about some of the nicer experiences she'd shared with Shade. Times like their early morning coffee that day in the kitchen, his dinner invitation, their lunch. She couldn't forget his kiss in the meadow. What had meant a great deal to her must have been nothing more than a playful flirtation to him before he and Vanessa married.

Pippa knew she didn't want to hang around when that uppity snob became the mistress at Wolfhaven, even if she hadn't already been asked to leave. It appeared Lila was going to end up doing her book alone, unless Shade got someone else to continue with her.

Tears dribbled in thin streams down Pippa's cheeks catching in tiny pools at the corners of her mouth. She scrubbed them away with the backs of her hands. She hated crying. It made her feel so infantile. She looked around the room. This was the nicest place she'd ever lived. But her time had run out, just as all the other places had, wherever she'd stayed while growing up.

She went to the closet for her suitcase and backpack. She began stuffing her belongings inside like the night of her aborted escape attempt. Too bad Shade hadn't let her go then.

She made the decision again not to take the clothes she'd bought with the money from Lila. It didn't take long to finish her packing. That was the easy part about her leaving. The hard part was writing a farewell note to Lila and another one to the Hendersons. But Pippa couldn't bring herself to go without letting them know how much she appreciated their kindness.

Once she'd finished the notes, she took one last look around. She flirted with the temptation to take something as a reminder of her stay here. Then she remembered Shade asking her if she'd stolen anything the night he caught her trying to leave. Happy memories would have to serve as souvenirs. At least no one could take those away from her.

Pippa set Lila's note on top of the shawl she'd finished for her. The Henderson's note lay folded on the scarves she'd crocheted. She gathered her things, walked downstairs, and out the front door. She almost wished Ross or Enid were there to say goodbye and wish her well.

Now that she was going, she realized how much they had become like surrogate parents to her during her stay. She'd never been able to break the habit of trying to look for people to fill the emptiness she felt because her own parents hadn't wanted her in their lives.

She tossed her things into the car and drove away without looking back at the house that held such a mixture of comfort and uncertainty for her. Pippa reached the point where she'd had her flat tire the night she arrived. She couldn't forget this was also the first time she'd seen her wolf.

Where was he now? Locked up in some cage? Lying on some steel table hooked up to an IV that dripped a noxious fluid into his vein? She hadn't dismissed the idea that there was a hidden place on Avalon land. She may have found it if that man hadn't made her go back to the house.

Had he told Shade about seeing her? Could that be part of the reason he wanted her gone? She almost felt like she owed it to the animals to go back and look again. Even if she didn't find anything it would make her feel better knowing she'd tried. She began to warm to the idea.

Shade probably knew by now she'd left the house, thanks to Vanessa. If everybody thought she wasn't there Pippa reasoned, she might be able to hide her car in the woods, sleep in it tonight, and set out at first light back to the area where she'd run into the man with the leash. It'd be dark, of course, but she did have a good flashlight to keep that particular fear under control.

She slowed down looking for a spot to pull off the road, when an animal suddenly leaped out of the woods and landed right in front of her. Pippa immediately pressed her foot on the brake pedal, but it was too late. She ran into the beast before she could bring the car to a complete stop.

She heard its cry of pain and instantly shut off the engine. Headlights beamed over the animal lying on the ground. Pippa gasped in alarm when she recognized her wolf.

"Oh my God, I've killed him!"

She shoved her door open, and jumped out. He surprised her by rising to his feet. Pippa watched helplessly as he took off in a limping run disappearing back into the woods. Her first thought was to go after him. She quickly abandoned the idea knowing he'd probably turn on her. The thought of him lying somewhere hurt and possibly dying filled her with anguish. She couldn't leave him out here all alone without telling someone.

Pippa scrambled back inside her car, turned around, and headed back to the house. The wolf would probably need medical attention. Secret or no secret, she had to get someone in the household to believe her. She drove back as quickly as she could. She ran into the house and raced down the hallway that led to the Hendersons' quarters. Ross answered her knock within seconds.

"Why Pippa, what's the matter? You're shaking."

"It's the wolf. I just hit him with my car. I didn't see him in the dark."

His hand squeezed the door handle. "Pippa, we've told you, there aren't any wolves here."

"Stop it! I know you're lying. Aren't you going to do anything to help that poor beast?"

The upsetting events of the evening had stressed Pippa to the breaking point. The fact that Ross was standing here unwilling to help made her desperate to force him to do something. The crazy idea that Shade may be the wolf entered her head, urging her on.

"I think you know it could have been Shade I hit."

Ross jerked back. "Mister Shade? I thought you said you ran into an animal."

"Did I? You tell me Ross. Was it an animal or something else?" she asked and held her breath.

"I'm sure I don't know what you mean. Is the beast still on the road?"

"No, he ran into the woods. But he was limping."

"You go to your room now, Pippa. I'll tell you the minute I know anything."

It wasn't the confession she'd hoped for, but at least he promised to get back to her.

She was too agitated to sit down once she returned to her room. She barely glanced at the things she'd left for Lila and the Hendersons, which seemed like a lifetime ago. Did Ross believe her or was he just pacifying her? She went to the window and peered into the darkness wondering if the wolf might have made his way to the garden out of habit.

She wasn't sure how much time had elapsed before Ross finally knocked on her door. She yanked it open to find him standing there with a tray in his hands.

"Enid sent you something to eat since you missed dinner."

Food? How did they expect her to be able to eat after what had happened? Pippa moved back; and he entered to set the tray on a table.

"Did you find the wolf? Is he going to be all right?"

"There wasn't any wolf."

She pressed her fingers to her temples for a moment. "Look, I understand if you want to keep his presence here a secret. I just want to know that he's going to be okay. Did you talk to Shade? I'm sure everything I say to you goes from your lips to his ears. Is he all right?"

"Calm yourself. Mister Shade is fine. I don't know why you think he wouldn't be."

"I told you what I think. I'm sure you know what's going on here, Ross. Won't you help me understand, so that I . . ." she stopped when he shook his head at her.

"Some things are best left alone. Please eat your dinner now, and try to get some sleep."

He left the room leaving Pippa trembling with frustration at what she saw as another dead end. She walked to the tray after several seconds and lifted the lids. A hot roast beef sandwich, green salad, and an apple tart with a carafe of tea. She replaced the covers. She didn't want to eat.

She didn't care about Vanessa's demand that she leave now. She wasn't going anywhere until she found out for herself that Shade really was okay. She knew she wouldn't be able to sleep if she didn't do something to work off some of her adrenaline.

What she needed was something that required more physical exertion. Swimming several laps in the pool might help to burn off some of the tension tearing at her. She undressed, put on her bathing suit, and slipped on a robe before making her way through the silent house to the pool.

Pippa just stepped into the gym when she heard the jets on the hot tub going. She hadn't expected to find someone else here at this late hour. She stayed back in the shadows wondering if she should give up her swim when the jets turned off. She pressed herself against the wall peering around the corner curious to identify the nighttime visitor.

She watched as Shade climbed gingerly out of the tub.

Pippa's mouth went dry at the sight of his naked body revealed in the glow of the lights surrounding the spa. He looked even more magnificent than she'd imagined. Water glistened on his shoulders and ran in rivulets over his hair roughened chest. Her eyes followed the narrow line of dark hair down the planes of his flat abdomen and beyond.

She saw that everything about him was large and well defined. The play of muscles as he moved caught her attention until she noticed the huge purple bruise covering most of one hip and part of his thigh. Her mouth gaped open. Ross had obviously lied about Shade being fine.

Pippa watched him wrap a towel around his narrow waist and limp through the doorway that led to his part of the house. She sagged against the wall. It wasn't her imagination this time. His injuries were real. The sight of his bruised body made her sick. Had she done that to Shade?

She stood while her brain tried to separate what she had seen from what she knew couldn't be real. Shade, a wolf? Impossible! She had to get out of here before she lost her mind completely.

Pippa rushed to her room, changed into her clothes, and left the house, determined to get as far away as quickly as possible. She kept a sharp eye out for any animals or men prowling around the Avalon land in the middle of the night. The last thing she wanted to do was run into one again.

She drove through the night arriving back in Los Angeles and her home above the bookstore. Chloe Bert, the owner was a friend of Pippa's last foster mother and had offered her a job in her store including a roof over her head.

She'd been gracious enough to let Pippa take the position with Lila while still holding her job. Chloe's nephew, Craig had been helping out in her absence. But it was time she returned to her responsibilities here. Not to mention familiarity and blessed normalcy. No more dark secrets. No more wolves – and definitely no more Shade Avalon.

Pippa pulled into her parking place behind the store. She trudged up the backstairs to her tiny apartment, which hadn't really been an apartment at all, but a storeroom. The fact that it had a bathroom had been a lucky break. She called from her car to let Chloe know she'd be returning sometime today. She collapsed onto the bed fully clothed, and fell into an exhausted sleep.

Pippa woke the next morning, confused until she recognized the watercolor painting of the unicorn hanging on the wall. It'd been a gift from Craig who was majoring in art in college. She focused on the whimsical picture, hoping to forget the reason she'd driven all night to get back to her lonely little abode. She crawled out of bed and headed for a shower before going downstairs.

Chloe greeted her with such warmth it made Pippa swallow down a lump in her throat.

"I thought you were going to be staying longer with the Avalons. Did you finish the lady's book sooner than you'd planned? You didn't mention it on the phone or why you chose to drive at night instead of waiting until today to come back."

"There isn't going to be any book – or, at least not one that I'll see to completion."

Chloe studied Pippa for a moment. "Sounds like something unexpected happened. I'm willing to listen when you're ready to tell me why you left. I set out coffee and Danish for you."

"Thank you. Coffee would be good."

"Have the sweet roll. You look like you've lost weight."

Pippa hid a smile. Chloe was plump enough to think that anyone thinner than her needed to eat more. She poured her coffee, slid a roll onto a paper plate, and climbed onto a stool next to a small round table wedged in between boxes of books. The aroma of coffee mingled with the scent of musty old books, and printer's ink, from brand new ones.

She sat sipping the coffee while she made a mental list of the things she needed to do. Buying Chloe flowers for being so patient with her came to mind right away. It made Pippa think about the first time she saw Shade carrying the bouquet for his grandmother that morning at Wolfhaven.

Would she ever stop thinking about him? Not likely.

It wasn't every day she met a person like Shade. The thought of him being part-wolf nagged at her, mostly because it annoyed her that she couldn't let the insane idea go. She recited the data inside her head supporting her wild theory that he might be some kind of transgenic creature.

70

She only heard or saw the wolf when Shade was home. The animal couldn't get into the garden unless someone left a gate open, or if the beast was already inside. Someone, such as a man. What about the bruises she saw on Shade's body right after she hit the wolf with her car? Was that just another strange coincidence?

The entire household insisted there were no wolves in the area when she knew differently. She'd told them from her very first day at Wolfhaven about her encounters and still they denied her claims. Why else would everyone keep that a secret, unless they were trying to protect Shade?

What about Shade himself? She'd given him enough hints to confess. Pippa sat with her chin resting on her palm, thinking. It could be that no one, especially Shade, wanted to talk about what happened to him because it was something so abnormal. The poor man. Rich enough to buy anything he wanted, yet helpless to cure himself of an unnatural double life. What a cruel twist.

She shook her head in exasperation, reminding herself yet again she had to stop allowing her rampant imagination to take over sane reasoning. What about her original theory? Did the residents of Wolfhaven deny the wolves were there because of illegal testing? Yes, that had to be it. No one, not even the very clever Mr. Shade Avalon could turn himself into an animal.

The little bell hanging over the store's door jingled, signaling the first customer of the day. She headed for work, determined to pick up the fragmented threads of her life.

Home for over a month without a word from anyone in the Avalon household had Pippa feeling well and truly forgotten. She hadn't really expected any word from them. But she supposed a part of her subconsciously hoped Lila might call or send a note to thank her for the hours she'd spent helping with the stories. What about the things she'd made for her and the Hendersons?

She realized the shawl wasn't much of a gift for a woman who could afford to buy anything she wanted. Ross and Enid may have so many scarves hers wasn't any big deal to them. What about Shade? Was he glad to have her out of his house as Vanessa claimed? The thought made her insides ache. She kept telling herself she wanted to forget about the Avalons. So why couldn't she get them out of her head?

Having trouble sleeping after her first night home didn't help. Adjusting back to the nighttime city noises after the quiet country was taking Pippa longer than she expected. It didn't help that she kept having dreams about Shade sometimes as a man and sometimes as a wolf. She walked the gardens with him in his wolf form. When he was a man they made love in the pretty little meadow as the sun blanketed their naked bodies with its golden light.

The love making dreams were very disturbing if her pulse rate and sweaty body were any indication. She often woke up with a physical longing so strong it left her trembling with need. She couldn't stop thinking about the way Shade kissed her or how it felt to be held in his arms. How was it possible to want and fear him at the same time?

Even more difficult to forget was when she recalled the way Shade looked when she saw him climb out of the hot tub. The image of the water trailing down his body was still very much etched in Pippa's mind. All she could do was endure the visions and hope they would fade away.

Craig came running in the store several weeks later waving a newspaper in his hand.

"Ava Lon is finally having another art exhibit here. Yes!" he hooted, pumping his fist in the air.

Pippa continued to repair the book she was working on and didn't bother to look up.

"And this news should excite me because . . . ?"

"You'd know if you looked at the arts section once in a while instead of the comics. She's a major artist. Her work is sold all over the world. Her paintings go for several thousand dollars.

She always paints scenes from nature, especially of forests and its animals. They're so real looking you'd swear you can smell the trees, or step inside and pet a deer. This one is a little different, though because she added people. Look at this photo."

Hearing his enthusiasm and knowing she should at least pretend an interest, Pippa glanced at the picture he shoved under her nose and thought her heart would stop. This couldn't be what she thought it was. She grabbed the article from him and peered at it more carefully. The more she looked, the more it felt as though all the air had left her lungs.

Craig chattered on, unaware of her reaction, as Pippa struggled to breathe.

"It isn't just her incredible talent that draws people. She's a mystery woman. Some say she's a recluse, while others say she's deformed and captures beauty in her paintings to compensate for her own ugliness. She doesn't have many shows. That's why it's so exciting when she does. I sure would like to go to one, but somehow my name keeps getting left off the guest list," he joked.

"Oh well, I wouldn't get to see her anyway. An agent always represents her. As far as I know no one's ever seen the real Ava Lon."

Pippa touched an unsteady fingertip to the newspaper photo.

"I have," she whispered.

EIGHT

"You want to run that by me again," Craig urged. "I think I must be hearing things."

Too late, Pippa realized she'd spoken out loud. The photo of a petite red haired woman and a tall dark haired man embracing in the middle of a meadow, surrounded by several forest creatures had caught her off guard. She knew with every fiber of her being that Shade had painted her with him; and he'd chosen the meadow where they'd kissed as the setting.

Ava Lon. She almost smiled at the clever way he'd divided his name, so people would think he was a woman. Now she knew what Lila had meant about Shade having another good reason to require time to himself. He obviously used it to paint, when he wasn't involved in company work.

Other bits of information began to come to her mind, as she stood there staring at the newspaper clipping. His paint splattered clothes the first time they'd met in the hallway outside her room, and Vanessa's revealing news that Shade's mother liked to paint. He'd clearly inherited his parent's genes. Cara apparently hadn't been very talented if Vanessa was to be believed. Shade was. Like everything else he did, he did it well.

Craig said he was a famous artist. How many other secrets had Shade kept from her? How many more talents did the man possess that might yet be waiting to be revealed? Now with this painting being shown in such a widely distributed newspaper in the city where he knew she lived, Pippa had to wonder if Shade had allowed this particular one to be advertised because he hoped she would see it.

Was this his way of showing her that he trusted her enough not to reveal his secret identity as the mysterious Ava Lon? Not that she would. Or did it mean he might be missing her as much as she missed him? Did he want to see her again? If that was the case, why hadn't he called her? Why had he left her wondering about him all these weeks?

Pippa's mind continued to churn with confusing questions until Craig took that moment to break into her thoughts.

"Hey, don't go all quiet on me now. Did you or did you not say you've met Ava Lon?"

His words hung between them while Pippa gave herself a mental shake knowing she had to cover her slip.

"Of course not. I teased you because you ribbed me about reading comics. Bad joke. Sorry."

"Well, you had me going there for a minute. Are you okay? I hate to use such a tired old cliché, but you look like you've seen a ghost. I'm sorry if I upset you with that crack about not knowing who Ava Lon is. You sure got even with me when you said you'd met her, though."

"You didn't upset me. I'm the one who should apologize for being so insensitive to pretend I'd met such a famous artist. As to how I look, I'm starting a migraine. You know how they sometimes just come out of nowhere. Would you mind watching the store while I go upstairs and take something before it gets any worse? I won't be long."

"I'm done with school, and have the rest of the day free. Why don't you lie down? I'll stay until Aunt Chloe gets back from her dentist appointment."

"Are you sure?"

"Yeah. It's almost closing time, anyway."

75

Pippa was so desperate to be alone and think things out that she could have thrown her arms around him at his willingness to fill in for her.

"Thank you, Craig. I owe you."

"I'll call it even and forgive your bad joke, if you'll make me a batch of brownies."

"You got it. Do you mind if I take this news article to read later?"

"Be my guest." Craig winked at her.

"I'll end up turning you into an Ava Lon admirer yet."

Pippa wondered what he'd say if he knew Ava Lon was a man who'd been the main focus of her dreams for weeks, none of which had anything to do with art.

"You never know."

She stepped out the door clutching the newspaper, as she ran upstairs to her room where she immediately read the clipping. Pippa devoured each word, starved for information about Shade.

Her eyes kept straying to the picture while she tried to focus on the words beneath.

She read what Craig had already told her about Ava Lon being a mystery woman and a major force in the art world. It mentioned how the paintings were coveted by serious art collectors. Admission to the exhibit was by private invitation only. In other words, don't bother coming without a fat wallet.

The last line of the article all but jumped out at her. It stated that although the artist herself would not be in attendance, Ava Lon's longtime representative, Ms. Vanessa Allan would be hosting the exhibit. Pippa's fist closed around the paper wrinkling it into a loose wad without realizing what she was doing.

That explained what Shade meant about their relationship being a business one. Pippa just assumed Vanessa lived off her family's money, since no one had ever talked about her actually having a career. They couldn't say anything without possibly revealing the fact that Shade was her most famous client.

Pippa let out an angry little hiss when she looked down and saw what she'd done to the article. She asked Craig for the paper because she planned to frame the picture. Now she'd ruined it with her carelessness. She laid the paper on the table trying to smooth out the wrinkles, only to end up tearing off one corner.

She'd have to go to the newsstand and buy another one. She only hoped the papers hadn't all sold out. Pippa hurried downstairs and saw Chloe closing the store for the day.

"Is your headache gone, honey?"

"Almost. I think a little fresh air would help. Did Craig leave?"

"Yes. He said to remind you about owing him a batch of your brownies."

"I haven't forgotten. I'll pick up the ingredients at the store when I take my walk."

"I'm going to close out the register and head home. I'll see you in the morning."

They said their goodbyes. Pippa hurried out the door, walking briskly in her anxiousness to reach her destination and get her hands on another newspaper. She breathed out a sigh of relief when she arrived at the store, and saw several copies stacked neatly in the rack. She bought three. It wasn't every day she found her likeness in a painting by a world renowned artist.

Pippa selected the ingredients she needed for the brownies, plus a frozen microwavable pizza, and a liter bottle of soda for her dinner. She'd never met a famous person before, let alone spent time with one. Craig's excitement flashed inside her head. It made her wish she could really tell someone that she actually knew the elusive Ava Lon.

What she wouldn't give to see Vanessa's expression when she looked at the painting for the first time. Craig said Ava Lon's paintings usually only had animals in them. Vanessa must have been royally ticked to see Shade had broken his rule by using Pippa of all people.

The sun began to set by the time she started walking back home. She watched as the pale gray sky absorbed the fading golden light until it disappeared. She wasn't worried being out alone. This neighborhood had always been safe. The well lit street lined with old houses, little mom and pop businesses run by families that had grown up here like Chloe, were scattered along the way.

The people knew how to take care of and appreciate what they had. Most of the yards were small and well kept – certainly nothing like the gardens at Wolfhaven, but pretty in their own way.

Most neighbors knew each other by first names and were quick to help out when someone got sick or there was a death in a family. They sat on their front porches or visited over back fences. Kids riding bikes or cruising along the sidewalks on skateboards were a common sight. You could always count on receiving a friendly wave when you walked by.

Pippa made her way around the back of Chloe's store taking the stairs up to her apartment. She balanced her grocery bag on her hip with one hand, while unlocking the door with the other. She wiggled inside, snapped on the overhead light, and almost dropped everything when she saw Shade sitting at her little table, with one ankle resting on the knee of his other leg.

"Hello, Pippa."

If she lived to be a hundred, Pippa knew no other man's voice would ever be able to cause her pulse to race with such force, and just as quickly make her body feel weak with longing.

"Shade! How did you get in here?"

78

He stood up, took the bag from her, and set it on the table. "Your landlady."

"Chloe? I can't believe she'd do that."

"I convinced her that you would be safe with me."

"Well, that remains to be seen. Why are you here?"

"I'm sure you already know the answer to that."

"The painting." She pulled a paper out of the bag. "I saw it in here. You're full of hidden talents – clever use of your name, by the way. Do you think you'll get a lot of money for this one?"

"It's not for sale."

"What do you mean? If you're not going to sell it, then why did you paint it?"

"I think you know the answer to that, too. We have some unfinished business between us."

Her nerves began to jingle like Christmas bells. "We do? Like what?"

"This," he said, drawing her into his arms.

He dipped his head and took her mouth in a searing kiss before Pippa had a chance to say another word. All the emotions she'd worked so hard to shut down during the last several weeks came roaring to life. It felt like having a bomb go off inside her. Desperate, she kissed him back with enough heat to set fire to them both.

It no longer mattered what secrets Shade kept from her. Artist. Animal tester. Part wolf. Need punched through her. Any woman with half a working hormone would desire him. She'd wanted him for so long, Pippa didn't care if she needed rabies shot, or ended up having pups.

She almost groaned out loud at such lunacy, inwardly cursing the lousy timing for her imagination. Sometimes she wished she could shut down her brain when these absurd ideas emerged. Especially when she wanted to concentrate on something more important, like having Shade take her to bed.

They were both breathing heavily when Shade raised his head.

"I've missed you."

"I guess it's obvious I missed you, too. I haven't been able to get you off my mind."

"That's nice to know."

She plucked at his shirt front. "Did that kiss mean you're going to make love to me?" She watched his eyes stray to her single bed. "I know my bed's too small for you. We can put the quilt on the floor."

"Don't you think you're rushing things a bit?"

She frowned.

"I don't know. Am I? It's not like we just met yesterday."

"Have you ever been with a man?" he asked in a gentle voice.

"Once." She squirmed. "Well, almost. It didn't work out. But I want to be with you."

"So you can use me to satisfy your curiosity?"

"It's not like that. I've been attracted to you from the moment you looked up at me from the garden that first morning I was at Wolfhaven. I don't think you would be here if you didn't care a little bit about me. And you wouldn't hold onto that painting if what happened between us in the meadow didn't mean something to you, either. I'm asking you to do this because I'd like my first time to be with someone who won't think of me as just another conquest."

When Shade didn't answer, Pippa began to worry that she'd been wrong about him having feelings for her. Could he be struggling to come to a decision because he didn't want to be with an inexperienced woman, or because he was afraid she'd expect some kind of long term commitment?

"I promise I won't ask for anything else if that's why you're holding back. This is a big step for me. I'm twenty-

three years old. That other time the man I was with, he . . "
She shook her head. "I'd rather not talk about it. I've been
afraid since then, but I'm not afraid of you."

Shade tucked a curl behind her ear.

"What you're offering is a precious gift. I don't want
to end up hurting you in any way."

"I know you don't. That's why I trust you to do
what's right."

"I've never been sure what is right when it comes to
you, Pippa. I didn't come here with seduction in mind. I
won't lie and say I'm not tempted to take what you're
offering. I'm flattered that you would choose me to be the
first man to make love to you. But I'm going to do the
gentlemanly thing and respectfully decline your generous
offer."

"I should have more pride not to beg you. I know
what I want. Please, Shade."

He drew her to him, and kissed her with something
very close to reverence.

"I can't."

"Why not? I bet you've made love to a lot of women."

His brows rose very slowly.

"Are you asking me about my love life, Pippa?"

"I just wondered. I guess it's not polite to pry. Chalk
it up to my lack of sophistication. I don't understand why
you don't want me," she persisted. "Is it because I'm
inexperienced?"

"Oh, sweet Pippa, I do want you. Very much. But
now is not the time."

"I hope that means you'll change your mind later. I
wasn't kidding when I said I've missed you. I left
Wolfhaven weeks ago. It kind of hurt me when no one
bothered to call or write. I thought maybe I might at least
hear from your grandmother."

Shade stepped back, and rubbed a hand around the
back of his neck.

"I'm afraid there's an unpleasant reason for that. I didn't want to tell you via phone. She had a stroke the night you left."

Pippa's hands flew to her mouth.

"Oh no! Is she all right? Please don't tell me she died."

"No. The stroke wasn't as bad as it could have been considering she's so frail."

"Is she doing better now?" Pippa asked unaware of the tears shimmering in her eyes.

Shade pulled her back into his arms and caught the first tears that fell with his fingertip.

"Yes. A physical therapist comes three times a week to work with her. We had a live-in nurse for a while. It depressed her so much that as soon as she was well enough Enid took over."

"That would be nicer. Sometimes I pretended Lila could be my grandmother."

"She'd like to know that. She misses you very much. Why did you leave, Pippa? Your polite little note gave no reason."

"You of all people should be happy I didn't stay. I saw you as someone I'd like to get to know, but you saw me as a threat. You were so busy trying to get me to say goodbye, I never really had a chance to say hello."

"I'm not proud of my behavior. I realize I wasn't as welcoming to you as I should have been. It wasn't your fault. I tend to become a bit of a recluse when I'm at Wolfhaven because of work. I value my privacy to the point of resenting any intrusion."

Pippa wondered if he was going to mention his engagement to Vanessa. But since he hadn't, she decided to give him the partial truth for her hasty departure.

"I needed to come back. I couldn't expect Chloe to keep my job open for me indefinitely. She let me go in the first place because she knew how much I loved the idea of being involved in helping to write an anthology of children's stories."

"She seems like a very nice person."

"She is. I owe her a lot. She not only gave me her friendship, she also gave me a place of my own for the first time in my life."

Shade's eyes quickly scanned the drab little room.

"So this is your permanent home?"

"This is it."

"No wonder you were so worried about getting lost when you came to Wolfhaven."

She pulled away from him.

"It must be a real comedown for you to be here."

"It isn't the size of a place that makes a home. It's the people who inhabit it."

"If you say so. Would you like something to drink? I don't have anything like you're used to. But hey, why not see how the other half lives, and get a sample of my life? I'll even feed you."

"Sounds interesting."

"Don't look so wary. I don't plan on poisoning you. Sit down and give me a few minutes."

Pippa laughed, when Shade took a bite of pizza and wrinkled his nose.

"What's so funny?"

"You are."

"When's the last time you've had a microwave pizza and drank soda pop?"

"This would be the first."

"I thought as much. Too bad you came such a long way for a mediocre meal."

"It's not mediocre; just different. Food wasn't the most predominant reason for my visit, as you know. I wanted to tell you about my grandmother. Another reason for my being here is that I'd very much like you to come back to Wolfhaven with me."

Pippa could feel her heart pounding extra hard at the thought that Shade may be getting ready to make some kind of a commitment to her after all. If only he could want her just a little.

"You do? Why?"

Blinded by the desperate wish to be needed, she stared at him in anticipation.

And waited.

NINE

He wiped his mouth on a paper napkin.

"Because my grandmother needs you."

Pippa retreated inside herself, silently chiding her naivety to think that Shade would make a declaration of love. She couldn't even get him to bed her, and she'd certainly thrown herself at him. The man could have easily taken what she insisted she was so willing to give. He was being nice to her only because of his grandmother. She should have known.

She also couldn't forget about Vanessa. She had the advantage of being a longtime family friend and a member of Shade's inner circle, while Pippa could only ever skirt the edges. Vanessa had made it clear Pippa would always be out of the loop, never fitting in at Wolfhaven or anywhere else as an equal in their privileged world. Sad to say, she was right.

"Please tell your grandmother I'm very touched that she wants me to return, but I can't. My life is here. It wouldn't be fair for me to take advantage of Chloe's generosity to go traipsing off. I won't do that to her, even if she was willing to let me leave again."

Pippa braced herself for an argument. Shade simply turned his head to look away from her. She studied his profile as he stared straight ahead, and thought how handsome he was. She wished once again that their worlds weren't so far apart, especially how she'd confessed to wanting him to be her first lover. That bit of artlessness had already made her wish she hadn't been so forthright.

The seconds ticked by, and his silence was becoming almost unbearable. Pippa felt her nerves grow taut. Her fingers kept flexing on her glass. She was about to plead with Shade to say something when he finally looked at her again.

"Would it help if I said I want you to come back, too?"

She hoped to hear him say that, but now she knew he'd only said the words because of Lila. As fond as she was of the older woman, Pippa knew it'd be better to break away from Shade now before he became so embedded in her life that it was impossible for her to live without him. She'd already struggled enough to forget him.

"You don't have to pretend. We both know you don't want me as much as I need you. I asked you to make love to me because I just wanted this one time for us to be together. Vanessa will have you to herself the rest of your lives."

"Have me in what way, exactly?"

"You needn't deny it. She told me about you two being engaged to marry. That's probably another reason why you turned me down, now that I think about it."

"Is that why you really left my home? If it is, you should know that she was lying."

"Well, someone is. Either way, it doesn't matter. Nothing can change the fact that I'm from the wrong side of the tracks, or more precisely, the wrong side of the dumpster. Sooner or later you're going to remember that and be embarrassed by it. I know you asking me to go back to Wolfhaven doesn't constitute any real obligation on your part. Just having me around is bound to eventually make you uncomfortable. I'm trying to save us both the embarrassment of that."

She had little doubt that when he stepped out the door he'd be walking out of her life for good this time. Pippa wanted to beg him to stay even as her words told him to go. The urge to give into temptation was especially strong when he turned and looked at her.

Their eyes met. She tried to read what she saw as his gaze swept over her. Pity? Anger?

"If you can set your concerns about pedigree aside for a moment, you should know that I would have asked you to come back even if my grandmother hadn't pleaded with me to try and persuade you. She misses you very much. You hurt us all when you left."

"I didn't want to hurt anyone, especially her. I'm not that uncaring. You're not being fair."

"You call sneaking off in the middle of the night without telling anyone an act of fairness?"

"No, but I did what I thought was best at the time. I never intended to upset anyone."

"Then at least come to visit. I'm going back in a couple of days. That should give you enough time to think about it. I'll send a car for you. You can stay at the house for as long or as little as you like. I'll leave that up to you. But I'd like you to consider one thing. We both know my grandmother can't have many more years left, and she'd like to finish her book before she dies."

Pippa saw the quick flash of pain in Shade's eyes and knew the prospect of losing Lila was very disturbing for him. She couldn't deny that she felt her own sense of sadness at the thought.

"Are you saying I have some kind of control over her health?"

Shade shrugged.

"All I know is my grandmother feels better when you're with her."

"It's probably just her wanting to do her book. You could get someone else to help."

"She doesn't want anyone else. She wants you. Don't you like to finish things you start?"

"Of course I do. If I should come back, and that's a big if, will Vanessa be there?"

"That's always a possibility. You already know she's a family friend. She also coordinates the logistics of making sure the sales from my paintings goes to various charitable organizations I support. Especially to the foundation I set up in my father's name for animal conservation."

Pippa recalled what Vanessa said about his father's love of animals. It made sense for Shade to carry on that work. Vanessa's extensive involvement in Shade's business life surprised her.

"I had no idea she did all that. I guess I owe both of you an apology."

"I don't need your apology, but it would be nice if you'd extend that courtesy to my grandmother. A car will be here the day after tomorrow at eight in the morning. Be at the curb if you change your mind."

He left before she could say anything else. Pippa told herself she'd made the right decision to ask Shade to go. So why did she feel like bawling her eyes out? He mentioned being confused about what to do with her. Now she could certainly relate to that dilemma in reverse.

She sat there until the pizza turned cold and her soda went flat, which pretty much matched how she felt.

"I think you should go," Chloe told Pippa the next day over their morning coffee.

"I've already spent enough time away from you and the store."

"Craig and I can handle it. I know you, Pippa. If you turn down Mrs. Avalon's wish to help her finish the book you'll never forgive yourself. Why would you deny her that small pleasure?"

"I want to help her. I'd just rather not be in such close proximity to her grandson."

"I don't know why not. He's a handsome devil. I certainly wouldn't kick him out of my bed if I was a young woman. I know you've been restless ever since you got back, and once I saw Mr. Avalon I had a pretty good idea he was the reason."

"Is that why you let him into my apartment – which by the way was a sneaky thing to do?"

"I let him in because I believed you two had things to settle. How'd that go by the way?"

"None of your business," Pippa mumbled.

Chloe slapped her knee, and grinned.

"I knew it! He looked like a man on a mission."

"He wasn't on that kind of a mission; and stop trying to embarrass me."

"Sweetie, if you could get a man like that to bed you, you don't have anything to be embarrassed about. You should be doing your happy dance right now."

Pippa was too embarrassed to say Shade turned down her offer to make love to her.

Pippa spent the rest of the day struggling to keep her mind on work while she kept tormenting herself, trying to make the decision whether or not to go back with Shade. Every time she thought about Lila she was swamped with guilt. When she thought about Shade she was filled with a longing so deep it made her body burn as though she suffered with a fever.

Lila won. Pippa knew she had to go back to Wolfhaven, when images of Lila holding her unfinished book with tears running down her cheeks, kept intruding into her thoughts. She packed her single suitcase, and stood outside in front of the store the next morning, when a black limousine purred silently to the curb like a sleek jungle panther.

A man dressed in a black suit got out.

"Ms. Scott?" he said in a gravelly voice.

"Yes. I guess Mr. Avalon sent you."

"Yes, miss." He reached for her suitcase. "May I?"

He took her bag in one hand, and opened the back door with the other.

"Make yourself comfortable. There's coffee in a carafe and assorted rolls. You'll be served a full breakfast on the plane."

"Thank you, Mr., um . . ."

"I'm Tim."

Pippa leaned back against the cushy leather seat. She may as well go along with whatever plans Shade had for her, and enjoy her first time in a limo. Even more exciting would be her first ride in a private jet after that. She could always turn her adventures into a story. God knows she had the imagination to come up with any number of plots.

It didn't take her long to appreciate it was a lot easier to let Tim negotiate the Los Angeles freeways instead of her having to fight the traffic on her own. She noticed people tended to have a lot more respect for a limousine than they did for her puny little car. Just one of the many perks of being wealthy she supposed.

Shade met her at the airport, and led her personally onboard his plane. It took Pippa a moment to accept that she was actually inside a private jet, and not some luxury home. She felt like she should have taken off her shoes before stepping onto the plush carpet.

"Thank you for coming. My grandmother was overjoyed when I called her."

"I'll stay two weeks. Then I need to come home whether the book is finished or not."

"I'm hoping you'll surprise us all by wanting to stay longer, Pippa."

Her pulse started doing the Cha-Cha, as his eyes ran over her.

"I won't change my mind."

"You sound very sure of that."

"I won't keep taking advantage of Chloe. She was in my life before Lila, you know."

Pippa prepared herself to argue with him if necessary, but her breakfast arrived just then.

"I took the liberty of choosing for you."

A young woman brought Eggs Florentine, honeydew melon with raspberries, sourdough toast and coffee. Pippa's eyes widened at the elegant China, silverware, and linen napkin.

"It's like being in a five-star restaurant. The plane is pretty big. Is there a galley onboard?"

"Yes. This area is used as a conference room. There's also a bathroom and a bedroom."

"A home away from home."

"Not quite Wolfhaven, but it serves its purpose on long trips. I hope you enjoy your food."

"Aren't you having anything?"

"I've already eaten."

"Oh. Are you going to be staying in the cockpit, then?"

"Not today. I've work to do."

Shade took out his laptop. He let her eat while he stayed absorbed in his work.

Pippa barely had time to finish her meal when the plane was getting ready to land. She couldn't help thinking what a contrast this was to the hours she'd spent driving to Wolfhaven.

Shade's big SUV stood parked nearby. "Does this airstrip belong to you?"

"Yes."

"It's not every man who has his own mountaintop airport."

"I didn't have it built exclusively for my own use. The area needed something like this for emergencies."

"Is there anything you don't have?"

"Naturally. No one can have everything." He held the car door open for her. "Ready?"

Pippa climbed inside. She watched as his capable hands guided the car along the narrow, winding road. She recalled the last time they'd been in this vehicle and how they had lunch before walking to the meadow. Her heart skipped a beat thinking about Shade's first exciting kiss.

"What are you going to do with the meadow painting?"

"What do you suggest I do with it?"

"I can't imagine why you'd ask my opinion. Vanessa must have also been furious when you told her it wasn't for sale. After all, it's her job to sell as many of your paintings as possible. According to my friend they're in great demand."

"Contrary to what you insist on thinking, making Vanessa happy is not a high priority for me. I don't want to spend your time here constantly talking about her, if you don't mind."

"Fine by me."

They drove the rest of the way in silence. Pippa hadn't realized how much she'd missed his home until they pulled up in front of the house. Despite some of her turbulent times here, she also had many fond memories.

Both Ross and Enid came out to greet her. Pippa had to hide a smile when she remembered how different Enid's behavior had been on her first introduction to Wolfhaven.

"Welcome back, Pippa," Ross said, taking her suitcase.

"Mrs. Avalon is waiting in the morning room," Enid added. "She's been so excited knowing you were on your way that she insisted on sitting by the window to watch for you."

"We'd better go inside before she tries to wheel herself out here," Shade suggested.

Two things brought a lump to Pippa's throat when she saw Lila. First, she was wrapped in the pink shawl Pippa had made for her. Second, she looked as though she had shrunk and was being swallowed up by her chair. Reed thin arms reached out. They embraced.

"I missed you very much, my dear."

"I missed you, too. I'm sorry you've been ill."

"It's vexing when I have so much I want to do and my body continues to sabotage me."

Shade came over and kissed Lila on her cheek.

"I'll leave you two to get reacquainted."

Lila reached for his hand. "Thank you for bringing Pippa back."

"She'll only be here for two weeks, Gram, so you'd better make the most of it."

Pippa felt like an ogress when she saw the disappointed look on Lila's face.

"I thought . . . never mind. She's here now. We'll indeed make the best use of her time."

"Use the house phone if you need me."

Shade held Pippa's gaze until she blushed. She turned to Lila as soon as he was gone.

"Do you have feelings for my grandson, Pippa?"

Did she have a neon signing blinking over her forehead announcing that she wanted to sleep with Shade?

"I think he's a nice man for caring so much about your welfare."

"Ah – an evasion. I've made you uncomfortable. Forgive me. You must ignore an old woman's wish to have two people who are special to her become more than just friends. You're right about Shade. He's very protective toward the people who are important to him."

Shade's look had held more than protection. Pippa was pretty sure she hadn't mistaken the hint of desire in his eyes. Apparently Lila caught the spark, too. Was he regretting not sleeping with her? Maybe he was about to rectify that. Now there was a thought to stir up one's libido.

Lila broke into Pippa's little fantasy.

"We'll do as much as we can on the book while you're here. It'll end when you leave."

"I'm sorry if I'm making you cut it short."

"It'll be the length it was meant to be. I did want you to be here when I added the next animal. I think you'll like it because you were the one to suggest him in the first place."

"Are you going to do one about the wolf?" Pippa asked, unable to hide her excitement.

"Yes, indeed."

Lila's stories about the woodland animals had all been fictional. She would undoubtedly claim this one would be as well. But she may be planning in a very subtle way to use ideas based on the truth. Pippa's mind filled with expectancy at the possibility of finally learning what was going on with the wolves of Wolfhaven.

"I can't wait to get started," she said with enthusiasm shining in her eyes.

"Neither can I. It's been a long time in coming. But first let me catch up on all your news."

They visited until Lila needed to rest before dinner. Pippa could barely contain her impatience at the delay in beginning the story. She decided to take a walk to work off some of her frustration. She knew just where she wanted to go.

She'd often wondered about the gazebo in the garden and the bench inside with the name "Cara" carved into the marble. Once Vanessa revealed that was Shade's mother, it wasn't too difficult to understand he had put up this tribute to the woman who loved flowers enough to create Wolfhaven's lovely gardens.

Pippa didn't know why she felt like going there. Maybe it had something to do with Shade having had a mother long enough to know her love. She was always a little envious of people that had good parents. She sat on the bench and ran her fingers over the smooth surface.

She recalled her first impression that stormy night; and thought how it reminded her of something out of a gothic novel. That wasn't the way she felt about Wolfhaven now. The sudden urge to explore made her leave the confines of the walled garden and go outside the compound.

Knowing how easily she could get lost, she reminded herself to keep the house in view. Pippa set off, lured by the aroma of pine that made her think of Christmas trees. She hadn't walked very far when she thought she heard what sounded like a puppy whimpering.

She listened as the cries became more piteous and hurried toward the sound following the increasingly distressful whines. After searching for several minutes Pippa realized she could no longer hear the little animal even though she had gone quite a ways into the woods now.

Waning sunlight crept among the trees with increasingly slender rays poking through thick foliage scattering patches of pale light on the forest floor. Cooler temperatures were beginning to make her shiver beneath her cotton shirt. It wasn't just from the cold.

Night was fast approaching. Fear crept in twisting like a knife in her belly. She hated the dark. Darkness brought bad memories. She bit her lip and turned in a slow circle studying the area.

She'd gotten herself lost.

And no one knew she had left the house.

TEN

What had seemed so beautiful during the daylight had taken on a whole new look now that the sun was signaling the end of the day. The woods began to emit strange sounds heightening her anxiety. Pippa liked sunsets, but not when she was lost in the middle of a dark forest all by herself. Too much imagination and too many nightmares as a child had convinced her long ago that she was definitely a day person. She wasn't a coward. She just had a thing about the dark.

She started back the way she'd come. Having zigzagged around so many trees and bushes, she wasn't sure if she was on the right track. She searched the area for a familiar landmark. A moss covered log, a broken branch, a couple of her footprints pointing in the right direction, anything to help. Why did the trees have to be so big and take up so much of the sky? Who knew foliage could look so innocent one minute and take on such weird scary forms the next?

Pippa reminded herself how childish it was to be afraid. But when the bushes started looking like hairy trolls with teeth and the trees resembled giants with multiple claws, she knew she was in trouble. It didn't matter that she was a grown woman. Age had not diminished old fears that had started when she had accidently locked herself in a cellar when she was five years old.

She fought down the nerves that rose inside her, making her heart hammer and her lungs labor to draw in each breath. She hoped the puppy was doing better than she was in finding its way to wherever it belonged. Or maybe she'd imagined the little animal. She began to hear subtle noises of emerging nocturnal wildlife. Hopefully any large animals around wouldn't be interested in preying on small dogs or short people. Pippa began to chant the words out loud that she'd made up when she was a little girl to chase away her nighttime fears:

"Nighttime monsters go away. Come back tomorrow and then I'll play."

Full darkness came with its sweeping mantle, cloaking everything with a black shroud so complete Pippa became disoriented. She stood still wringing her hands wondering what to do when a small light appeared in the distance. A flashlight?

"Shade, is that you?" She squinted into the darkness, watching as the waving light moved closer. She called out again. "I'm over here. Can you hear me?"

A tall figure loomed next to her, raised a hand, and hit her on her forehead. She cried out in pain, as stars burst inside her head before she slid into unconsciousness.

Strong arms scooped her off the forest floor and carried her to an ancient mud splattered Jeep, where she was laid gently on the backseat. The driver drove out of the Avalon woods heading for one of the many narrow back roads hidden in another part of the forest.

Pippa lay unmoving, as blood seeped from her wound, staining the torn seat cover.

Shade wheeled his grandmother into the empty salon. He made sure she was comfortable before pouring her the one glass of sherry she was allowed per day. He picked up a crystal decanter and splashed a couple fingers of Scotch into a glass for himself before taking a seat near Lila's chair. She smiled and reached over to pat his hand.

"I'm glad you took my advice and left your tie off. I promised Pippa we wouldn't dress so formally while she was here. I told Enid to leave the clothes in the closet Pippa bought when she was here before, so she'd have something to wear. I want to do everything I can to put her at ease."

"As do I."

"I had no idea she felt so uncomfortable about the way we dressed when she was here until she asked to dine with Ross and Enid. Have you noticed how naïve Pippa seems despite her age?"

"Yes, I have."

"She's so sweet, almost childlike."

Shade heard the wistfulness in her tone, and realized how much she must miss his mother and sister. Pippa had obviously begun to fill some of that emptiness for her, which made him all the more determined to keep Pippa here longer.

"She reminds me of a rose bud waiting to open and bloom. She just needs the right encouragement. You'd think all that shuffling around she went through as a child would have toughened her. I think it made her unsure of herself. I imagine she lives a simple life at home."

He thought of the storeroom that had been converted into her tiny apartment.

"She does."

"I know you saw her when you were there. I hope your meeting wasn't too awkward considering it's been a while since she left us. Were you careful with her?"

"Yes."

She let out an exasperated sigh.

"My dear boy, you shall make me run out of conversation if you continue to be so miserly with your own words."

"I'm sorry, Gram. I didn't mean to be impolite. My visit with her went fine."

"Not impolite, but preoccupied I suspect. I'm going to be a nosy old woman and ask you if everything is all right between you and Pippa. I thought I detected a bit of tension between the two of you this morning. I've been trying to decipher whether that was a good thing or not. Perhaps you weren't being entirely truthful with me when you said your visit with her went well."

He reached over, took her hand in his, and brushed his lips over the paper thin skin that stretched over her knuckles before laying it gently back in her lap.

"You are being nosy."

"Only because I love you. You know I would do anything to make things right. I want you to be happy. When you're not, that makes me unhappy."

"I know, but I'm an adult now. There are some things I have to work out for myself." Shade looked at his watch and frowned. "Pippa should have joined us by now."

"She may have forgotten what time we dine. It might make her feel self-conscious if one of us calls her. Why don't you have Enid do it? That way if Pippa should need any help with a zipper or something, it can be taken care of without causing her too much embarrassment."

"You are a wise woman."

"Not as wise as I'd like to be when it comes to finding out what's going on between you and Pippa. I'm working on becoming sneaky, though," she said, making him laugh as he picked up the house phone.

"Did Enid talk to Pippa?" Shade asked when Ross appeared a few minutes later.

"No, Mister Shade. My wife called her room as you requested, but there was no answer. She went there and knocked on the door without receiving any response. That caused her some alarm, so she took it upon herself to enter Pippa's room without her permission."

"And?" Lila prompted.

"No one was there."

"Perhaps she was in her bathroom."

"My wife thought the same thing. That room was also empty."

"Oh, dear. This doesn't sound very good."

"Have you searched the house?" Shade demanded pushing by Ross to enter the hallway.

"We're in the process of doing that right now. I've told whoever finds Pippa to let you know immediately."

"What about the grounds?"

"I've sent people out there, too."

"Have your wife come and stay with my grandmother. Make sure she doesn't let anyone say anything to upset her further."

"Yes, Mister Shade."

"Are you certain no one has seen Pippa? There are enough people working around here that it seems reasonable someone might have gotten a glimpse of her."

"I've finished questioning the inside staff when I thought I should report to you that she wasn't in her room before I started calling the people who work outside. "

"If Pippa's gone off on a walk she has to be found as quickly as possible now that it's dark. She may have gotten herself lost."

They received information moments later from one of the gardeners. He happened to be raking pine needles away from the compound walls when Pippa disappeared into the nearby woods.

"Damn it," Shade stormed, as he dragged both hands through his hair. "What the hell was she thinking of going off on her own? She knows she can't find her way out of a paper bag."

"Should I call the sheriff's Search and Rescue unit, sir?"

"Yes. While you're doing that I'll take some of our men to begin looking."

Shade stood at one of his bedroom windows watching the sun making its slow descent. The movement matched the sinking sensation of his heart. He didn't need Mother Nature to remind him that Pippa had been missing for over twenty-four hours now. His bristled jaw ached from clenching his teeth. What could have made her go into the woods on her own so late in the day?

Hounds traced her movements to the base of a large oak tree, but her scent ended there. The handler had allowed the dogs to follow another scent that led to a set of vehicle tracks. There was always the possibility that someone had simply been exploring in his woods or even doing a little hunting, despite the fact that it was posted as being private property.

The sheriff had reported poachers in the past. Shade wasn't about to put some old timers in jail for taking a few rabbits or even shooting the occasional deer out of season. He was aware that many of the people in the little mountain community lived on tight budgets. As long as they didn't carry their hunting activities to the extreme, he was willing to let them take their illegally gotten game, and not notify the authorities.

He asked the sheriff to check out anyone that he'd ever suspected of poaching in the area. Shade knew they had to follow any lead they could to try and find out what had happened to Pippa.

He'd just gotten her to come back to his home. He couldn't lose her again.

Not now.

Not ever.

If someone had found her in his woods why hadn't she been brought back here to Wolfhaven? Could it be possible that no one knew she belonged here? Shade's biggest fear was that Pippa had somehow hurt herself and wasn't able to communicate where she belonged. Surely if that was the case, whoever found her would have contacted the sheriff by now.

Two men stood by the single bed where Pippa lay, silent and ghostly white.

"You shouldn't have brought her here, Jerry," a slightly built elderly man admonished.

A larger, younger man shook his head.

"I told you, I had to be sure she didn't see me."

"In the dark? Well, she's going see you now if she ever wakes up."

"No she won't. She's going to see you. I'll be waiting outside, while you find out if she knows about me being on Avalon land."

"Why do I have to be the one to question her?"

"Because you ain't the one who violated his parole."

"None of this would have happened if you hadn't gone back to the Avalons. There are plenty of woods around here. Why'd you go messing around on their land again?"

"You know why. I always get good game there. I don't hear you complaining when you're shoveling down the meat I bring back, Harv."

"Okay, okay. I don't want to argue." He stared at Pippa more closely. "That bump on her head looks pretty bad, and she's been out an awful long time. If she was on their land she probably works at their place, which means they'll be looking for her. We gotta get her out of here."

"What if she wakes up and tells someone I was poaching?"

"I don't think she will by the look of her. If she does, you just say you don't know what she's talking about. I'll tell people you've been with me here in the cabin the last few days. That ought to cover enough time to put you in the clear. It'll be our word against hers."

"I guess your way is best. I can't risk taking her to the Avalons, and I ain't going to just dump her in the middle of the woods with her still being knocked out like this. The poor little thing could end up being a puma's dinner."

"Jeez, I didn't mean for you to do that. Why'd you hit her so hard anyway?"

"I didn't think I did. I was aiming for the back of her head. I kinda misjudged in the dark."

"Sometimes you don't know your own strength."

"I guess not. So what should we do now?"

"I got an idea. I'll go start the Jeep. You bring her out."

"Okay. I'm sorry about this, Harv."

"No harm done as long as someone else takes her on, especially if she ends up dying."

People often accused Marcie Cook of being too softhearted. She didn't mind. She liked to help people who had been cast adrift by their families or society. They came to her in various stages of physical or emotional distress. She did her best to meet their needs with a combination of compassion, a strict code of ethics, and the belief that everyone deserved to have somewhere they could go when life threw them curves they couldn't navigate on their own.

Her two guestrooms were empty at the moment, making Marcie feel a bit lonely.

Although she was still unmarried at forty-one, she hadn't given up hope. Right now she had her eye on Samuel Arnold, the nice looking widowed doctor who had moved here last year.

She met him when she'd cut her finger while slicing tomatoes and had to have a few stitches. The dance and pot luck supper coming up next week at the grange seemed like a good way to get better acquainted. She just had to work up the nerve to invite him. The phone rang.

Much to her delighted surprise it was the man himself calling.

"Thank you, Jesus," she whispered under her breath.

"Ms. Cook, this is Dr. Sam Arnold. I don't know if you remember me, but I . . ."

"Of course I remember you," she cooed. "You did a great job stitching up my finger. It healed beautifully. The scar's barely noticeable."

"I'm pleased to hear it. The reason I'm calling is that I've been told you sometimes let people stay with you that don't have any place else to go when they're released from the hospital."

"That's right." All thoughts of flirting vanished. "Do you have someone that needs me?"

"Yes I do. It's a young woman with a head injury. She's well enough to leave the hospital, but I'd like her to be nearby while she convalesces. May I bring her to your house?"

"Absolutely. I'll take good care of her. May I ask how she ended up at your hospital?"

"Someone dumped her, and left without a word," he replied in a voice tinged with anger.

Pippa sat propped up on lace trimmed pillows in a comfortable double bed. She looked out the window before her gaze switched to the woman standing next to Dr. Samuel Arnold.

"The view is nice."

"I thought you'd like it better here than the hospital."

She smiled at him.

"I do. This room is pretty. I like the wallpaper. Where exactly am I?"

"You're in my home," Marcie said taking over. "My name is Marcie Cook. I'm going to be taking care of you while you stay here. Anything you need, you just let me know."

"I need to know how I got hurt, and how I ended up in the hospital."

Pippa had been missing for a week. Not a day went by that Shade didn't go to her room to remind himself she had actually been in his house. He was there now standing at the windows overlooking the garden when Ross came to the door. He cleared his throat breaking the silence.

Shade turned.

"What is it?"

"I'm sorry to disturb you, but there's a call for you from Mrs. Bert. She says it's urgent."

A mixture of hope that Pippa was safe mingled with fear that something bad had happened to her, stirred in his chest. His face showed none of this in his expression when he nodded to Ross.

"Thank you."

He walked quickly to his office, closed the door, and snatched up the telephone receiver on his desk.

"Mrs. Bert."

"Oh Mr. Avalon, my prayers have been answered. I've just received news about Pippa."

He closed his eyes, and inhaled a deep, shuddering breath.

"Tell me."

"A Dr. Samuel Arnold just called. He works at a hospital in a small town up your way." She told him the name. "Is it near you?"

"Close enough. You said he's a doctor." His body clenched. "Is Pippa all right?"

"She ended up outside his hospital, unconscious with a gash to her forehead. No one knows how she got there. She regained consciousness, but she doesn't know what happened."

"Jesus."

"I told the doctor Pippa disappeared from your home. He'd like to talk to you."

She recited the number while Shade jotted it down. He couldn't help wondering why Pippa didn't have the doctor call him, since he was so much closer to the hospital than Chloe.

"Thank you. I'll get back to you as soon as I can."

He made his call to receive directions to Marcie's. Sam and Marcie came out to meet him, as he pulled up in front of her house. Shade barely took the time for introductions and quickly exchanged handshakes, before heading for the front door in his anxiousness to see Pippa.

"Mr. Avalon, wait!" Sam called out. "I need to tell you something before you go in there."

"Later," he yelled back and dashed into the living room where Pippa sat on the sofa.

She glared at him as soon as she saw him.

"I'm not going back with you. Get away from me and stay away!"

Sam and Marcie rushed into the room. Shade stared at them, his face a study in confusion.

"That's what I wanted to tell you," Sam said.

Eleven

Shade wasn't prepared for this devastating disappointment after worrying about Pippa's safety the last several days. He expected to be embracing her right now, not facing a hostile glare.

"What the hell is going on here?"

Sam took a chair, while Marcie left to make coffee.

"Please sit down, Mr. Avalon."

Shade lowered himself onto the sofa next to Pippa, who instantly got up to take another chair. The action made him suck in a deep breath, and look angrily at Sam.

"What have you been saying to her? Is this some kind of a bad joke?"

"No one's joking here. She really is holding you responsible for her situation."

Shade looked at Pippa, who folded her arms over her chest, and continued to scowl at him.

"Why, for heaven's sake?"

"She's been through a traumatic experience. It happened at your home. She blames you."

"That's absurd."

"But true. It may help her if you could explain what you know about her disappearance."

He turned to Pippa again. The guardedness in her expression felt like a stab to his heart.

"You apparently decided to take a walk without telling anyone. A gardener saw you go into the woods just before dark. We went looking for you, but you were gone."

"Gone, how?"

107

"I don't know."

"How did I get hurt?"

"I don't know that, either. I can only assume you must have fallen and hit your head."

"Wrong. Someone hit me. I bet you know who did it," she said giving him an accusing look.

"Pippa, stop this. I do not know anything of the sort."

"Well, someone clobbered me, and I have the scar to prove it." She snapped her fingers. "I bet it was the guy who made me go back to the house the day I tried to take a walk."

Shade's forehead furrowed into a frown.

"When was this?"

"When I was at your house before. I saw this path going into the woods. It looked well used, so I thought it'd be okay. A man came and stopped me."

"What man?"

Pippa puffed out an exasperated breath.

"I didn't ask his name. He insisted I go back to the house, so I'm sure he works for you. He said it was too dangerous because of wild animals. If that's the case, what was he doing out there, I'd like to know?"

"I'm sure he was trying to protect you. Why else would he make you turn back?"

"Don't pretend you don't know. You can't let anyone else find out about your secret."

Shade's eyes flickered toward Sam. He shrugged, as if to communicate that he had no idea what Pippa was talking about.

Marcie returned.

They sat drinking their coffee in silence until Shade asked if Pippa would be willing to return to Wolfhaven with him.

"You must be kidding. Why would I want to go back there after what happened to me?"

"For my grandmother's sake. She's the reason you came back, if you'll remember."

She caught her bottom lip between her teeth.

"I don't know if I should. Someone doesn't want me there. I'm convinced it has to be someone who works for you."

She touched her head.

"How do I know they won't try to bean me again – or worse?"

"You have my word you'll be safe. All I ask is that you let someone accompany you if you decide to go for another walk. Please! Do this for my grandmother. It'd mean so much to her."

Pippa agreed to return to Wolfhaven when Marcie offered to go with her. Shade called Ross to alert the household about Pippa's fear, and how they must be prepared that she might be suspicious of them.

She sat in the back with Marcie, staring nervously out the window as Shade pulled up in front of the house. He got out, and opened the car door for them.

"Welcome to my home – again."

"This isn't a house, it's a town."

He smiled. At least she hadn't lost her sense of humor.

Pippa merely nodded when the Hendersons ran out to greet her.

"Come inside. My grandmother is waiting."

Shade nodded to include Marcie, who still stood gawking at the mansion. Ross and Enid followed in somber silence, obviously disappointed at Pippa's coolness toward them.

Shade led them to the salon where Lila waited. Pippa was polite, but not her usual friendly self in response to Lila's warm greeting. Shade guided them next to the bedroom.

"This will be your room again tonight. We'll put Ms. Cook across the hall."

Pippa sucked in a breath.

"Across the hall? Can't we share? I . . . I don't want to be alone."

Marcie put her arm around Pippa's waist.

"She's frightened of the dark. I think it'd be best if I stayed with her. Would it be possible to put a cot in here for me?"

"Of course."

The drive tired Pippa. The two women ate in their room. They went to bed with both the bedside lamps on, but she still cried out in her sleep.

Plans were made in the morning to fly Pippa and Marcie to Los Angeles where Chloe awaited. She hoped, like everyone else, that being Pippa's old friend, she would be able to comfort her; but most of all, she needed to convince Pippa to relax while at Wolfhaven, and not to hold its occupants responsible for her injury and disappearance.

The trip proved to be an exercise in futility, when Pippa refused to change her mind.

"I may as well stay, as long as I'm here. I'm sure Shade will see you safely home, Marcie."

But when Marcie called Sam, he recommended Pippa return with Shade to his home to give him and the Avalon household a chance to regain her trust.

"It'd be better coming from you."

She handed Pippa the phone.

"Sam wants to tell you something."

Pippa listened.

"I don't see how that will work as long as my mind's convinced Shade knows what happened to me."

"Hopefully being around him will prove you wrong. You may even discover the real culprit. It's worth a try.

Think of it as getting back on a horse after you've taken a spill."

She looked doubtful, but agreed, knowing she needed to do this for herself as well as Shade.

She stood with Shade in her old room looking down at the garden.

"So much beauty."

"My mother loved flowers."

"It shows. She left you all a wonderful legacy. I'm so sorry you lost her. At least you had a mother for a few years. I envy that, being an orphan. But I'm very thankful to have Chloe."

"You also have me," he reminded her in a quiet tone.

"We'll have to see how that goes."

She looked around the room.

"I don't want to be more difficult than I already am, but I know even with the lights, on I won't be able to stay in here."

"Choose another room. I'll have it prepared for you."

"It isn't the room." Pippa's fists clenched at her sides. "I'm afraid of being alone."

"I can have one of the young girls that come in to clean, share a room with you."

"It'd be a stranger I'd have to get used to. It sounds contradictory after all the things I've said about not trusting you, but would it be okay if I slept with you? Your bed is big enough to land an airplane on. We wouldn't have to touch. Just knowing you were close would help me a lot."

Shade almost groaned aloud at the thought.

"I don't think that's a very good idea."

"Please! I . . . I see things in every shadow, whether something is there or not." Tears began to sparkle in her eyes. "Sam and Marcie said you would take care of me. That's why I agreed to come back here. Maybe you don't want to help me because I'm right about you knowing what happened to me here that night."

"I'll have your things moved into my quarters right away; because I do want to help you."

Shade lay, mindful of Pippa's earlier claim that they wouldn't have to touch. They'd started out on opposite sides of his large bed. Sad to say, her good intentions didn't last for long. He'd ended up instinctively pulling her into his arms in an effort to comfort her when she woke up sobbing about monsters attacking her.

She fell asleep again nestled up against him while he laid there stiff as a board, especially in a certain part of his anatomy. Shade didn't know how long he'd be able to continue with this sleeping arrangement before he went crazy. He felt like a starving man surrounded by food, unable to partake of the nourishment within his reach.

He knew he must keep his hands to himself, while Pippa struggled to regain her trust in him.

Not an easy task with her sweet body pressed so close it felt like torture. She moved innocently nudging a silky thigh near that vulnerable body part making Shade break out in a sweat.

He had a feeling it was going to be a very long night.

Shade had taken so many cold showers, it was a wonder he hadn't turned into an icicle by the end of Pippa's second week sleeping with him. He called Sam with his daily report.

"Good morning. What's up today?" Sam asked in a cheery voice.

"I am, as usual. I never expected her to ask to sleep with me; not when she acted like she hated my guts."

Sam chuckled.

"Still status quo with the sleeping arrangements, I take it."

"Yes. She also follows me around during the day."

"Pippa is probably trying to test her feelings toward you. That should make you feel good."

"It might if my staff would quit looking at me like I'm some kind of pervert taking advantage of her. How much longer do you think this is going to go on, Sam?"

"I wish I could tell you. I talked to Mrs. Bert. She said Pippa has been afraid of the dark since childhood. You have to also remember she has some real fear issues with your house and the woods there now. Did you try my suggestion that you sleep in separate beds in the same room?"

"Yes. She couldn't even make it for an hour before she was crawling in bed with me trembling in terror. Every time I even hint that she might try it again those big green eyes of hers fill with tears, and she looks at me in panic. It kills me to see her like that."

"I can imagine. As I've just said, this fear of being alone might subconsciously be connected to her being lost and alone in the forest the night she wandered off. She may be thinking if she's alone, especially at night, she'll somehow become lost again."

Shade snorted.

"Inside a house filled with people? That doesn't make sense."

"Not much about you and Wolfhaven is making sense in Pippa's mind right now."

"You're right, but Jesus, I'm not made of stone. Do you have any idea what it's been like sleeping in the same bed with her and not being able to do anything about it?"

"You have my sympathy. Is Pippa getting friendlier toward the rest of the household?"

"Better, I think. My grandmother says she's warming up to her a little more every day. The story writing has helped them."

"Good. Hopefully given enough time more things will change in your favor."

"Sam, I'm going to ask you something, and I don't want you to think that I'm being as disgusting as everyone else around here seems to believe I am."

"Okay, shoot."

"What would happen if I stopped acting like some teddy bear Pippa can hug to sleep at night, and try something a little more intimate?"

"That depends. How intimate are we talking here?"

"A little stroking. Maybe a peck on the cheek. If that goes okay, a light kiss on the lips."

"Let me ask you something before I answer. Have you and Pippa ever made love?"

Shade paused a moment.

"No, but she wanted to just before her return to Wolfhaven."

"What happened?"

"I turned her down."

"You obviously want her now."

"I wanted her then, too. She said she'd only had one encounter with a man before. Apparently it didn't go well, and she's still a virgin. It didn't seem right to take advantage of her innocence."

"That was pretty chivalrous of you."

"I don't know about that. In any event, she ended up deciding we shouldn't have any kind of a relationship because I'm rich and she's poor."

"So you gave up completely on the idea of sleeping with her?"

"If you must know, I was rather hoping we'd get our sleeping arrangement worked out to where we'd both feel comfortable. She wasn't here long enough for me to get to that point."

"The fact that she's following you around may mean she still feels an attachment to you, but just hasn't connected the dots yet. Try some light petting and see what happens. She could end up enjoying it enough to want to have sex with you."

"It'll be more than sex."

"I certainly hope so for her sake, if she's a virgin as you say. Don't push her. Good luck, and if you can carry this off without blowing a fuse, you're a better man than I am."

Shade climbed into bed. Pippa already lay curled up on her side. They smiled at each other. The one thing he had to be thankful for was that she always wore flannel pajamas and not some short transparent nightgown.

Of course, the way he felt right now she'd look sexy in a flour sack. As for himself, since he usually slept in the nude he'd had to dig out a T-shirt and a pair of sweatpants from his dresser.

He cleared his throat.

"Comfortable?"

He couldn't believe how nervous he felt. Sweat dewed his body like a virginal teenager getting ready to test his virility by diving into a forbidden sexual pool.

"Yes, thank you. Are you?"

"Well, now that's a good question."

"What do you mean?"

Pippa sat up.

"Are you ill? Should I call Mr. Henderson?"

"Lie down. Please. I didn't mean to imply that I'm not feeling well. In fact, I'm feeling pretty much like any normal male would, who found himself in bed with a beautiful, desirable woman."

Shade watched her cheeks turn a lovely pink, as she settled back against her pillow.

"I'm not beautiful."

"Yes you are, and you forgot the desirable part."

She began to pleat the top sheet between her fingers.

"I'm aware that my sleeping with you hasn't been easy for you. You cannot know what your patience has meant to me. Every morning when I wake up I promise myself I won't put you through this again. Then night comes, and all I can think about is being in your bed with you. You make me feel safe, Shade."

"Is that all I make you feel, Pippa?" he asked softly.

She looked down at her hands, and let the bedding slip away.

"No."

"What do you feel when you're lying next to me? Are you sexually attracted to me?"

"What woman wouldn't be? You're very handsome, and your body is magnificent. I enjoy falling asleep in your arms. I have no doubt you'd make a wonderful lover."

"You must have thought so when you asked me to make love to you in your apartment."

"I did. I think I still do. I'm just not sure."

"Will you let me kiss you, then? Just a kiss," he said when he saw her bite her lip. "If that's all you want, then that's all we'll do. You said I was beginning to make you feel safe."

She leaned her head to one side and studied him for a few seconds.

"Just a kiss?"

He nodded.

"Okay."

Twelve

Shade slid his arms around Pippa. He brushed his lips across her mouth. That little taste made him want to take so much more. She shuddered against him, and for one heart stopping moment he thought she'd been repelled by his touch, until she leaned forward to kiss him back.

He continued to toy with her lips nibbling at their softness, encouraged by the low whimpering sounds she made. Using more restraint than he thought he would be capable of, considering all his blood had rushed to his groin area, he deepened the kiss.

Pippa clutched his shoulders. He rubbed her back before slowly easing his hands beneath her top to caress the velvety flesh beneath. He skimmed the pads of his fingertips along her spine lingering just inside the waistband of the pajama bottoms. Her mouth, sweet and delectable lured him closer promising more, when she startled him by suddenly pushing herself away.

"Pippa?"

"I can't."

Shade silently cursed himself for rushing her.

"I'm sorry, Shade. I don't want to be a tease. It's just that I'm nervous about you. About things here that I don't understand. Things that no one will tell me."

He rolled onto his back.

"You know everything you need to know."

She shook her head.

"You know very well I don't. You want everything from me. Is it too much that I should expect the same courtesy from you?"

117

"We're in a bed, not a confessional."

"Why won't you . . ."

He moved to his side of the bed turning his back to her.

"Go to sleep, Pippa."

A sound woke Pippa in the middle of the night. She jerked into a sitting position, surprised that she'd managed to fall asleep after her frustrating conversation with Shade. She sat there gradually becoming alert to the distinctive howl. She looked for Shade, already suspecting he would be gone. How could she think otherwise when he was so much a part of the mystery surrounding Wolfhaven's wolf?

The howl came again, making her skin prickle with nerves. Shade must be thoroughly sick of her being such a big baby, cowering at every odd shadow or strange sound. Pippa knew many important demands filled his time. Yet he'd spent hours trying to help her conquer her fears about him and his home, including letting her share his bed.

He'd done everything he could, except tell her the truth.

She scooted over to his side of the bed burying her face in his pillow breathing in his scent that lingered there. She closed her eyes only to have them snap open when she heard the wolf's howling again, closer to the house now. The animal sounded so lonesome and forlorn she ached inside, because it reminded her so much of the lonely times in her own life.

She forced herself not to look out the window knowing the sight of her wolf would only make her feel sadder. Pippa thought of her little room above Chloe's bookstore. What a pathetic testimony to the way she lived. Tears slid unbidden down her cheeks. She ended up crying herself to sleep, just like the baby she'd compared herself to earlier.

Pippa sat with Shade and his grandmother at the breakfast table the next morning. She plucked a slice of toast from a basket, and began to scoop up marmalade from a little china dish.

Always trying to get them to slip up and tell her about the wolf, she decided to test their reactions. She may be putting herself in danger trying to find out more, but she had to know. She just had to.

"Did the wolf howling bother either of you last night?"

Shade set his coffee cup carefully back on its saucer.

Lila shot him a quick glance.

"Pippa, not the wolf issue again. I thought we were done talking about that."

"You are. I can't say the same about myself. How can I when the howling keeps waking me up? I wondered if it bothered you because you weren't in bed. Or maybe you're just used to it."

"I didn't hear anything myself. The wind sometimes makes a moaning sound when it blows through the trees," Lila said before concentrating on the soft boiled egg in front of her.

"I know the difference between the moaning wind and a howling wolf."

"Perhaps you were having another nightmare," Shade suggested.

"I wasn't having a nightmare because I wasn't asleep. The reason I know I was awake is because you were gone, like I said."

"I thought you'd appreciate some time on your own after our . . ."

Lila cleared her throat.

"Shade, must you discuss such things in front of me?"

"Forgive me."

"It's okay, Mrs. Avalon, we just exchanged a few kisses."

Now it was Shade's turn to clear his throat.

"Would you mind changing the subject?"

"Sure. I want to tell you something else, and don't laugh."

Now she'd drop her bombshell to see if any chinks would appear in Shade's armor.

"When I saw you lying in bed this morning with your dark hair and the black stubble of beard on your face, I began to think you're like the wolf – a big, strong male animal with dark fur."

Lila choked on her tea. Shade reached over to gently rub her on the back.

"You're comparing me to a wolf? It sounds like the stories you and Gram are working on have definitely stirred up your imagination. This book ought to be very interesting reading."

Pippa couldn't help admiring how Shade kept his cool after her startling comment.

"Hmm, especially if we could write about wolves. They're very intelligent, you know."

"Then I suppose I should be flattered to be compared to one."

He stood.

"If you ladies will excuse me, I have some phone calls to make."

"Shade?" Lila asked, as her eyes darted toward Pippa and back to him.

He patted her hand.

"Don't worry, Gram. Everything will be fine."

Ross appeared later that morning to tell Pippa she had a phone call from Chloe. She excused herself and went across the room to pick up the receiver there.

"Hi."

"How are things going? Any closer to forgiving Mr. Avalon?"

"It's still a work in progress."

"Oh, well that's something I guess. I hope I'm not interrupting anything important."

"I'm working, actually. Was there something you needed?"

"I need you to come see me. I've missed you and as it happens, Mr. Avalon has business in Los Angeles today. He offered to have you fly down to spend the day with me."

"Really? He never said anything to me."

"No, but he's saying it now," Shade announced from the doorway before coming fully into the room. "It'll be good for you to get away for awhile. You've been cooped up here too much. A little time away won't hurt."

"He's right," Lila quickly agreed. "You should go."

It seemed to Pippa, Lila sounded a little too anxious to have her leave.

"I thought you wanted me to help finish your stories."

"You'll be back."

Would she? Pippa wondered. Maybe her latest grilling about the wolf made them a little too uncomfortable this time. She could have earned herself a one-way ticket out of here for good.

She turned back to the phone.

"Looks like I'm being ganged up on. I'm all yours, Chloe."

Shade left his plane and got settled into one limousine for his meeting, while Pippa rode in another limo to Chloe's.

The chauffer smiled at Pippa. "I don't know if you remember me. My name is Tim. I had the pleasure of driving you once before while you were in Los Angeles."

"I do remember you. How are you, Tim?"

"Very well, thank you."

Chloe rushed out to meet them when they pulled up in front of her house.

Tim opened the door for her.

She climbed in back and gave Pippa a kiss on the cheek.

"This limo sure is snazzy, isn't it? I could get used to this mode of transportation." She opened her purse and pulled out a piece of paper. "Now then. Let's go over the list before we start."

Pippa raised her brows.

"What list?"

"These are the things Mr. Avalon faxed to me. He wants you to be outfitted from head to toe."

"You've got to be kidding."

"He also wants you to have a manicure, a pedicure, and get your hair done. He loves your hair, by the way, but says you need to have it trimmed. I'm supposed to warn the stylist if he cuts off too much Mr. Avalon will personally shave him bald."

She laughed.

"I bet he would, too."

Pippa stared at the length of the list.

"Heavens, is there anything he didn't put on there?"

"Yes, he explicitly said we were not to buy you any sexy nightgowns."

Chloe's list included which stores to patronize. Each one so exclusive they actually made Pippa feel ill at ease. But no one gave a hint if the salespeople thought she wasn't their usual type of client. She had a feeling Shade must have called to tell them to expect her. They fawned over her as though she might actually be a famous celebrity.

Or a wealthy man's mistress. The very idea of that made her feel ill at ease.

By the time they'd finished their shopping, the limo's trunk was filled with bags and boxes, each with the individual store's fancy logo. Shade left instructions on what he wanted her to have right down to her silk lingerie. She would have protested his high-handedness if he didn't have such good taste.

He even chose where she and Chloe would have their dinner. The restaurant looked so exclusive Pippa had a feeling she wouldn't be able to afford a crouton. But she needn't have worried because Shade made arrangements to pay for their food like everything else.

"Thank you so much for going with me today, Chloe. I couldn't have done it without you."

"My pleasure. What an adventure for me. I've always wanted to go into some of those boutiques. You certainly have a lot of beautiful clothes now."

"I have no idea where I'll be wearing most of them. I can't understand why Shade wanted to buy me so much. Living here or in a house in the middle of a forest doesn't exactly lend itself to the kind of clothes he picked out. It doesn't make sense."

"It does if you think about the kind of life he lives away from his house."

"What does that have to do with me?"

"Maybe since you don't want to go back to your old life with him, he wants to create a new one for the two of you."

Tim dropped Chloe at home before taking Pippa to the airport. Shade waited for her on his plane. They took off once all her packages were loaded, and they were settled in their seats.

"Did you enjoy yourself? I like your new hairstyle, by the way."

"Thank you. You spent too much money on me, though," she said, touching her hair.

"I'll be the judge of that."

Pippa decided to test Chloe's theory. "I don't need all those clothes unless you're expecting me to wear one of those fancy gowns while your grandmother dictates her stories to me."

"Wolfhaven isn't the only place in the world. I intend to see that you have the opportunity to experience what's waiting for you beyond its borders."

"What kind of experiences are you talking about?"

"We'll take them as they come. I thought we'd start with a charity dinner I'm expected to attend tomorrow evening in San Francisco. I've already booked a suite at a hotel I like to use."

"So I won't be going back to your house, then?"

"You will, but not right away."

"I'd rather not go to this charity thing. I have a feeling I'll feel out of place."

"It's just dinner, Pippa, not a coronation. You may find it interesting to meet new people."

"I can't see how being introduced to a bunch of strangers is going to excite me."

"How do you know until you try? Where's your sense of adventure?"

"I guess I lost it, along with my way in your forest one dark night."

Thirteen

Pippa looked stunning in her short black dress with spaghetti straps that showed off her creamy shoulders to perfection. The diamond pendant Shade clasped around her neck flashed in the hollow at her throat. Her hair flamed as red as molten lava while her eyes sparkled like emerald gems beneath the glow of the overhead lighting.

Shaky legs made her cling to Shade's steadying arm. No matter where she looked eyes scanned her from head to toe making her feel like a sideshow freak put on display for their entertainment. Her heart hammered, beating against her ribs, as her stomach clenched with nerves.

Shade turned out to be the main benefactor of this charity. Too bad he hadn't told her ahead of time to prepare her for people coming up to him all evening. He introduced her to each of them. They treated her with the same artificial politeness as the salespeople in the boutiques, making her wonder what they really thought about her behind their reserved expressions.

Dinner turned out to be another ordeal. Pippa couldn't understand why these people found it necessary to have so many different pieces of silverware and myriad of dishes for one meal. She thought they did a lot at Wolfhaven. The table setting here boggled her mind. If it hadn't been for Shade's subtle gesturing she wouldn't have known what utensil went with what course.

Shade couldn't be in a hurry to leave as the guest of honor. Pippa only hoped it wouldn't be much longer, as the endless dinner finally finished. She supposed this part of the evening would be considered networking, since practically every person who greeted him wanted to talk about some kind of business or charity. No matter what the reason, money ended up being the main topic.

Several more minutes ticked by. Pippa knew she had to get out of her shoes if only for awhile. Her feet throbbed in the unfamiliar high heeled silver sandals that matched the dainty silver clutch purse. She didn't care how pretty they looked or how much the shoes cost. A pair of comfortable sneakers sounded like heaven right now.

She whispered to Shade she needed to go to the ladies lounge. He gave her a vague nod before continuing his conversation with two men. The walk to the lounge made her feet ache even more. Pippa sank down onto one of the cushy upholstered benches as soon as she reached the room. She slipped the tortuous shoes off to rub her poor abused arches

She sat enjoying the solitude for a few minutes until the sound of voices made her grab her shoes and dash into a stall seconds before two women entered the lounge. Pippa ignored their conversation until one of the women said Shade's name. She listened, senses on full alert.

"Who's the little redhead with Shade? Why is he here with her instead of you?"

"Ugh! Don't even get me started on that con artist."

Pippa's hand tightened on her shoes at the blatant insult delivered in its venomous tone.

She knew that voice.

"Con artist? Are you saying she's scamming Shade? I can't see anyone getting beneath his radar, especially a woman. So what's the deal? Come on Vanessa, give with the juicy details."

"Her name is Pippa Scott."

"Pippa? Well, there's a name you don't hear every day. But then the Avalons are used to that kind of thing. So what's her connection to them?"

"Shade hired her to help Lila write silly stories. I got rid of her, but the conniving twit wormed another invitation back to Wolfhaven. Supposedly someone hit her on the head while she was walking near the house. She's blaming Shade, so she says he has to win back her trust."

"Surely he doesn't believe such a preposterous story."

"Of course not. Why would he care whether or not she trusted him? She's just a hireling."

"Maybe she threatened to sue him?"

"I doubt it. She can't prove anything. I'm convinced he's finding it amusing to see how far she intends to go with this act of hers."

"In the meantime, he's obviously spending money on her if that pendant or her outfit is anything to go by. Do you think he's sleeping with her?"

Vanessa sniffed in disgust.

"Oh, please. He'd never stoop so low."

"How long do you suppose he plans on keeping up with the charade?"

"I don't know, but I'm getting fed up with the whole farce. He's so busy playing nursemaid to her, we've barely had any time alone."

"Well, I think it's appalling he's with that charlatan. People are wondering if you two are split up. Having her here hanging all over him is fueling the rumor."

"I can see that, which makes me furious that he's put me in such an awkward position. He's also embarrassing himself by bringing that little nobody here tonight."

"Everyone thinks she's sleeping with him. You know, for services rendered."

Pippa swallowed the protesting gasp that rose to her lips.

The lipstick tube in Vanessa's hand clattered to the counter.

"How revolting."

"But true. It's time you set Shade straight. You'd be doing him a favor."

"I know."

Pippa stayed inside the stall long after their voices faded away. The fact that Shade might only be amusing himself at her expense made bitter bile rise in her throat. He didn't care about her feelings. The only reason he wanted her to come back to Wolfhaven was for Lila's sake. He probably decided as long as she was there he may as well make a game out of her presence.

And she'd made it so easy for him. They shared a bed thanks to her cowardice. No wonder he was being so nice to her. He wanted to have sex with her. She had wanted that, too, at one time – but not now. She supposed she should be flattered that he'd bought her all those expensive clothes and the jewelry first.

Well, the charade, as the woman had called it was about to come to an end. Pippa refused to spend another minute at Wolfhaven just so Shade could use her as a play thing. She slipped into her dreaded shoes, wobbled out of the lounge, and marched up to him. She didn't care if the elderly couple talking thought she was rude. She didn't care what any of these people thought about her.

"I want to leave."

Shade's brows rose at her sharp tone.

"We will when I'm finished here."

"No. You will go now," she said through clenched teeth. "Or I'm calling a taxi."

Shade's nostrils flared at her mutinous expression before he excused himself from the man and woman. Taking Pippa by the elbow, he steered her out of the room toward the bank of elevators. His grip tightened when she tried to jerk her arm away as soon as they were inside.

"Do not ever use that tone of voice to me again in front of people."

"I'll use whatever tone I darn well feel like. Dragging me to this shindig was your idea. I don't know what you hoped to accomplish. But I'm sure all those snobs are having a field day talking about the little nobody hanging on the great Shade Avalon. Oh, and let's not forget the way you made sure I was decked out tonight, jewels and all, so they'd be sure to speculate that I'm trading sex for everything."

Pippa tugged at her arm again. Shade released her when the elevator arrived. She moved to stand as far away from him that the limited space would allow.

"I bought you the outfit you're wearing because it was appropriate attire for tonight."

"Or you didn't want to be embarrassed if I chose my own clothes."

He shook his head.

"It wouldn't matter to me what you wore, but I knew you were worried about fitting in this evening. I hoped to make you feel more comfortable."

"What about all the other stuff you had Chloe help me buy? Why did you do that?"

"Because you seemed upset after Vanessa's disparaging remarks about your clothes."

"And this?" she asked lifting the diamond away from her throat. "What's your excuse for this extravagance?"

"Does someone need an excuse to buy a gift from one friend to another?"

She softened for a moment, knowing she was being rude after he'd given her so many lovely things. "I appreciate that, but a simple piece of costume jewelry would have been enough."

"I don't think this is about your wardrobe. What's really wrong?"

"Nothing!" she snapped, temper taking over again.

"When a woman says 'nothing' in that tone of voice it usually means the opposite."

"You would know considering you're so experienced when it comes to women."

"I'm not a mind reader, whether it involves a woman or not. I have no idea what brought on this change in your mood. Are you feeling ill?"

"I'm fine!"

"Fine? That's another misnomer if ever I heard one."

He didn't question her again until they entered their suite of rooms where she immediately kicked off her shoes. Shade leaned against the door and folded his arms across his chest.

"What's bothering you? Tell me, Pippa."

"I don't have anything to say to you except I'm going to bed and I don't want you sharing it with me. If you don't take the sofa, I will."

She would have walked away, but he grabbed her by the arm and spun her around. She saw he fought anger, barely held in check beneath the surface.

"Well that's a switch since I couldn't kick you out of my bed back home. You're not going anywhere until you tell me what the hell is wrong, and don't try to pull that PMS excuse on me that your gender is so fond of doing."

"See, you do know about females." She pulled her arm free.

"Pippa," he warned. "We're having this out if we have to stand here all night."

She suddenly felt weary. And hurt – and too wounded to want to continue arguing with him. She'd started this storm, and she'd have to ride it out. Anger would be the only way she'd get through it without dissolving into a puddle of tears. She did not want to cry, especially in front of Shade. She didn't want to give him that power over her.

"Did you know that Vanessa would be there tonight?"

"Of course. She's the one in charge of arranging these events. When did you see her?"

130

"I'm asking the questions here. Why did you take me with you tonight instead of her?"

"Because I'd rather be with you. I've told you before Vanessa and I are friends, not lovers."

She snorted.

"Yeah, right. That's not the way I heard it."

"Then why don't you explain what you heard because obviously something happened when you went to the ladies lounge."

"Is she your mistress?" Pippa demanded.

"I believe a man has to be married in order have the term mistress applied to any female he's supposed to be having an affair with, which in my case neither applies. How many times must I keep telling you that Vanessa is a longtime family friend? She manages my art exhibitions and takes care of the logistics regarding the charity organizations I sponsor. Period."

Pippa slapped her hands on her hips.

"Do you think I've been faking my blaming you for what happened to me?"

"No, I do not."

"That's not the impression some people have."

"The problem with impressions is that they aren't always correct. Why would you think I don't believe you? Did someone say something to you tonight to make you doubt my sincerity? You mentioned Vanessa. Did you talk to her?"

"As if she would lower herself. You know how she feels about me. I heard her talking to another woman. Vanessa said you were only amusing yourself with me. They both agreed that I was an embarrassment, and your friends think I'm sleeping with you for money. Do you have any idea how humiliating it is to know they think I'm a . . . a whore?"

Shade's nostrils flared.

"Anyone who is truly my friend would not be thinking that."

"Well, I'm not being a very good friend to you. I should never have gone back to Wolfhaven. I wish to God I'd never taken that walk in the woods. Nothing's been the same since."

"Then forget about the night in the forest and concentrate on the future. It's easier to plant an acorn than cut down an oak tree."

"My acorn would be a tree with weak branches. I'm sure you thought you were doing the right thing in taking me with you tonight, but I didn't fit in there. I felt out of place. I told you I would. I don't belong with you and your blue blood friends. And I don't belong at Wolfhaven. I can't be what you want, Shade. Let me go back to where I really belong. Let me go to Chloe."

Was she imagining the emotions working through him? What did she see that he was obviously trying so hard to control? Anger? Worry? Regret?

"You may feel differently in the morning."

"I doubt it. I tried your way and I'm tired of trying to be someone I'm not. I want to go back to the bookstore and be around people I know. I'm not asking you to let me go because I want to deliberately hurt you. You've been pretty decent to me considering the bad time I've given you. I'm going to call Chloe and ask her to pick me up in the morning. Please don't try to stop me."

A muscle twitched in his cheek.

"Why wait until morning? I'll take you to her tonight."

Chloe handed Pippa a mug of coffee. "No good usually comes of gossip. What you heard in that restroom last night was nothing more than a couple of catty women so bored with their lives they have to invent ways to entertain themselves."

"Most gossip is based on some truth. I heard enough to make me know I did the right thing by letting Shade go back without me. I didn't even know what fork to use at the dinner, Chloe. If I'm not an embarrassment to him now, I'm sure I would be eventually if I let him continue to take me out in public with him."

"Good lord, girl, you make it sound as though you have a communicable disease."

"My malady is being born poor. I'll never fit in with someone like Shade Avalon."

"I'd say that's for him to decide. This isn't the first time he's shown you what he thinks about your opinion of yourself. You said the same thing to him before and he still wanted to be with you enough to take you back to Wolfhaven. He wanted to prove to you he didn't care that you weren't born with the proverbial silver spoon in your mouth. That's why you were at his home when you got lost in the woods."

"He really just wanted me there to help his grandmother write her stories."

"That, too. He wasn't the only one who wanted you back. Mrs. Avalon is very fond of you."

"I know." Pippa set her cup down. "God, I don't know what to do."

"Why don't you try adhering to the old saying, 'Go with the flow'?"

"Because sometimes going with the flow leads you in the wrong direction."

Pippa enjoyed working in the bookstore and being on familiar turf again. Unfortunately the scare in the woods still had her afraid to stay alone at night. Chloe solved the problem by taking her home with her after closing the store at the end of each day.

She knew Shade called Chloe every day to check on her. His thoughtfulness touched her enough to make her think about going back to Wolfhaven. She supposed it was a good sign that she might be getting closer to being comfortable around him again. But not quite yet.

Indecision made her feel so restless one afternoon that Chloe suggested she take the afternoon off and go to a park for a couple of hours. After packing a sack lunch, Pippa rolled her car windows down, and set off with the wind blowing in her face and a smile on her lips.

The little park with patches of green grass and some well established trees had a couple of picnic tables, and a few benches near a tiny play area for children. Both of the tables were occupied with families. Pippa sat on a bench intending to eat her lunch, but ended up giving it to a homeless man digging through a nearby trashcan.

The weather turned warm, bathing her face with sunlight. Pippa closed her eyes letting her thoughts stray to the future. She knew Shade well enough to realize he wasn't going to allow her to stay away much longer without coming to some kind of decision about their relationship.

She couldn't understand why he kept troubling himself for her. She wasn't a great beauty, and other than being able to write a little, she didn't have any real talent. What about her questionable background? Being an orphan without a clue to her birth parentage left a big void.

She could be carrying the genes of some messed up people. The thought made her shudder. She didn't want to be like them, cold and uncaring. She wanted to love and be loved. Maybe her birth father hadn't even known about her, but her mother did. And she hadn't wanted her.

Sometimes when she'd see a woman with her coloring and body shape, Pippa wondered if she was the one who'd carried her all those months in her womb, only to end up leaving her in a dumpster to die. How could anyone do that to a defenseless little baby?

The painful reality made her want to think about something else. She switched her thoughts to Shade. She knew it wasn't possible for him to be part wolf, but she knew wolves roamed around his home. It continued to bug her that he and everyone else at Wolfhaven lied about that.

She sat there listening to children laugh as they played on the swings, watched a couple of young mothers pushing baby strollers, and a man tossing a ball back and forth with a young boy.

She got up to leave, when her stomach rumbled reminding her she hadn't eaten since breakfast.

The man left the boy and came up behind her so suddenly she gasped, and dropped her purse

"I'm sorry. I didn't mean to scare you, lady."

Pippa patted her hand over her heart.

"You did frighten me for a second."

"Sorry," he said again. "My car won't start. Do you have jumper cables I could borrow?"

"As a matter of fact I do," Pippa said, picking up her purse and glancing around her to be sure other people were still in the area.

"Great. My car is over there by that tree. If you could drive close I'll take care of the rest," he said, pointing to an old faded blue sedan that looked as though it had been driven through a mud puddle, then scraped dry with a wire brush.

He jogged off. Pippa followed in her car and opened the trunk.

"Help yourself."

"Thanks. Let me just try one more time to see if I can get my old heap started." He put his key in the ignition and the engine fired to life. "Well, I guess all I needed to do was give it another chance. I appreciate you being so willing to help."

"You're welcome. I'm glad everything worked out."

"Yeah, so am I. Thanks again." He raised his hand in a wave before going back to his car.

Pippa waved back just as her cell phone's digital music signaled a call. She dug the phone out of her purse. A text from Craig urged her to come immediately to a house where he'd be. He gave directions. She mustn't tell anyone, including his aunt. She frowned. What did the message mean? She texted him back for an explanation. His reply sent a chill racing up her spine.

Avalon in danger. Hiding here. Hurry!

Pippa didn't understand how Craig could be involved with the Avalons, but she wanted to help if Shade was in some kind of trouble. She climbed into her car as quickly as she could and drove for several miles, leaving the freeway behind until she ended up at a deserted homestead.

Nearly barren with anemic looking soil, there wasn't a tree or flower in sight. A few straggly clumps of weeds and small cactus dotting the yard seemed to be the only living things in sight. Mother Nature must have gotten tired of designing the landscape, tossed a length of ragged burlap over the land, and left it in this desolate state.

Remnants of a wooden fence skirted the property. Pieces of what had once been someone's home lay scattered about. A cracked terra cotta flowerpot and a broom with a split handle lay side by side half buried in dust. A wooden chair with one leg missing leaned against the sagging porch.

She couldn't imagine why Craig or Shade would be here. She looked at the house. The front door gaped open. Leaving her purse and phone in the car, Pippa hurried into what must have been the living room. Rodents scurried from her path, insects scattered, and birds flew out the windows narrowly missing the shards of broken glass.

"Craig? Are you in here? Shade? Anybody?"

Walking through the house, she found a small bedroom with a rusted bedstead, a tiny bathroom with a broken toilet, but no sink, and a kitchen with a few pieces of smashed crockery.

Growing more anxious by the second, she stepped outside again. She started to walk around the side of the house when someone grabbed her from behind. The weight of a hand pressed hard against her mouth, as she struggled to break away. Pippa tasted sweat and heard a man's harsh breathing next to her ear, as she was forced to walk up a little knoll to a storage shed. Strong arms shoved her inside with such force she fell to her hands and knees.

She scrambled to her feet and caught a glimpse of the ski mask covering the man's head just before he slammed the door in her face. The unmistakable click of a lock echoed like a thunderbolt inside her head. She pounded her fists against the rough wood.

"What are you doing?" The sound of retreating footsteps made her heart pound harder. "Hey! Let me out of here!"

Pippa called out several more times only to have each plea met with silence.

Her eyes darted around the small enclosure. Trapped and alone!

So much for trying to help.

Now who would come to her aid?

Fourteen

Pippa watched in dread, as all the tiny beams of sunlight slowly stopped peeking through the crevices in the walls. Oh how she wished she could capture one of the sunbeams in her hands to keep the darkness at bay. Her head throbbed from growing tension accompanied by a terrible thirst. Her mouth tasted like she'd licked a box of fuzzy peaches.

She took in deep breaths trying to keep from having a full blown panic attack as she moved her fingertips in small circles against her temples. The pounding inside her head felt like a couple of blacksmiths wielding dueling hammers using her skull as an anvil.

Who pushed her in this shed? Why did they do it and what did they plan now? Where was Craig? What about his message? Was Shade still in danger? Had she arrived too late? Pippa paled at the thought that either of them may have been hurt by the same person who locked her in here.

She used to wish something would happen to add some excitement to her dull life. This definitely wasn't what she had in mind. Now that she thought about it, Pippa realized things began changing for her the night she arrived at Wolfhaven the first time.

She should have recognized her flat tire as a bad omen, not to mention the wolf standing there at the side of the road staring at her. Black cats were supposed to be bad luck. She wondered if black wolves fit into that category.

She pushed such thoughts from her mind, knowing it was more important to concentrate on this dilemma. Chloe must be fretting by now wondering why she hadn't returned. Not to mention Craig. What a worry for the poor woman to have both of them missing, if he'd ended up being trapped somewhere around here, too – and how about Shade? Lila's fragile health wouldn't stand up to something happening to her grandson.

She'd tried jiggling the door handle several times without any good results while she still had daylight. She made an attempt to get out by shoving her body against the door, followed by a few kicks. All that did was to give her a sore shoulder and aching foot to match her headache.

Pippa finally eased herself down onto the dirt floor when all the sunlight disappeared. She didn't have any other choice but to wait for dawn and start yelling at the top of her lungs, or try to dig her way out. She wondered if anyone besides Chloe would be worried about her. She closed her eyes against the night and began to chant her old childhood mantra in a trembling voice.

Shade answered his private phone line to the sound of Chloe's sobbing.

"Mrs. Bert? Whatever is the matter?"

"It's Pippa. I'm . . . I'm afraid something's happened to her. She's been gone for hours."

His fingers gripped the phone tighter.

"Are you saying she ran away?"

"No. She felt restless. Too much being cooped up, I guess. I sent her to a park. I thought the outing would do her good. I should never have let her go alone."

"Did she have her cell phone with her?"

"Yes. I've called and called. She's not answering. I drove to the park. No sign of her. She's been through so much; I can't bear the thought of something else happening to her especially knowing it's my fault."

"It's not your fault. Have you notified the police?"

"No. I didn't think she'd been missing long enough for them to get involved, and I thought you'd want me to call you first."

"I appreciate that. But you should let them know now. Did Pippa seem depressed? Upset?"

"No. Just restless."

"All right. Call the authorities. I'll get to you as soon as I can. Be sure to notify me if you hear from her. You have my cell phone number."

"Yes, all right," she sniffed.

Shade cut the connection to call and have his plane made ready. He dreaded having to tell Lila and the Hendersons about Pippa's latest misfortune. But he couldn't take the chance of them hearing it from anyone else, as much as he hated to cause them to worry.

Thoughts of her missing again filled him with a sense of gut churning déjà vu. Chloe wasn't the only one feeling guilty. He shouldn't have let Pippa out of his sight, either.

Shade piloted the plane himself, forcing him to concentrate on issues other than Pippa's disappearance. He hated that he hadn't kept her from harm – again. He prided himself on taking care of the people who mattered to him.

Even as a child when he'd lost his family, he'd blamed himself for not dying with them. He'd stayed strong for Lila's sake. He used that need for control to run the family business and make it more powerful than ever. Work filled his time, but it hadn't filled the personal void.

Having his loved ones ripped from his life made him put up walls and shy away from close relationships. He never wanted to let anyone else get inside him, allowing only Lila to touch his heart. Pippa's entry into his life had begun to slowly break down those barriers. Although he still wasn't sure how to define his feelings, Shade did know he didn't want to lose her.

But first she had to be found.

Both Chloe and Craig greeted him with worried frowns when he knocked on their door.

Craig crossed sinewy arms over his chest.

"This probably makes Pippa look like she's accident prone or that she goes looking for trouble. Well, she's not like that. This isn't her fault."

"Have you heard me say that?"

"No. I'm just clarifying how it is. No offense, Mr. Avalon, but before she met you, Pippa never had anything worse than a sliver in her finger. Since then her life's turned into a soap opera."

Chloe touched his arm.

"You mustn't say such things. Mr. Avalon isn't to blame for this."

"It's all right. Part of me feels I have failed her. But short of keeping her locked in a cage, I'm not sure how I could prevent the things that have occurred."

"Of course you couldn't. I can't stand this waiting. I'll go make some coffee."

Craig watched her go.

"My aunt's taking this pretty hard."

"Can you blame her?"

"No, but Pippa's going to get out of this. You'll see. We just have to wait."

Shade finished his coffee and left a short time later to check into a hotel where he stood now at the windows of the suite looking out at the street below. Even at this late hour the city teemed with activity. Traffic lights, vehicle lights, neon lights, all made a mockery of the night sky. Every time he had to travel, he couldn't wait to get back home to Wolfhaven and the serenity of his woods.

Shade knew he'd never get tired of the scent of pine after a spring rain and the pale morning mist that hung around the trees like gossamer veils. The deep rich green of the forest in summer, its brilliant autumn colors mingling with the evergreens, and the dazzling white snow of wintertime had inspired ideas for many of his paintings over the years. He wanted to be back there now – but not without Pippa.

He'd kissed her in the meadow, embraced her in his bed. He'd had his taste. Now he realized he wanted the entire feast.

Shade practically pounced when his cell phone rang the next morning, willing the call to tell him Pippa had been found. Disappointment at the caller's identity filled him with frustration.

"What do you want, Vanessa?"

"Well, good morning to you, too."

"You have three seconds before I'm gone."

"Oh for heaven's sake, Shade. I have some papers I need you to sign."

"Fax them to the house."

"I had planned to do that until I called, and Lila told me where you were. I don't want to have them sitting around the house waiting for you to return. I'm in town as it happens. I thought you wouldn't mind if I came by. We could have lunch together."

"You thought wrong."

She huffed out an impatient breath.

"Must you be so difficult? I have to have your signature. Look, I know the reason why you're here. Lila told me. I'm not totally insensitive to your situation. Has there been any news about Pippa? I hope she hasn't come to any harm."

"Don't waste your breath or my time pretending that you really care. We both know you don't give a damn about her."

"That's not true. I'm not so coldhearted. While I admit we didn't exactly hit it off, I certainly wouldn't wish something to happen to her. I'm a little hurt that you'd think such a thing."

"Maybe it's easy for me because of the way you treated Pippa when you were at the house. You made it very clear you thought she was beneath you. You did everything you could to get rid of her including telling her I planned to marry you."

"Well, surely you didn't expect me to act as though she's my social equal and pretend we were girlfriends. Nothing can change the reason you had her at Wolfhaven. A hireling is a hireling, Shade. I'm surprised that you and Lila were willing to share your dining table with her."

Indignation blazed in his eyes.

"You speak of Pippa as though she was a pet dog we'd allowed in the house. You still haven't answered my question about our so-called engagement. Perhaps it was Pippa herself, and not just her being an employee that had you worried we were treating her as our equal."

"What nonsense. I would certainly never be jealous of someone like her, if that's what you're suggesting. I tried to prevent you from making a fool of yourself, which by the way you were perilously close to doing when you brought that little nobody out with you."

"Be careful what you say about her, Vanessa. But as long as we're talking about people making fools of themselves, what do you think your friends are going to say when they find out there aren't going to be any nuptials between us?"

"You're being very cruel. We've been friends for a long time. Our parents expected us to be married some day. You had to be aware of that. I merely precipitated their wishes by saying we were engaged. It's about time one of us did."

"You're wrong again. I've never intended to marry you, nor did my parents ever indicate that would be their wish. But it's because of our parents that I've allowed you to be in my employ. You should think about what that really means to you."

"I'm not sure I understand what you're implying."

"I'm not implying anything. I'm stating a fact. You are my employee, just as much as Pippa is when she helps my grandmother. I suggest you keep that in mind the next time you put yourself up on a pedestal."

Her hissing breath sounded loud in his ear.

"I can't believe you'd compare me to her."

"Facts are facts. I can fire you just as easily as I hired you. Fax the papers to me here at the hotel. I have no wish to see you at the moment," Shade snapped, before ending the call.

Vanessa glared at her phone for a few seconds before hurling it, along with everything else on her desk to the floor with an angry sweep of her hand.

Pippa rolled over and groaned. If she thought she'd been thirsty before, she couldn't work up enough spit right now to lick an envelope. The persistent hammering inside her head from last night had settled down to a muted ache. Unfortunately, just about every other part of her body hurt at the moment. Sleeping on a hard packed dirt floor didn't exactly make a comfortable bed.

She stumbled to her feet and grimaced at her miniature prison. The idea of trying to scream for help probably wouldn't do much good because of her dry throat. She also didn't want to encourage the headache. The option of digging her way out would be tough given she didn't have anything to dig with except her hands.

Could she find another way to escape? She began to turn in a slow circle examining every minute detail of the walls. She noticed splits in a few of the wooden boards. Pippa realized the sun's rays peeking through one of those openings had spread across her face wakening her. She walked slowly along the walls testing each gap trying to find a weakness somewhere in the wood.

She found what she was looking for halfway around in a board with a large rotted area. Kicking the door hadn't worked yesterday. Hopefully she'd have better results with this spot. Pippa looked down at her tennis shoes wishing for hobnailed boots.

"Well, let's hope this works."

She kicked at the board with her best imitation of a karate move. "Ouch! Talk about rattling the bones. How the heck do those Kung Fu guys stand this? It might help if I was built more like an Amazon babe instead of Tinker Bell."

Pippa kicked at the damaged board, alternating feet. Sweat soaked her body when the wood finally cracked with a loud splintering sound opening up just enough for her to crawl through. She didn't miss the fact that a larger person wouldn't be able to fit through the hole.

"Okay, I admit, sometimes it's good to be Tinker Bell," she panted.

She collapsed to the ground the moment she crawled completely free. She lay there with her eyes closed, while the world around her spun in a sickening spiral inside her head. She breathed in mouthfuls of fresh air filling her lungs, after her hours in the stuffy shed.

Pippa allowed herself a few minutes before she dared to open her eyes. She pushed herself into a sitting position and could have kissed a lizard when that action didn't bring any ill effects. Standing on her poor, abused feet turned out to be more of a challenge.

She noticed while the shed itself had obviously been there for quite a while like the rest of the buildings on the property, the padlock on the door looked new. Pippa knew she needed to get back to civilization and let Chloe know she was all right. She also didn't want to be here if the person who left her in the shed decided to come back and check on her.

She looked around hoping to spot her car. It had either been taken, or driven into the barn. Little clouds of dust rose around her feet as she limped across the yard, praying every step of the way that she would find her car inside. Relief leaped in her chest when she stumbled inside and saw the vehicle parked there. It didn't take long for that happiness to vanish when a thorough search left her empty handed of car keys and cell phone.

She ran her tongue over dry lips. She couldn't ever remember being this thirsty. Every swallow felt like a coarse file abrading her throat. Pippa leaned against one side of her car. The urge to cry tightened her chest even though she knew crying wouldn't do any good. She reminded herself to think like a survivor, not a victim. She'd learned early in life if you fell down, you got up. Sometimes you had help, and sometimes you didn't.

Movement from a nearby pile of rags caught Pippa's attention seconds before a large rat burst forth to run within milliliters of her feet and out through a hole in the wall. She shuddered, instinctively jumping back so quickly she banged her head hard against the car's window.

Pain exploded. The room spun around leaving her shaking and dizzy. The fear that other rodents may reveal themselves made her stomach churn with revolution. She staggered outside and scanned her surroundings. Still no sign of Craig or Shade.

Knowing what a resourceful man Shade was, Pippa couldn't imagine what kind of danger he'd be in that he wouldn't be able to handle on his own. And why would he enlist Craig's help? She hoped they weren't relying on her, because right now there wouldn't be a lot she could do. Being in charge of her own rescue meant she had to get to the main highway, and try to flag someone down.

She may have driven here; but now she'd have to walk, if she wanted to get away. Crawling could also be involved given how much her feet hurt. She put her hand up to shade her eyes against the sun, and stared at the dirt track. It looked a lot longer than it did yesterday.

Maybe she'd get lucky and someone would find her before she had to end up going all the way to the main road.

Unfortunately, she and Lady Luck had never had a very close relationship.

FIFTEEN

The boy sat on a scarred wooden bench next to his mother, clutching his hand in hers. A gap from two missing front teeth and a sprinkling of pale red freckles scattered across his nose, made the detective crouching in front of them smile. He reached over to tousle the boy's mop of sun streaked sandy hair.

"How you doing, Sport?"

"My name's Ronny."

"Okay. Ronny, it is. How old are you?'

"I'm eight."

"Then you're old enough to know the difference between a made up story and a real one, right?" Ronny nodded.

"Good. Now tell me who you saw."

"The picture of the lady on TV this morning is the one I saw at the park."

"You're sure about that? It's very important, Ronny."

"I'm sure. I remember her because she kind of looked like Aunt Julie."

"My sister," his mother added.

"Okay. Go on."

"A man saw me tossing my baseball in the air. He asked if I wanted to play catch. My mom said it was okay, as long as we stayed where she could see us."

"Did you know this man?"

Both mother and son shook their heads.

"It wasn't old Charlie," Ronny added.

The detective raised his brows at the woman.

"Old Charlie?"

"An old man – homeless – comes to the park looking for scraps sometimes. He's harmless."

"We'll check him out." He looked at Ronny again. "What happened next?"

"The lady started walking to her car. The man told me he had to go."

"The same man playing catch with you?"

Ronny nodded.

"He ran over to her. Then Mom said we needed to get home."

Ronny's mother continued his story.

"The guy talked to her for a few seconds before he went to what I guess must have been his car. She got in her car, and drove over to him. I don't know what happened after that because we were walking away by then. I wish I would have paid better attention, so I could tell you more. You know, get his license plate number or something."

"You've been very helpful. I'm going to have you go into another room now and talk to one of our artists. I'd like you both to describe what the man looked like and his car, too. I also want you to describe the homeless man."

"That poor woman – it scares me to think she was kidnapped right there in broad daylight. I've been taking my kids to that park for a couple of years. It's always been safe."

"Ms. Scott is missing. No one is saying she's been kidnapped."

He left them with the artist before pulling out his phone.

"Mr. Avalon."

Shade couldn't stop the adrenaline rush when he heard the detective's voice.

"Have you found her yet?"

"No, but we may have a suspect. A boy and his mother saw some guy talking to Ms. Scott at the park. I'm having a sketch made up as we speak. I called Mrs. Bert. Her nephew's in class right now. She's going to text him, and have him pick her up. I want all of you to look at the drawing, and see if any of you recognize him. Come down to the station as soon as you can."

"I'm on my way."

Shade sat in Chloe's modest living room watching Craig pace the room.

"Just because none of us recognized the guy doesn't mean he's innocent. I bet a hundred bucks he took Pippa. What about the homeless bum? He could be in on this. The police need to talk to him, too."

"I'm sure they will. Come sit down now," Chloe said.

He hesitated a moment before dropping into a chair. She caught Shade staring at the paintings hanging on the walls. Anxious to talk about something more pleasant, she proudly explained they were Craig's. The conversation turned to art, as she'd hoped it would.

Shade kept his expression blank when Craig commented on Ava Lon being one of his favorite artists. He confessed to wanting to see one of her private showings. He talked about attending a certain prestigious art college to further his studies, and how he was awaiting news on his latest application for a scholarship through a program funded by Ava Lon herself.

"I've applied before and got turned down. I'm about to get my break, though."

"You sound pretty certain of that."

"Yeah. I found out that old saying it's not what you know, but who you know, to be true."

"Well, good luck." Shade stood up. "I have some phone calls to make."

"You'll call us if you hear anything?" Chloe asked, twisting her fingers together.

"Definitely." He nodded to Craig. "Take care of your aunt."

"She's usually the one taking care of me," he said unfolding his lanky frame from the chair.

Shade drove back to his hotel. He could afford to have several homes anywhere he chose in the world, but preferred to stay in hotels when he traveled. The only real home for him would always be Wolfhaven. Hotel suites usually suited his needs. Not this time. Fear for Pippa's safety made his stay unsettling. Missing her emphasized his aloneness.

He called Sam with an update. Neither man mentioned their concern on how Pippa's disappearance might bring back the fear she felt after her ordeal of being lost in Wolfhaven's forest.

Shade heard Marcie's anxious voice in the background questioning Sam.

Shade knew they saw each other on a regular basis now. He felt happy for them. It amused him when Sam confessed that Marcie seduced him first with her kindness to Pippa. Then she'd pulled out her heavy artillery with her apple pie, and finally hooked him with her unexpected talent in the bedroom. He agreed when Sam commented it was rare to find a woman that felt so right.

Phoning Lila proved more difficult. Shade tried to soothe his grandmother's fears, even as he struggled to relieve his own. He preferred not to call her at all until Pippa could be found. But it ended up stressing her even more when she didn't hear from him and began to imagine the unthinkable. He ended the conversation with a few words to Ross to keep close watch on her.

Shade paced the room, his troubled thoughts making it impossible to relax. He couldn't stop thinking about Pippa. Had she driven somewhere and got lost? Did the vehicle break down? Trying to get hold of her on her cell phone proved worthless.

She could be injured and unable to help herself. The thought made his gut wrench. He sifted through his mind dissecting facts, conversations, and people who might have some connection to her. Had someone taken her? If so, why? Who would benefit the most? Did they plan to use his friendship with her as some kind of leverage to get something they wanted from him – a favor, money? What? No note; no contact. How could he know? How could anyone know until someone broke this nerve-racking silence?

He stopped pacing to pinch the bridge of his nose between his thumb and forefinger.

Many people wanted things from him. He went back to wondering if Pippa's disappearance could have something to do with him. He'd have to concentrate on the people who figured in the equation with them both, beginning with their mutual acquaintances.

Shade knew that list could be narrowed down to a very few people. He stood there with his eyes closed, trying to bring up something inside his head that suddenly seemed very important. His eyes snapped open after a few seconds; then he hurried over to his laptop.

Pippa swayed falling to her hands and knees in this miserable piece of landscape God had forsaken. And speaking of the Almighty, her prayers that someone would rescue her didn't seem to be getting through to the man upstairs. She grew weaker by the minute. The need for some kind of liquid had become desperate. Her eyes kept playing tricks on her making her believe shimmering waves of water lay up ahead. No matter how far she walked, relief remained out of reach.

Her legs gave out completely sending her sinking down until her body lay flat with her cheek resting on the dusty earth. She closed her eyes against the sun's glare and drifted off to a cool, green forest with the sound of a lone wolf's sorrowful cry.

"Pippa. Can you hear me?" Shade skimmed the back of his knuckles down her cheek. "You're safe now. Come on, how about giving me a sign that you understand?"

She looked so fragile lying in the hospital bed; he had to say the words out loud to remind himself she was here, and that he'd found her in time.

Shade led the procession of police cars and the ambulance to the area, once he'd discovered where she'd been taken. When he spotted Pippa's still form lying on the ground, a part of his world slipped away. He'd expected to find her in a storage shed, not out in the open unprotected from the sun. He barely gave himself enough time to stop his car before jumping out and running to her.

He held her, choking out her name through the lump rising in his throat. It had taken all his strength of will to let go of her while the paramedics took over. The police drove further and found the deserted homestead with the shed where Pippa had been kept. They told him later about the board being knocked out, which explained her bruises and slivers.

He said her name again, speaking softly. Her eyelids fluttered open.

"Water, please. I'm so thirsty."

Relief in hearing her talk was like music to his ears even, if she did sound like a hoarse frog.

"That's being taken care of." He pointed to the IV hanging by the bed. "I hope this will help in the meantime."

He slipped a small ice chip between her cracked lips.

"Hmm, that feels good. I'm so glad you're here. I tried to find you. Why were you in danger?"

"No danger. Rest now."

She blinked at him.

"I think there's something wrong with my eyes because you have two heads. They both look very handsome, though. Shall I kiss them both?"

Shade realized she was still suffering the aftereffects of her harrowing experience and prolonged exposure to the sun.

"How about I kiss you instead?" He brushed a light kiss across her forehead.

"Am I at Wolfhaven?"

"No, but you're going to be as soon as the doctor releases you. Right now you need to get your strength back."

"I thought I was a goner. How did you know where to find me?"

"We'll talk about that later."

"Everything's kind of fuzzy. Craig sent me a text. Said you were in danger. I couldn't find him, either. Oh God, is he okay?"

She tried to sit up, but Shade pressed her gently back onto the pillows.

"He's fine. Go back to sleep now. Hopefully when you wake up I'll only have one head."

"That would be good, especially if it's human."

He frowned at her strange remark. What did she see if it wasn't human?

Pippa sat up in bed two days later thumbing through a magazine Chloe left when Shade entered the room carrying a large bouquet of flowers in a tall glass vase. She put the book aside.

"Oh Shade, they're lovely. Thank you. They remind me of the flowers at Wolfhaven."

"Probably because that's where they came from. I decided as long as you can't go to the garden yet I would bring a little bit of Wolfhaven to you. One of the gardeners picked them this morning, and I had them flown here."

"Do not tell me you had your plane sent here just so I could have these particular flowers." She shook her head in disbelief. "Sometimes I forget how rich you really are. I appreciate you being so thoughtful, but you shouldn't waste your money on me like this."

"The expression on your face when I walked in here made it worth every penny. But if it will make you feel any better, a woman in the area having chest pains needed to be flown here to be checked out. I offered my plane."

"Oh. Now I don't feel so guilty."

"I didn't have the flowers sent to make you feel guilty. I'll have to be sure and tell the gardener what a good job he did in selecting them."

"Please do. Remember how I thought you were a gardener the first time we met?"

"How could I forget? You certainly put me in my place."

"Funny, I thought it was the other way around."

She touched a flower.

"Thanks again."

"You're welcome."

"I thought I heard a puppy whimpering."

Shade's brow rose in question.

"Excuse me?"

"That's the reason I went into your forest. I heard what sounded like a puppy crying. Leave it to me to turn a simple animal rescue into a major search operation."

"Well, the main thing is that you were eventually found. I know this has been another ordeal for you. I don't want to suggest anything that may upset you further. So, would you rather stay with Chloe for a while longer, or are you ready to come back to Wolfhaven with me? Before you answer, please understand that I want you to do what will make you feel the most comfortable."

155

"I don't want to cause extra work for your staff. What do you think about me sharing your bed again? That way they'll have one less set of sheets to wash."

"I'm all for laborsaving practices."

A blush rose high on her cheekbones.

"I meant really sharing."

"I certainly hope so."

"You said you'd tell me why I ended up in that shed. But before you get on my case, I didn't make that up about receiving a text message from Craig saying you were in danger and hiding out. He gave me directions to that broken down place, but warned me not to tell anyone."

"I know. Thank you, by the way, for wanting to come to my aid."

"You're welcome. But what was Craig talking about? Have you seen him? I haven't had a chance to talk to him. He hasn't been to see me. Chloe says he's too upset."

Shade pulled in a deep breath through his nose and let it slowly escape through his mouth, thinking how she was so ready to help even if it meant putting herself in jeopardy.

"I need you to wait a little while longer before I tell you anything else."

"Why can't I know now?"

"I have to take care of a few things first. I promise to tell you as soon as I can."

"The fact that you're stalling worries me. I can't help wondering if Craig's warning about you being in danger was true. Is there something bad going on at your home, Shade?"

She gave him a shrewd look.

"Is that what he meant about you being in danger?"

"Craig didn't know what he was talking about. Everything is fine at Wolfhaven."

Pippa stayed in the hospital for another day before being well enough to travel. As much as Shade wanted to take her back to his home, he knew Chloe needed to spend more time with her. He had Tim drive the limousine to collect Pippa at the hospital. The things he told her he had to take care of lay like a heavy weight on his shoulders, and hadn't lifted by the time Tim took him to his own destination.

Shade wouldn't be recognized by the people who staffed any of the prominent art galleries where Vanessa kept offices, and showed his paintings. The ruse became necessary in order to maintain his anonymity as Ava Lon. He walked into the large modern gallery, and stood.

No money had been spared to create the luxurious interior befitting the well-known artists who displayed their work here. Glass and marble united, with chrome and expert lighting, to generate an aesthetically pleasing backdrop. Shade knew an entire room had been set aside for his paintings. He didn't bother going there.

The sound of high heels clicking on the marble floor made him turn toward the thin young woman dressed in a cherry red suit who approached him. Her teeth were blindingly white against a slash of red lipstick. The color reminded Shade of a bloody wound. He ignored the spark of appreciation flickering in her eyes when she looked at him.

"Good afternoon, sir. My name is Wanda. May I be of assistance?"

"I'm here to see Ms. Allan."

Her brows lifted.

"Oh? I don't have anyone listed for an appointment. Is she expecting you?"

Shade started toward the hallway leading to the back of the gallery.

"No, but she'll see me."

157

"If you'll just give me your name I'll let her know you're here," she said, hurrying after him.

"She doesn't need my name. We're old friends."

"Ms. Allan doesn't like people dropping in on her unexpectedly, whether she knows them or not. She's a very busy woman. Please let me announce you."

"I'll announce myself."

"But sir, you can't."

Shade stopped so abruptly she almost ran into him. His intimidating stare sent her stumbling back a few steps.

"I'll . . . I'll call security."

"You do that," he said, and left her standing there with another protest frozen on her lips.

Sixteen

Shade found the office he was looking for, and silently entered the room. Vanessa sat at her desk with her back to the door, listening to Wanda's frantic warning.

"Why are you bothering me with this? Get rid of him. That's what I'm paying you for," she scolded before cutting the connection. She twirled her chair back to face the door.

"Why Shade. What a nice surprise. I had no idea you were the person my secretary meant."

He stood by the closed door with his legs slightly apart and his arms folded across his chest.

"Not all surprises are nice."

"Oh dear. Has something happened to Lila?"

"My being here has nothing to do with my grandmother."

"Then I must say it sounds as though you're still in a temper. I'm sure it's probably due to that bungling assistant of mine. I'll deal with her more fully later as to who I will and will not see without an appointment. Perhaps an espresso would help to melt your frostiness. Let me buzz Wanda. That's the least she can do for you."

"She didn't announce me because I didn't give her my name; and no, I do not care for an espresso. I'm not here for refreshment."

"Well, what do you want? You snapped at me on the phone, and now you've come here ready to snap at me again. I can't imagine what I've done to cause you to be so rude. Quite frankly, I'm getting tired of your boorish behavior. You owe me an apology, Shade."

"I'm not in a very apologetic mood at the moment."

"Obviously. I would have expected you to be in a better frame of mind now that Pippa has been found safe. I saw it on the news. It's such a wonderful thing when a missing person is returned to their home unharmed."

"You wouldn't be saying that if you saw the condition she was in when I found her."

"Oh? I didn't realize she'd been injured. I do hope she's going to be all right. I even thought about sending her flowers to the hospital."

"Did you?" he said in a deceptively quiet voice. "What made you change your mind?"

"I decided it would have been a waste of money and effort knowing how she feels about me." She pointed to a chair. "Why don't you sit down and tell me what brings you here?"

"This is not a social visit, Vanessa. I'm here to tell you that you'll be going away."

"Really? It sounds like you're sending me on a vacation. While that's very sweet of you, darling, I'm afraid I don't have the time right now. You'd know that if you bothered to take a few moments and check the schedule I faxed to you."

"You'll be taking the time."

"You sound very sure of that."

Her mouth suddenly lifted in a slow smile.

"Oh, Shade. Forgive me for being so obtuse. You want us to go on vacation together." She started to rise from her chair, but he motioned for her to remain seated.

"Is that what this surprise visit is about?"

"I'm afraid not. While you'll be going away, I won't be with you."

"I see. What about my agenda?"

"You'll be following an agenda, but it'll be quite different than what you're used to."

Vanessa's forehead pleated in a frown. "I'm not following your innuendoes. If this is some kind of game you're playing I have to say I am not amused." She started shuffling papers on her desk. "I'm very busy. Are you quite finished now? I have several phone calls I need to return."

"You needn't worry about your busy schedule. That's about to end."

Her hands stilled.

"Are you by any chance firing me?" she asked, narrowing her eyes at him.

"Let's just say you might want to start cleaning out your desk."

Vanessa shoved her chair back and surged to her feet.

"It's because of Pippa, isn't it? You've been like a man possessed ever since she came into your life. What a person of your wealth and breeding, not to mention talent, sees in such an insignificant person like her is beyond me. She isn't the right person for you."

"But you think you are."

"Well, certainly more than she'll ever be. We come from the same background, the same mold. We have our kind of people. Pippa has hers. You're deluding yourself if you think you two can ever really be compatible."

"I don't remember asking your opinion."

"That's because her poor me act has blinded you. I'm sure your grandfather has been rolling over in his grave seeing how you've behaved with Pippa. Since he's not here to save you from yourself someone has to do it. Our families go back too far for me to ignore what's been going on."

"So you decided to take on the task yourself. Did it ever occur to you that I don't need saving, as you put it?"

"That's the problem in a situation like this. Most people who do, don't usually realize it."

"Cut the drama, Vanessa. You don't care about saving anyone except yourself. Once you realized I wasn't ever going to marry you, you were determined to get Pippa out of my life. You can't stand that I prefer her to you. You almost pulled it off when she left after you convinced her we were engaged. I'm sure you were overjoyed when she got lost in the woods near my home."

"That's not true."

Shade went on as though she hadn't spoken.

"You thought your way would be clear, but then Pippa showed up at that hospital. You never expected me to take her back, did you? It must have galled you when I did."

"I don't think she's your responsibility, which only proves my point about you being obsessed with her."

Shade shoved his hands into his pockets and leaned his shoulder against the wall. "As long as we're on the subject of obsession, have you looked at yourself lately?"

"What's that supposed to mean?" Vanessa asked before sitting down again.

"What do you call your fixation on trying to get Pippa out of my life?"

"An act of kindness from one longtime friend to another."

"A real friend would know when they'd overstepped the boundaries of friendship, as you did when Pippa was lured to that deserted farmhouse."

She picked up a pen and began to tap it on the desk in quick, jerky movements.

"Not only has she made you obsessed, it seems she's also made you delusional."

"Unfortunately for you, I am not delusional. I know everything, Vanessa. I have little doubt the others will talk to save their own skin."

"I have no idea what you're going on about," she insisted before tossing the pen aside.

Shade came over to lay his hands flat on the desk, thrusting his face close to hers.

"Your scheme came close to ending very badly. Pippa may not have made it if I hadn't found her when I did. If she had died, I would have personally made your life a living hell."

Vanessa scrambled out of her chair.

"You really are insane. I'm going to call the police."

"Be my guest. They're looking forward to having a conversation with you and your accomplices."

"What are you talking about? What accomplices?"

"Let's start with your assistant, shall we?"

"Wanda? What does she have to do with your ridiculous accusations?"

"The gallery in New York needs a new manager. She wants the job."

"So?"

"She knew she'd be a shoo-in, if she could do something to really please you. What better way to win your approval than to come up with a prank to scare the woman you despise?"

Vanessa sat down again, and leaned back in her chair.

"That's quite a tale you've got going. Perhaps you should be the one helping Lila with her stories."

"Wanda knew she couldn't do it alone," he continued. "She needed help from someone close to Pippa. She also figured out she'd have to have something to entice that person into joining her; something that would benefit them, too."

Shade took a step back from the desk, his eyes never leaving Vanessa's face.

"That's how Pippa happened to be contacted at the park."

"Ha! Now you've tripped yourself up, if you think I sent that text. I'm quite willing to let you or anyone else, including the police check my cell phone records, and the phones here. You won't find anything like that."

"I said contacted. How did you know the message came as a text?"

A tiny muscle quivered at the corner of Vanessa's right eye.

"I just assumed."

"I know you didn't send it. You bought another phone for the person who did, and had them throw it away, so the text couldn't be traced. You should have picked more reliable people for the job, Vanessa. Someone who would be more loyal, and less greedy for what they wanted. But you don't know much about loyalty, do you?"

"Look who's talking about loyalty. You'd choose someone like that little mouse with no breeding and no background, when I'm so much better than she could ever be. Did you think I'd stand by while you continued to humiliate me?"

"You've done a pretty job of humiliating yourself without my help. People who live in glass houses shouldn't . . ."

Vanessa sliced an impatient hand through the air, cutting into his comment.

"I'm aware of the cliché. People who live in glass houses shouldn't throw stones because they might end up having stones thrown back at them with disastrous results. What does that have to do with me?"

"Actually, I was going to say people who live in glass houses shouldn't walk around naked, because they may reveal more than they want others to see."

"What a crude thing to say."

"But in your case, accurate. You've exposed too much, Vanessa. I know what you did."

She lifted her chin at him.

"All right, so what if I did take part in helping Pippa to be taken. No one is going to believe you. The police wouldn't dare accuse me with my family name, not to mention my reputation in the art world. You'll never get me to confess to the police," she jeered throwing caution aside.

"Thanks to your temper, you just did," Shade said, as he walked over to open the door.

The detective, accompanied by two uniformed officers walked in.

Vanessa frowned at Shade.

"What are they doing here?"

"What do you think?"

"You brought the authorities? How dare you."

"I dare a lot of things when someone I care about is put in danger."

He looked at the detective.

"What about the others?"

"We have the assistant. I'll wait on the other suspect as you requested, but not for long."

"Thank you."

Shade left the gallery with Vanessa's screams of protest ringing in his ears. Deluged by his conflicting feelings, he told Tim to drive around rather than go back to the hotel. He wasn't ready to face anyone else just now. He knew in her own warped way, Vanessa really did believe she was doing him a favor by trying to force Pippa out of his life.

Shade knew, despite her betrayal, he would miss their happier times. They'd played together as children, attended social functions their wealthy parents thought were essential to their upbringing, and shared secret wishes and dreams. He'd given her her first chaste kiss, her first driving lesson, and comforted her when she'd given her virginity to a boy who quickly dumped her.

Their relationship started to change as they got older, and he began to realize she wanted to be more than friends. Shade never felt any romantic feelings toward

Vanessa, and did his best to keep their friendship platonic. But she refused to give up the idea that they would be married some day. Pampered and spoiled all her life, she was used to getting whatever she wanted.

When Vanessa's parents died within six months of each other from cancer, she'd been hysterical, lost, and alone. Shade gave her the coveted job of representing his paintings, and keeping track of his charitable affiliations, more as an act of pity than anything else.

He'd kept their contacts strictly long distance for months at a time. The arrangement worked well for him because he preferred to spend as much time as he could at Wolfhaven, and Vanessa hated the isolation. On the occasions when he did have to meet with her, he often felt as though he was dragging their friendship around like an anchor hung on his neck.

But he'd instigated her last couple of trips to his home for the worst possible reason. He wanted to test Pippa's reactions. She'd already made him too aware of her. What did she think of him? It shamed him to remember it, especially when Vanessa had been her true self, and treated Pippa like some beggar who had wiggled her way into his and Lila's personal lives.

Something about Pippa struck a chord in him from the very first moment he looked up from the garden and saw her standing at the window looking down at him. The quick flash of emotional current had been brief, but forceful enough to set his heart knocking against his ribs.

A smile tugged at the corners of his mouth now, as he thought about their encounter in the hallway later that morning when she'd mistaken him for the gardener. He enjoyed their brief bantering. That flicker of emotion she generated earlier had deepened into something more tangible, and had all but engulfed him as he'd stood so close to her. The clean, sweet scent of the floral soap she used stirred his nostrils, while the urge to run his hands through all that flaming hair and to taste the soft looking mouth had nearly undone him.

Shade shook himself free of the old memories to stare out the window at the passing scenery. Tim left the freeway behind and took them into the hills high above Los Angeles. Shade asked him to pull over as soon as he found an area large enough to accommodate the long vehicle. A few minutes later he found himself standing at the top of a long sloping hillside, while Tim remained by the car respecting Shade's need for privacy.

The afternoon sun spread its golden warmth over the ground, touching the long strands of ivy that covered the hill, making the leaves shine as though each leaf had been hand polished. He lifted his eyes and stared beyond the houses below to look straight ahead at the far horizon, where the gray line of the ocean blended harmoniously with the soft blue sky. A few thin clouds hovered overhead like delicate pieces of gauzy lace, lending their beauty to the scene.

He thought of Vanessa. Her outer beauty could never make up for the flawed inner person. Shade knew it'd be a very long time before he would be able to erase the vivid picture of how she clawed at the officers. No longer the cool sophisticated socialite, she had turned into a wild snarling animal, fighting to break free of her captors.

The thought of a wild animal made Shade realize the time was drawing ever closer that he would have to address the wolf issue with Pippa, especially if he could convince her to stay at Wolfhaven, as he hoped. She'd made repeated references, questioned his grandmother, and the Hendersons enough for him to know he wasn't going to be able to keep his secret from her much longer. The big question was, would she be able to accept living with a wild animal that was as much a part of Wolfhaven as he was?

Only time would tell.

167

Shade had Tim drive him back to the hotel where he shed his suit coat and tie before settling in for an afternoon of work. Although he had every confidence in the people he hired to manage the various divisions of his family's business, he didn't bury himself away at home to the point that he didn't know what was going on.

By the time he finally shut off his laptop, evening shadows were beginning to filter into the room, softening the décor with a pale lavender hue. He called his private secretary in the central office with instructions to field any calls for him, barring any emergencies for the rest of the day.

Shade sat there in the semidarkness for several minutes staring into space. Now that his mind no longer focused on business, his thoughts switched back to Vanessa. He had walked away from her as the police took over, while fighting his conflicting feelings of her betrayal. Now the reluctant need to take care of her would not be silenced.

He called the detective for an update, and learned she insisted she be released. No shock there, but a surprise, however, to discover she hadn't called her attorney. Shade expected that to be the first thing Vanessa would have demanded. He gave the name and phone number of her lawyer.

They hung up. Shade sat thinking how ironic and twisted it was that he should consider aiding Vanessa in any way, after what she had done to Pippa. But their friendship hadn't been all bad. Memories of better times couldn't be so easily denied.

He sat brooding. Shade knew he had to make another call. He'd been putting it off all day. It couldn't wait any longer. The detective reminded him that time was running out. To heap more hurt onto people who had already suffered through no fault of their own, made his chest tighten with regret. Sometimes being the messenger really sucked.

Having Vanessa arrested had been difficult for him. This was going to be a lot worse.

He raked long fingers through his hair and with a weary sigh, picked up the phone.

Seventeen

"Hi," Pippa answered in a cheerful voice. "How was your day?"

"Busy."

"Trying to catch up I bet. You've been spending way too much time fussing over me."

"Men do not fuss. They stay occupied."

"If you say so. I hope you haven't fallen behind with your work. Did you get things taken care of that needed doing? If you get too far behind you'll have to end up firing yourself."

"Sometimes firing is the only solution to a problem."

"I guess so."

She hesitated.

"I have a feeling we're not talking about you. Are you all right? You sound kind of down."

"I'm just a little tired from staring at a computer screen all afternoon."

"I think it's something more than that. Is it me? Have I done something wrong again?"

"No, my sweet, you've done everything right. But then, not everyone is you."

"Probably a good thing they're not. I'm not sure what this call is really about. Should I be concerned if I see Vanessa's silk stockings hanging on your bathroom shower door?" Pippa said, attempting to add humor to the personal query.

"I haven't been entertaining her in my hotel room if that's what you're implying, although I did spend some time with her this afternoon."

"Well, sure, you'd have to, being as how she's so involved in your, um, business life."

"Relax. It wasn't the kind of business you're obviously thinking about."

"I wasn't . . . okay, I was. Sorry about that. Did you and Vanessa have a falling out?"

"You could say that. Pippa, I need to talk to you."

"We are talking."

"But not saying what I need to. I have something important to tell you."

"I'm listening."

"I don't want to do it over the phone. If I send a car will you come to the hotel?"

"Tonight?" she squeaked.

"That would be preferable, yes."

She let a few seconds of silence elapse before she answered.

"All right."

Shade drew Pippa into his arms the moment she walked into his hotel suite. Her heart thundered with anticipation feeling certain that he was about to confess something big. Whatever he wanted to tell her clearly gave him trouble. Could her crazy, out of this world, insane theory that he was part wolf, be true? Is that what he was getting ready to tell her?

She eased back after several seconds when he continued to just stand there holding her.

"Shade, please tell me whatever is bothering you. I won't be judgmental. I promise."

"Sweet, Pippa. Always so caring – always so willing to please."

He cupped her face before sliding his hands down her neck, to her shoulders, and finally to rest at her waist. His mouth touched her lips, gently, then with more pressure, drawing a surprised little gasp from her. They closed their eyes, wrapped their arms around each other and settled more deeply into the kiss.

Shade's hands roamed, discovering Pippa's tender curves, filling himself with the feel and scent of her. She pressed against him, drinking him in, innocently signaling her desire. Their heavy breaths filled the room, as emotions spiraled, swirling in a cloud of heat, surrounding them. He leaned back to stare at her. His blood hummed, raw passion clawed, as he fought for control.

"Pippa, I . . ." A shudder went through him. "I need you."

She reached up, touched his face, and looked into his eyes.

"Then take more. Take it all."

Shade paused a moment before lifting her in his arms and carrying her into the quiet dark of the bedroom. He headed unerringly toward the bed where he laid her gently down. She watched as he began to quickly remove his clothes. She kicked her shoes off, tugged her top over her head, and unsnapped her jeans before he bent down to finish undressing her.

Shade lowered himself to the bed, took Pippa into his arms, making her suck in a breath at the first contact of naked flesh. His chiseled body pressed along the length of her while he tenderly stroked her soft skin. Fingertips grazed and soothed her nervousness, even as they aroused.

He continued to glide his hands and mouth over her, finding secret places, nudging her toward the peak, that pinnacle of pleasure waiting to burst free. The thrill of discovery. The need too long denied began to build sending wave after wave of desire washing over them.

Eyes flashed with hunger, muscles tensed, poised to surrender. Electricity sparked, snapping like a thunderbolt spearing through them. Shade dragged her beneath him and looked into her eyes.

She touched his face again and whispered, "Yes."

He took her gently. She gasped out her pleasure and gave him what he needed in return.

Minutes later, Shade eased away.

"Are you all right? Did I hurt you?" he asked in an anxious voice when tears dampened her cheeks.

"I'm fine. This was what I wanted, if you'll recall."

"I know, but you're crying. Are you sure you're . . ."

She pressed a fingertip to his lips.

"These are tears of happiness. What just happened had to be one of the most beautiful experiences of my life."

He hauled her into his arms and buried his face in her hair.

"You have no idea how much I've wanted you."

"If it's half as much as I've wanted you, then it's a lot. But I don't think that's the only reason you asked me here tonight."

"You're right. Let's clean up first, and then we'll talk."

Shade pulled on his slacks and tossed his shirt to her when she came out of the bathroom. "You'd better put that on, and come into the living room. The bed is too damn inviting if we stay in here."

He took her by the hand, and led her to a couch. Pippa sat down, but Shade didn't join her.

Sensing that this appeared more difficult than he must have anticipated, she decided to steer the conversation to Vanessa, as much as she loathed talking about the woman.

"I knew you were upset on the phone. I'm sorry for whatever's happened between you and Vanessa. I'm sure you'll patch things up," she said, clenching her fingers together at the thought.

"That's highly unlikely."

He sat next to her and taking hold of her hand, rubbed the tense muscles.

"Pippa, Vanessa knew about that text message you received at the park."

Her sharp intake of breath sounded very loud.

"Are you sure? How do you know?"

"It began with my suspicions about someone else, and eventually led me to her. That's why I went to the gallery this morning."

"I knew she didn't like me. I just had no idea her hatred went so deep. I really am sorry, Shade. I may not care for the woman myself, but I know you two have been friends for a long time. It makes me sad to think that you lost your friendship because of me."

"Vanessa is the responsible one. Ours hasn't been what I would call a comfortable friendship for a long time now."

"Because she wanted you to marry her?"

"Yes, but I have never given her any indication that I would be putting my ring on her finger. I'd managed to avoid the subject because I made it a point not to encourage her. The time we spent alone at Wolfhaven was business. She knew better than to press me on any other level."

"She made it pretty obvious she didn't like you and Lila being friendly with me. That must have convinced her she had to get me out of the picture."

"When Vanessa decided she wanted to become my wife, the idea of failure never occurred to her. She doesn't take no very well. She's also extremely class conscious."

"Oh yeah, I got that loud and clear."

"She believed it was her responsibility to make sure you didn't become a part of my life."

"That makes me sound like some kind of contaminant."

"I'm sorry for the way she treated you. I challenged her about that this morning. She admitted she felt you were beneath me. I can understand the logic behind her sick motive to keep us apart, because that's how she was raised. Having you put in that shed, is something I won't forgive."

"I can't imagine how hard it must have been when you confronted her."

"It wasn't pretty."

"Where is she now?"

"Jail."

"I almost feel sorry for her. She's got to know the life she took for granted is falling apart."

"I doubt if she's come to that conclusion yet. Don't waste your pity on her. Believe me when I say if the situation was in reverse, she'd be out drinking champagne and celebrating."

"I suppose. What do you plan to do now? I mean, are you going to postpone going back to Wolfhaven, and stay here in the city to see what happens with Vanessa?"

"No. I'm sure it's going to be quite a while before this is over."

He looked down at their joined hands and played with her fingers for a few seconds before looking up again.

"Vanessa wasn't the only person involved in setting you up."

"I didn't think so. A man shoved me into the shed. Wait a minute. A guy at the park asked me for jumper cables. He ended up not needing them. That could be a ruse. Maybe it was him."

"No. The police brought him in for questioning. He's been cleared."

"Well, I can't think of anyone else who'd want to do such a thing to me. Or why."

"You were a means to an end. The gallery in New York is going to need a new manager. Wanda, Vanessa's assistant wanted the job. She knew there would be a lot of competition, so she decided to do something to gain favor.

Vanessa made it no secret you weren't her favorite person."

Pippa made a face. "It's a wonder she didn't take an ad out in the newspaper. That Wanda did this to me, so she could suck up to Vanessa for a job? Brother. Has she been arrested, too?"

"Yes."

"Serves her right."

"A job wasn't the only thing Vanessa could provide. A third party was involved."

"Yeah, the guy who pushed me into the shed. What else was she going to dole out?"

"A scholarship to one of the art schools I support. Vanessa promised she'd make sure the person got it if he helped Wanda. You weren't supposed to be hurt."

"You just said he. Do you know who it is?"

"Yes." Shade stared at Pippa, his eyes mirroring his misery. "And so do you."

He waited, watching as her expression slowly changed from bewilderment to realization. Her body went rigid. He let her ease her hand away from his. She walked across the room, keeping her back to him.

"So it really was Craig who sent the message, after all?" she asked quietly.

"I'm sorry."

She whirled to face him.

"That means he waited for me, when I followed his directions."

"That's right, but as I said, he didn't mean for you to be hurt."

"If that's true, he shouldn't have shoved me in the shed, or left me without water. He did that for a lousy scholarship? Why didn't he apply like everyone else, for Pete's sake?"

"He did apply, but was turned down. Part of the acceptance has to do with talent. The 'lousy' scholarship, as you called it is worth quite a bit of money. That's why the competition is so tough. Unfortunately, Craig's enthusiasm doesn't match his ability as an artist."

"Why did he leave me in that shed all night? He knows how much I hate the dark."

"Vanessa's orders – she wanted to make you suffer. I'm sure he didn't."

"God." Pippa rubbed her forehead. "I can take this in. I supposed he's been arrested, too."

"He'll be picked up tonight."

"Poor Chloe – this is going to be very hard. I think I better go back, and be with her."

Shade stood.

"I'll go with you."

Two police officers were escorting Craig out of the house as Shade pulled behind their patrol car. The tears flowing down his cheeks matched the ones seeping from Chloe's eyes. Pippa hurried out of the car, and ran up to them.

"I'm sorry, Pippa. I'm sorry! I never meant for you to get hurt."

"How could you do this?"

"I had to. She wouldn't give me the scholarship if I didn't. I needed the money."

"I'd advise you not to say anything more until you can talk to an attorney," an officer said.

Shade waited until they left before guiding Pippa up the stairs where Chloe still stood.

"He's a good boy, Pippa. He loves you. He really does. Please don't hate him for this."

"No Chloe, I won't hate him." She put her arm around the older woman's trembling shoulders.

"Come inside now."

Pippa offered to stay and help Chloe run the store. But because things were so awkward between them right now, she insisted Pippa should go back to Wolfhaven with Shade for a while.

She finally agreed, when she realized Chloe really wanted the time on her own.

Pippa also had to accept that she loved Shade, even though she still wasn't sure what to do about the secrets he hadn't shared with her. She'd forgotten her wolf questions with so much else going on in her life. Perhaps he feared that telling her about the wolf situation would send her away from him for good. He'd made it obvious on more than one occasion he wanted her to stay with him at Wolfhaven.

But in the meantime, they were still in his hotel suite.

They were eating breakfast when Shade's cell phone rang drawing his attention away from her. He listened to Sam issuing an invitation from Marcie and himself to stop and see them on their way back to Wolfhaven, if they were planning on driving instead of taking the plane. Shade held the phone away from his ear to ask Pippa what she would prefer.

"Oh, could we stop, please? I've talked to them via phone, but I'd love to have an actual visit. I told Marcie I would try to arrange something in the not too distant future. I'd also enjoy seeing some of the countryside again, especially near where they are."

"We'll compromise and take the plane to the nearest major city and drive from there."

He told Sam. The two men made plans while Pippa slipped away to the bedroom to dress. They were going to have time on their own in the plane and car. She wondered what she could say to Shade that would let him know just how much he had come to mean to her. She'd have to be careful not to hurt his feelings by saying she was a little frightened at the prospect of making a commitment to a creature who might be part man and part wolf.

She immediately wrinkled her nose at the idea of thinking of him as being a creature. It made him sound like some kind of monster. She couldn't accept that description. No man who could make her feel the way he did could possibly be considered a beast.

Pippa was determined not to think of Shade as an animal. Her sensible side still warned her that what she was thinking had to be all wrong. She'd been so fixated on him being a wolf that she'd almost forgotten about her animal testing theory.

But no one could deny that he certainly was a very unique individual. Soon she would have to decide whether or not she really wanted to spend her future with him. She couldn't continue to go on like this with so much unsaid between them.

If only he would trust her enough to tell her about himself. He clearly wanted to be with her when he was a man. What would happen when he turned into his wolf form? She didn't have anyone to turn to for answers to help her know what to do.

Maybe if Lila or Ross and Enid would confide in her, Shade wouldn't have to bear the burden of telling her everything by himself. Surely if that was the case they would have at least given her a little bit of information after the night she'd hit the wolf with her car.

Pippa rubbed her temples feeling a headache coming on from so much conflict going on inside her. She did love Shade. Would that love be enough to accept what had to be the most bizarre way of life anyone had ever been expected to embrace?

She also had to worry about something else.

If her theory about Shade being part wolf turned out to be wrong, that would make her one of the stupidest people on the planet.

Shade's phone rang as they boarded the plane. "I have to take this."

Pippa assumed it was probably about business. She smiled at him.

"You go right ahead. I have a book to read," she said digging the novel out of her purse and holding it up for him to see.

He nodded and walked to the back of the plane either to spare her from having to listen to his conversation, or clearly intent on having his privacy. Pippa opened her book. She barely got through a half dozen pages when the words begin to blur in front of her.

She struggled to stay awake. Shade could be coming back to join her any minute. She assumed they'd be getting to take off soon. He certainly wouldn't expect to find her dozing in her chair. But she decided she had to grab a quick nap when she simply could not keep her eyelids from wanting to close. She set her book aside, leaned her head back against the cushioned headrest, and fell asleep within seconds.

Shade stood looking down at Pippa. The sight of her curled on the seat asleep filled him with such tenderness he had to stop himself from taking her in his arms. He realized that was how he felt every time he looked at her now.

He'd never wanted to do so much to give pleasure or feel the need to be accepted for being himself. Not as the head of a highly successful international company, nor a famous artist. Not for his money or even for his looks that he'd been aware over the years had caused many females to make fools of themselves around him.

He'd rejected most women because he knew they wanted him for those things, especially his wealth – but not Pippa. In fact, he'd almost lost her because of his money. He'd found himself regretting his financial position for the first time in his life.

Knowing she'd been thrown away at birth filled him with sadness, thinking of how she'd had to fight from her first breath. Life hadn't been easy for her. She'd never had much to call her own. The tiny place she considered home, the fact that she could fit her entire wardrobe into a backpack and small suitcase gave testimony to that.

He knew she sometimes used sarcasm to protect herself. He had a feeling her imagination and good humor were mainly what made life as pleasant as possible for her, while she was shuffled from one foster home to another during her growing up years. Chloe had finally given Pippa her first stability, and the closest thing to a mother she had ever known.

Shade hoped to make sure Pippa would never again have to want for any material things, or someone to love and cherish her. He leaned over and pressed his lips gently against her forehead.

She stirred and opened her eyes.

"I fell asleep."

"That you did. Feel rested now?"

She smiled and stretched.

"Hmmm, yes. Are we there yet?"

"Just about. We'll be landing in a few minutes."

"Oh, good. I'd better hurry to fix my makeup and hair."

"You don't need to fix anything."

A car awaited them at the airport as usual. Pippa had discovered that no matter where he landed, it seemed Shade had transportation available, whether he chose to drive himself or take a limousine. Once again she knew with his wealth and position, it wasn't all that surprising.

Pippa also learned that Shade favored heavy duty SUVs when he drove, especially up in his mountains. Today's charcoal gray vehicle boasted a black leather interior and smelled as though it'd just rolled off the assembly line.

He drove away from the airport as soon as their bags were transferred to the car, and headed for the route that would lead them to Marcie's house. Pippa sank back against the comfortable seat looking out the window at the passing scenery.

"It's so beautiful here. All these trees make me sad to think that in some areas of southern California the buildings have taken their place. Of course if you look hard enough you can find beauty anywhere, even in the middle of a big city."

"How does one do that?"

"There are always sunsets and sunrises."

"Which do you enjoy the most?"

"I like them both."

"But not the darkness," he reminded her.

"True, but it's the beauty before and after the dark that I'm talking about."

"Tell me."

"When the sun sets, and the sky is bright red and orange, it reminds me of fire. Other times it's all pink and lavender with smoky clouds scattered about like fluffy feather plumes. The rosy blush can make even the ugliest buildings look good when they're covered in that soft glow."

"I never thought of that. When I look at a building, all I see is the structure."

"Well, you probably don't have a lot of time to stand around watching sunsets."

"Perhaps I should take the time. What do you like best when the sun rises?"

"Mother Nature gives us the loveliest way to wake up. It's so beautiful when the sun rises and turns everything to amber and gold."

"True, but what about the mornings when it's raining and you can't see the sun?"

"You just have to be patient and wait, because you know it will come back. It kind of reminds me of life. Some days things seem gray and murky. You're not sure if anything's ever going to be right again. But if you wait it out, the gloominess lifts and everything is bright and cheery again. Plus, you can always hope for a rainbow."

She laughed.

"Oh lord, I must sound like Pollyanna."

He shook his head.

"No."

"I didn't mean to go on. You're an artist. You know more about color than I ever could."

"I paint colors; you absorb them. Listening to you makes me feel very humble."

"I don't think I said anything all that amazing."

"The fact that you don't think so is what makes it so special. You're an extraordinary young woman, Pippa."

"Because I like sunsets and sunrises?"

"No. Because you've had so little in your life, but appreciate so much."

Eighteen

They rode on in silence each lost in their own private thoughts. By the time they pulled into Marcie's driveway they both knew they had added another layer of admiration to their relationship.

Sam came out to greet them, explaining that Marcie left for the grocery store to pick up the whipped cream she'd forgotten, to go with the strawberry shortcake she'd made for their dessert.

"Pippa, let's have a look at you. None the worse for wear I'm happy to see, after having to endure another upsetting incident."

"Leave it to me to be the pawn in other people's nasty schemes."

"We can't always control the strange things that sometimes happen in life, that's for sure. Come on in. I'll get you something to drink. Marcie left lemonade or iced tea for you, Pippa. I'm betting a beer might sound better to you right now, Shade."

"I wouldn't say no to a cold one."

"Lemonade sounds good to me," Pippa said, smiling as Sam held the door open for her.

Shade inhaled.

"Something smells wonderful."

"Marcie put a roast chicken and potatoes in the oven. A salad's in the fridge."

Pippa looked around the tidy living room.

"Although you all took good care of me in the hospital, this place felt more warm and inviting."

"Just like Marcie. She has that way about her. As you probably already know, I'm her latest houseguest. Along with a three legged dog, a one eyed cat, and a donkey that thinks he's a rooster."

Shade snorted out a laugh, and Pippa giggled.

"You're making that up about the animals."

Sam joined in their laughter.

"I am. But she did tell me she once owned a donkey that woke up the entire neighborhood by braying at dawn. Have a seat while I get those drinks."

"Let me help you," they both offered at once.

"Thanks, but I have strict orders from the lady of the house to wait on you."

He came in a few minutes later carrying a couple bottles of beer by their necks in one hand and a glass of lemonade in the other. They sat and talked, comfortable with each other until Sam looked at his watch and frowned.

"Marcie's certainly taking a long time. I know she wanted to be back as soon as possible. She felt bad enough as it was, not being here to greet you."

They visited a little while longer, filling Sam in on Pippa's recovery and answering his questions about her escape, until they all began to be concerned about Marcie's continued absence.

"Maybe she's having car trouble," Pippa said, but even as she suggested it, she knew they all thought Marcie would have called the house on her cell phone to let Sam know, if that was the case.

"Why don't we take a drive and check?" Shade asked, earning a grateful look from Sam.

Pippa stood.

"You two go. I'll check on the chicken and set the table. We don't want her having to worry about that when she comes flying in here. Don't worry, she's probably visiting with someone and lost track of the time."

185

But they knew that was unlikely since Marcie wanted to get home to her company as quickly as possible. Pippa thought her voice sounded overly bright even to her own ears. She couldn't speak her fears out loud that the dreaded thought something must be terribly wrong to cause Marcie not to contact them. She watched the men leave before heading for the kitchen.

"I'll drive while you look," Shade offered.

Sam spotted skid marks on the road that disappeared into the thick brush growing alongside the roadway less than a mile from her house.

"There!" he pointed. "Car tracks."

Shade nodded. "I see them."

He pulled onto the shoulder. Sam leaped out of the car to scramble down the embankment. Shade hurried after him. They followed the jagged path that ripped through the foliage.

"Dear God," Sam sucked in a breath when he saw Marcie's car wedged between two trees. He skidded to a halt beside the vehicle and peered inside. "Marcie?"

"Oh Sam, I knew you'd come. A darn bee flew in the window, and starting buzzing around me. I tried to shoo it out when I lost control of the car. I would have called you, but my cell phone is in my purse in the backseat. I can't reach it. I'm sorry."

"It's okay, love. Let's have a look at you."

He tugged the damaged door open.

"I think there's something wrong with my right leg. It really hurts and my head is buzzing like that bee must have somehow snuck inside."

"I'll call for an ambulance," Shade offered.

Sam recited the direct number. "It'll be quicker than 9-1-1."

Pippa had never cared for hospitals, and since she'd been forced to stay in them because of her recent problems, she liked them even less. She recalled all too well her stay in this same place after her misguided walk in the forest. She ached inside knowing Marcie lay closeted behind a door someplace out of sight having surgery.

Sam arranged for her and Shade to wait in a private waiting room, when he became aware word had gotten out about Marcie's accident. The regular waiting area quickly filled with several concerned townspeople wanting word on her condition. Pippa knew she should be thankful they didn't have to sit with people gawking at them. Waiting, made her pace. How long had they been here? When would they have news? Sam stayed in the operating room, or he might have given them periodic updates on Marcie's progress.

"There's enough people running around here to start a circus. Why hasn't anyone come to tell us what's going on?" Pippa complained to Shade for the umpteenth time.

"I expect they will when they know something. Come and sit down."

"I can't. I'm too upset. The pacing helps."

"If you ask me, it's making you more agitated." He took her by the hand, and tugged her down onto the little couch next to him.

"Believe me, I speak from experience."

Pippa realized he was referring to the times he'd had to get through the long hours waiting for news about her when she'd been lost, and then again after her disappearance.

"Marcie never would've been out driving and having a bee dive bomb her, if she hadn't gone for the whipped cream."

"I suspect Marcie wanted to make everything perfect for our visit."

"Look what happened because she did. Stupid bee! Stupid whipped cream. For a woman who only tries to

187

help people, you would think she'd have a guardian angel riding on her shoulder."

"Perhaps she did. Otherwise she may not have survived the crash."

Pippa pulled her bottom lip between her teeth.

"You're right. I'm sorry for being such a grouch. It's just that I really do hate hospitals."

"I imagine very few people actually can say they enjoy them."

She almost mowed Sam over when he entered the room a short time later.

"How is she?"

"She'll do. You know Marcie, she's a real trooper. They're moving her into a room now."

"When can we see her?"

"She's going to be out for a while yet. The leg was a mess. I knew as soon as I looked at it that she'd need a skilled orthopedic surgeon."

He looked at Shade.

"Dr. Hunter is one of the best. Thank you for sending your plane to San Francisco, so he could get here so quickly."

"I'm happy to be able to help."

"Marcie will want to see you when she wakes up and remembers that you're here. Why don't you two go to her place now, and come back in the morning? I'll call to let you know when she's ready. I know she'd want you to stay at her house."

"All right. What about you?" Pippa asked.

"I'm going to stay here for the rest of the night. I want to be around when she opens her eyes."

He scrubbed a hand down his face.

"It's never easy when a person's in surgery, and you know people are sitting in a waiting room, worrying and wondering how things are going. But it's a whole lot worse, when the person lying on that operating table is someone close to you. I thought I'd go crazy even knowing she had a damn good surgeon working on her. I'm still not going to feel right until I hear her sweet voice actually talking to me."

Shade stepped up to him, and gave his shoulder a comforting squeeze. "We'll head back to Marcie's place now and wait for your call."

"Try to get some rest if you can," Pippa urged before giving him a hug.

"I will. But first I have to go out there and tell the rest of the people how she's doing. I think half the town showed up. Someone said the mayor's even out there."

"That says a lot about Marcie."

"Yes it does. I'll talk to you later," he said and left the room.

Shade turned to Pippa and reached for her hand, locking their fingers together.

"Let's go."

She waited until they were in his car and driving to Marcie's, before she spoke again.

"Why didn't you tell me you'd sent your plane for that doctor?"

"You knew he was here."

"Yes, but I didn't know you were responsible for his transportation. I should have known you had a hand in it when he got here so fast. You're a very caring man, Shade."

"I have my moments."

"More than moments – I looked your company up on the Net. Your corporation is very generous when it comes to donations, and I'm betting that has a lot to do with you."

"I'm no hero, Pippa."

"You are to me."

"I hope you'll remember that, when I have to say or do something you may find upsetting."

Pippa's mouth went dry at the thought he might be trying to prepare her for when he revealed his dark secret. She'd certainly thought about it long enough. Would she be ready to hear him talk about his strange circumstances? She had to be. Her future depended upon it.

They rode in silence the rest of the way to Marcie's. Shade unlocked the door, and stood back for Pippa to enter the house. She couldn't help thinking it didn't seem as warm and inviting as it had this morning, now that their friend lay injured in a hospital bed.

"I'm going to make myself a cup of tea. Would you like one?"

"All right."

Pippa pulled out a couple of mugs, stuck in tea bags and nuked them. They sat at the kitchen table. Shade reached over to stroke the top of her hand.

"I'm sure everything will look better tomorrow."

"I hate to break it to you, but according to the clock it already is tomorrow, and things don't look all that rosy for Marcie."

"Not yet, but they will. It could have been worse. She's alive, and the doctor was able to save her leg."

"Thank God. It's just that it breaks my heart to think of her in such pain."

"I'm sure with Sam's love and support she'll make a full recovery. They'll probably be out dancing in no time at all."

"I never knew they liked to go dancing. Who told you?"

"No one. I just thought it sounded like a nice thing to say."

"It does. You're much better at being optimistic than I am. Do you like to dance, Shade?"

"It depends on my partner. How about you?"

"I don't know. I've never danced with anyone, unless you count the couple of times Craig gave me a quick twirl when he was excited about something."

"I've noticed you two appeared to be pretty in tune with each other."

"Well, we used to be anyway."

"It'll be up to you if you want to be again. He's very sorry for what he did. He got himself on the wrong track for a while. But as Chloe said, he's still a good man."

"I know. But it's very upsetting to think he let those women talk him into betraying me for money. He's the nearest thing to a brother I've ever had, thanks to Chloe."

"She's been hurt by this, too."

"Oh lord, yes. The thought of him going to prison is devastating for her. It hurts both of us that he broke his loyalty like this. She brought him up to know better."

"Tell me about them."

"She never had any children of her own, and even though she was pretty young when her husband died, she didn't remarry. Craig's mother was her younger sister. A wild child according to the things Chloe told me. She came crying to Chloe when she discovered her pregnancy."

"What about the father? Was she married at the time?"

Pippa shook her head. "No marriage. She wasn't even sure who the father was. She didn't want the responsibility of raising a child. Her sister agreed when Chloe asked to adopt Craig."

"Chloe sounds like another Marcie."

"I never thought of that, but you're right. Chloe helped her sister with other problems through the years. Craig may have ended up in foster care like I did if she hadn't."

"I imagine hurting Chloe is a big part of the guilt he's feeling right now."

"For sure."

"Getting back to the dancing thing, why is it that you never had a real partner?"

"The opportunity never presented itself. I remember hoping that some boy would ask me to my senior prom in high school. When no one did, I decided it was better I didn't get to go, because I probably would have stepped all over their feet."

"I doubt that. I'll give you your first lesson to prove it when we get back to Wolfhaven."

She smiled at him.

"Thank you. If you're as good at dancing as you are at everything else, I know you'll be an excellent teacher."

They drank their tea, while sounds of crickets chirping outside joined tiny frogs in a nightly chorus of song. Pippa picked up the mugs, and walked to the sink. Shade pushed back his chair to stand with his hands shoved in his pockets, watching as she rinsed the dishes in hot water.

"I guess we should go to bed," she said, keeping her back to him.

"It's been a long day."

"I don't have any idea what you're thinking about our sleeping arrangements, or if you're thinking about them at all. I'm sure I don't need to remind you that we haven't made love since that first time at your hotel."

"I dreaded having to tell you Craig would be arrested that night. You looked so sweet when you walked in I couldn't resist kissing you. I didn't mean for things to go any further. But I'm not going to lie and say I didn't enjoy myself. I'd like to think making love helped to soothe you before I gave you the disturbing news."

"It did."

She turned around to face him.

"I'm disturbed about Marcie's accident. I wouldn't mind some of that same kind of soothing right now."

Shade drew his hands slowly out of his pockets. The kitchen light bathed his features with its bright glow, emphasizing every angle, each sharp blade of flesh and bone, as he stood there watching. Pippa stared back, determined not to flinch as his eyes dragged over every inch of her.

For one terrible, humiliating moment she thought he would refuse her. Maybe she hadn't pleased him enough to want her again. She thought she'd have to say something about them both being tired, when he suddenly reached out, took her by the hand, and pulled her from the room.

Shade tugged her down the hallway into a bedroom where he flipped on the wall switch. He drew her into his arms. His kiss was tender, almost feather light. She pressed herself against him, vibrating with need, seconds before his mouth became more insistent.

Impatient hands shoved at clothing, baring heated flesh. Their bodies hit the bed, entwined, mouths clinging. Hungry need began to claw, fighting for release. The room filled with the sound of desperate pants drawn from lungs struggling to draw each breath.

Tight as a bowstring, Pippa's body arrowed up to welcome Shade, as desire pounded through them and moans of pleasure cut through the air. Her gasps mingled with his groans, sending surges of heat burning through their bodies until they collapsed together.

Shade gradually moved them to their sides where they lay hip to hip. He touched a fingertip to Pippa's mouth, while another pushed a damp curl off her forehead.

"I thought you were going to turn me down because I didn't please you enough before."

"On the contrary, you please me very much, Pippa."

"The feeling's mutual."

She pressed against him enjoying their intimate closeness.

"I suppose we should try to sleep now."

"Not just yet," he said, and plundered her mouth with another breath robbing kiss.

Nineteen

They ate the strawberry shortcake for breakfast. It didn't seem right not to, after what Marcie had sacrificed to make it perfect for them. Pippa finished putting their dirty dishes in the dishwasher when Sam called to let them know they could come see her. He met them as soon as they walked into the hospital's main entrance.

"It'd be best if you kept your visit short. Don't be alarmed if she nods off. She's still feeling the effects of the anesthetic, plus she's on some pretty powerful painkillers."

Pippa felt like crying when she saw Marcie's bruised and swollen face. Instead, she made herself smile, as she bent to give her a light kiss on the forehead.

"Hello, Marcie. I'm so sorry about your accident."

"Who would think a little thing like a bee could cause so much trouble?" she mumbled. "Ruined my dinner and our visit."

"Don't worry. We'll make up for it just as soon as you get out of here. Just promise me there won't be any running back to buy whipped cream."

"I should have fixed my chocolate cake."

Shade stepped forward to touch her lightly on the hand not attached to the IV.

"We'll definitely take a rain check on that. Sam told me your recipe won a blue ribbon at the local fair."

"Three years running," she said and tried to smile. It looked more like a grimace of pain.

"We'll leave you now. You need to rest," Pippa said kissing her again.

Marcie's eyes were slowly closing.

"Come back. 'kay?"

"Every day," Shade assured her. "My home isn't that far away."

They found Sam in the hallway and bid him goodbye with their promise to return tomorrow. Pippa looked at Shade, as he drove out of the parking lot.

"Sam looks like he's been trampled on, poor man. I had no idea how much he loves her."

"I'm not sure he realized how deep his feelings went until now. Situations like this often have a way of making a person face their emotions head on."

Pippa wondered if seeing her lying in a hospital bed had caused Shade's feelings to change toward her. And if they did, how deep did they go?

Pippa's reunion at Wolfhaven brought tears to her eyes. She knew a big part of her emotion came from being greeted with such genuine enthusiasm from Lila and both Hendersons. Growing up, she'd felt like a waif drifting from one foster home to another, always on the fringes and never feeling she really belonged as a member of anyone's family unit. What a precious thing to know she now had several people who truly cared about her.

Enid outdid herself with dinner that evening, including lobster tails, fresh asparagus, rice pilaf, and a perfect caramel flan. Pippa joined Shade and Lila in the salon after dinner to answer Lila's questions. They made plans to once again pick up where they'd left off on their wolf story.

"You're doing a wolf story?" he asked, raising his brows at Lila.

"Yes, we are. Do you have any objections?"

"Should I?"

Pippa wished she could interpret the look they exchanged between them. Had she imagined that hint of defiance in Lila's tone – the suggestion of concern in Shade's query?

"I suppose you won't know until the story is finished."

"Then I hope you'll grant me the privilege to be the first reviewer."

Was he giving her a subtle warning? She knew it wasn't like Shade to deny his grandmother. Pippa shifted in her chair feeling uneasy with the sudden tension in the room.

"We can always do another animal," she suggested looking from one to the other.

Lila wagged her head back and forth.

"No, I'm looking forward to writing about the wolf. But I know you'll want to visit your friend while she's recovering. Please don't worry that I'll make too many demands on your time, Pippa dear."

"I would never think that, Mrs. Avalon."

"You must call me Lila now. We've been friends long enough."

Pippa felt a little thrill of excitement thinking how this was one more step to making her feel like she was becoming closer with the family.

"Thank you. I'd like that very much. I've actually been thinking of you by your first name in my mind for a while now. I never had a grandmother. I think you make a lovely one."

"Oh, my dear. What a sweet thing to say, and what a delightful granddaughter you would be to anyone lucky enough to have you in their life. You cannot know how disturbing it's been for me hearing about all the terrible things that have happened to you."

She glanced at Shade.

"Knowing my grandson, he probably didn't tell me all of it."

"I'm sorry I caused you so much worry. Everything is fine now."

"I certainly hope so. I don't know very many details because everyone around here seems to think I'm made of glass. They conspire to keep me from watching the news on television or reading the newspaper if they know there might be anything in them that would upset me."

She looked at Shade again.

"I'm sure you're the one responsible for that."

"Why clutter up your life with bad news? I certainly wouldn't be paying any attention to the media if I didn't have to know what's going on in the business world. By the time the news has given every exhausting detail on whatever the story of the moment, you're sick to death of it."

"Well yes, but one does get tired of watching cooking shows and children's cartoons."

"You'll make Pippa think I'm a tyrant."

Pippa laughed.

"You watch cartoons?"

Lila patted her hair in a gesture of embarrassment.

"I only watch the ones with animals to get ideas for my stories. How else can I keep up with what children are interested in today?"

"I love cartoons. Now I won't bother sneaking while I'm here. We can view together."

"Bless you. I'd like that. Now, since I'm forbidden from watching any real news, perhaps one of you can answer a question I've wondered about. Did the man who took you act on his own, or were others involved?"

Pippa sent a quick, stressful look toward Shade. The slightest shake of his head told her he had yet to tell his grandmother of Vanessa's participation. Perhaps he never would. She'd be more than willing to leave that decision up to him. She certainly didn't want to mention Craig.

"As far as I know he acted alone."

198

"I'm happy to hear that. I wouldn't like to think there was some elaborate plot going on with multiple accomplices. You must stay here with us, so we may keep an eye on you."

"No one can be completely safe anywhere; and I'll have to go out sometimes on my own."

"Not on my watch, you won't," Shade insisted.

"I don't need a babysitter."

"No? Your past speaks for itself enough to make me justified in wanting to protect you."

She opened her mouth to protest.

Lila stopped her, before Pippa had a chance to say more.

"Now – now, children. You mustn't argue. If I may put in my two cents worth, I do hope you will consider that my grandson may have a valid point, Pippa."

"I don't want to be a bother to anyone, that's all."

"As if you could be. In any event, I'll leave you two to work things out on your own. I'm feeling a bit sleepy now. Will you let Enid know I'm ready to retire, Shade?"

"Of course. I also need to talk to Ross. I'll be back in a few minutes."

Pippa waited until he walked out the door before she complained to Lila.

"Your grandson can be very bossy."

"I know, my dear. I feel that way sometimes myself. But in my case, and yours, he acts that way because he loves us so much."

"What makes you think he loves me?"

"Because I know him. I've waited a long time for this to happen. I couldn't be more pleased that you're the one he's chosen."

"My gosh; I don't know what to say."

"You don't have to say anything to me, but if I'm not mistaken, I believe you love him, too. Just follow your heart. All will be well. You'll see."

Pippa's heart began to beat so fast now it was difficult to control her breathing. Hearing Lila say that Shade loved her was playing havoc with her system. Wishing for his love was one thing, having his grandmother be so certain of his feelings filled her with a sense of hope. Had he actually confessed his love for her to Lila? The thought thrilled her until the usual doubts crept in.

Were his feelings toward her genuine, or a ruse to please Lila? Just because he made such beautiful love to her didn't mean he was actually in love with her. Pippa knew she had little experience with men, but being good together in bed didn't necessarily guarantee a compatible future together. Of course she couldn't very well discuss their sex life with his grandmother.

"I do love him. I haven't told him, and he hasn't said anything to me. Maybe he wants to keep his feelings a secret for now, because I also think he keeps other secrets from me, too."

There! She'd said it out loud and waited for Lila to deny her accusation.

"The words will come when you're both ready. The same thing will happen when it's time to reveal whatever secrets there are. I think everyone has a bit of mystery about them, don't you? It's what makes life so interesting. I have every confidence you'll work things out. Love has a way of making people adjust and learn how to cope with most anything."

Once again Pippa's elation was tinged with uncertainty. Shade made it clear he wanted her here, and that he intended to protect her. He'd given her enough compliments to let her know he respected her, even if he hadn't come right out and told her he was in love with her.

Would Shade go so far as to ask her to marry him? If he did, should she give him a ring, or would he prefer a nice juicy bone? She almost groaned at such an absurd idea.

Pippa waited for Shade to bring up the things Lila had told her when she was alone with him in his bed that night. He pulled her into his arms and kissed her with such tenderness, she felt her heart and body open to him. But although he made love to her until she lay quivering and completely spent, he did not declare his feelings in words.

Obviously he wasn't ready to tell her what she longed to hear. Getting answers out of this man was proving to be one of the most difficult things she'd ever had to do. She held in a sigh.

"I'm glad I didn't slip and tell Lila about Vanessa's involvement with Craig's scheme. I can understand why you wouldn't want her to know. Look what his part has done to Chloe."

"I should have told you I'd kept Vanessa's name out of it when she plied me for details."

"How will you manage to keep it from her forever? Even if she doesn't accidently see it on the news, isn't she going to wonder why Vanessa won't be visiting here?"

"Not necessarily. Not soon, anyway. Vanessa only came to Wolfhaven when I'm ready for her to select the paintings and make arrangements for one of my art shows. Everything else I needed her for could be done via phone, fax, or computer. My grandmother knows Vanessa didn't like being here. She's used to not seeing her for long periods of time."

"You're going to have to tell her eventually."

"And so I will, when the time is right."

"I can't see Vanessa keeping your true identity out of the public eye now. She's going to want to do anything she can to get revenge for you having her put in jail. What are you going to do when she blabs about who the real Ava Lon is?"

Shade shrugged.

"She already has. So far she hasn't been able to convince anyone that Ava Lon isn't a woman. The fact that she's been ranting on about so many things is in my favor, because everyone pretty much thinks she's fabricating her claim about me."

"I still have trouble believing she's behind bars, and I'm here in your bed."

"Vanessa wasn't ever going to end up in my bed, no matter what she did."

"But she looked like such a perfect match for you."

"Looks can sometimes be deceiving."

He kissed her.

"Enough about Vanessa."

Darkness cloaked the room, when Pippa felt Shade leave the bed.

"Is something the matter?"

"No. I just need some fresh air. Go back to sleep."

She watched him pull on a pair of jeans and a sweatshirt. He was going outside to turn into his wolf form. She just knew it. Well, if he wasn't going to invite her to join him, she'd have to do it herself. Pippa reasoned it would be a good time for Shade to finally give up the burden of his secret, and share his unnatural condition with her. She hoped he would, so she could stop the endless speculating and confirm her suspicions.

"I'd like to keep you company."

She started to get out of bed. He laid a hand on her shoulder, stopping her.

"I'd rather you didn't. I have things on my mind. I need the time alone to work them out."

Shade left Pippa sitting there, staring at the closed door. She scrambled out of bed and ran over to the windows, as soon as he was gone. She waited, barely remembering to breathe when the sound she expected vibrated through the night like a throbbing moan. The howl sounded lonelier than usual. She pressed her forehead against the glass, suddenly feeling just as lonely herself.

Pippa spent the next few days working with Lila's story in between going with Shade for their visits to see Marcie. He spent the rest of his time at home working in his office. She didn't think he was doing any painting. He had too many other obligations, including finding someone to take Vanessa's place.

If she expected some heartfelt admission of undying love from him, each day folded into the next without any such declaration. He seemed restless, often distracted, and more moody than usual. They hadn't made love since the first night back at Wolfhaven. Perhaps Lila misinterpreted Shade's feelings, because her own were clouded by what she wanted for him.

Pippa couldn't bear being around Shade when she felt as though she had to look, but not touch. Once again her solution involved getting away from his home. Only this time she wouldn't be climbing out the window or losing her way in the forest. Marcie's accident provided the excuse she needed to put some space between her and Shade.

They were walking to his car after one of their visits when Pippa let him know her plans.

"Marcie's going to be released to go home in a couple of days."

"I know. Sam told me. It's wonderful news that's she doing so well."

"She's not well enough to be on her own yet. She'll have to have help bathing, dressing, getting her meals, things like that. Sam has to work and can't spend every moment with her."

"I'm sure he's made arrangements for a nurse to come in when he can't be there."

"Marcie doesn't really need a nurse fulltime. That's why I volunteered to stay with her."

Shade waited until they were both settled inside his car.

"When did you decide that?"

"I've been thinking about it for a while. I know how you feel about me not being away from Wolfhaven, but Marcie was there for me when I needed help. Now I want to be there for her."

"Naturally. If there's anything I can do to make things easier, you have only to ask."

Pippa had expected him to try and talk her out of going, or at least offer a token protest.

"Then you don't mind?"

"How could I? I'm sure she'll be pleased to have your help rather than a stranger's. I know that's how my grandmother felt after her stroke."

She tried not to be hurt that he didn't seem to mind her being gone. Then again, he'd have the opportunity to come and go during the night without having to worry about her tailing along.

Could Shade be thinking what was best for Marcie?

Or was he relieved that he'd be on his own again?

Twenty

"Isn't Sam just the sweetest man?" Marcie gushed to Pippa. "Look how he built ramps at the front and back doors, and removed the molding to widen the doorways in the house to make my wheelchair fit. Of course I'm planning on being out of this thing just as soon as I can. My therapist says I'm coming along really well. He expects me to be using a walker before too much longer."

"I bet you will. It's no fun feeling helpless."

"That's for sure. I'm certainly looking forward to getting my old life back."

"I don't blame you. I'm here to help in any way that I can, which reminds me. It's time for your lunch. Your friends have brought enough food to keep me from having to do much cooking. You have quite a nice variety of casseroles in your freezer."

"Not to mention all those lovely flowers and colorful balloons, encouraging notes and cards. I feel truly loved. Speaking of love, I'm going to burst if I don't share my wonderful news with you."

Her eyes sparkled with excitement.

"Sam proposed to me last night."

"Oh Marcie, I'm so happy for you." Pippa hugged her. "When's the wedding?"

"Sam suggested we elope and have a reception after I'm out of this chair. I told him I'd like to wait until I can walk down the aisle without a walker or cane. I guess it sounds silly at my age, but I've always wanted a church wedding, with the dress and the other things that go along with it."

"I'm sure Sam understands that."

"He does. I'm so lucky to have found such a wonderful guy. I almost got cold feet when he proposed because I got to thinking I didn't have what it takes to be a doctor's wife."

"What do you mean?"

"Oh you know; the prestige, and all that goes along to being married to a professional person. Sam assured me he's just a country doctor now, and I won't have to worry about the fancy trappings that went along with his job when he lived in the big city. I bet Shade must get tired sometimes, having to be in that rat race."

"I couldn't say."

"It'd be quite a task for any woman to take on if he ever married, don't you think?"

"Knowing Shade, I'm sure he'll find the perfect wife. I'll get your lunch started now."

Pippa went into the kitchen thinking about weddings, and the things that were expected of brides because of their husband's positions. The demands on Shade's wife would be tremendous in order to compliment his status in life. She didn't need Marcie to tell her that. She knew it'd be like marrying into a royal family of the rich man's world.

Even if he did propose to her, that same old nagging thought entered her head about his dubious genetics. Could he be a normal husband for any woman?

As much as Pippa didn't regret her decision to stay with Marcie, she did miss Wolfhaven as the days went by. Seeing her friend struggling with her recovery, especially when she knew Marcie suffered pain, filled Pippa with a pain of her own. But as Sam had pointed out earlier, Marcie was a trooper and although the therapy sessions often brought her to tears, she never complained.

Knowing a wedding awaited her friend at the end of her ordeal, created a huge incentive for Marcie to get well as quickly as possible. Planning the nuptials also helped to keep her mind off of her discomfort in a pleasant way.

Pippa had never been involved in helping make the arrangements for a wedding before, and at times found it almost a daunting experience with all the myriad of details that Marcie insisted she had to have. And she wasn't alone. It seemed the entire population of the little town found ways to be a part of the big day, until it was taking on all the earmarks one might find while celebrating a national holiday.

She often wondered what Sam thought of this invasion into his private life. He never complained, probably because he couldn't help being thankful to have Marcie well. He seemed willing to do anything, including wearing a pink bowtie and cummerbund with his white tux.

But Pippa suspected as understanding as he tried to be, Sam must feel frustrated not to have more time alone with the woman he loved. So whenever he arrived, she tried to make herself as scarce as possible by working in Marcie's garden, visiting with the neighbors, or going for walks.

Sam wasn't the only one longing for time alone with the person he loved. Pippa missed her lack of privacy with Shade. He came to see her less often, which made him grow increasingly distant in his behavior toward her. Could it be because they weren't alone enough, that he didn't want to make the drive? Or did all the wedding talk, make him worry she would get ideas for them?

Pippa simply could not figure the man out. Why did he act like he wanted her back at Wolfhaven, and then end up being so aloof around her? She wondered which one of them felt the most conflicted. Besides cutting back on his visits, he didn't even bother to call her all that much.

She did, however, spend quite a bit of time on the phone with Lila, as she took down the notes for the wolf story. Pippa hid her disappointment when Shade's grandmother continued to avoid revealing anything about how, or if he actually did transform himself into a wolf.

She wondered sometimes if Lila gave her discreet messages, though. Her tale involved a lone wolf who lost his family and pack. The solitary animal went searching for them every night, howling into the darkness hoping to receive an answer in return.

The weeks slowly slid by, and the big day for Marcie and Sam finally arrived. She had to lean heavily on the mayor's arm when she walked down the aisle to meet her groom. But it didn't diminish that special moment for her, or anyone else watching.

No one could say she didn't look lovely in her white satin gown and antique lace veil. The church overflowed with people standing along the sidelines, and peeking in through the windows, when there simply wasn't any more room inside. It seemed everyone showed up.

Everyone that is, except Shade. He'd called Sam that morning wishing them well. He apologized for not being able to join their celebration, explaining that an emergency made it necessary for him to fly to Washington, D.C. right away.

He called Pippa as he was getting ready to board the plane.

"They're so disappointed. It must really be some emergency for you to miss their wedding."

"It is, but I don't have the time to explain now. I've got to go. I'll try to call you later."

"You sound like you have a lot on your mind. I know you're in a hurry, so I'll make this quick. I won't be here when you get back."

"What are you talking about?" he snapped in a voice filled with impatience.

"Marcie no longer needs me. Chloe does. She sprained her ankle. I'll be working in the store."

"You never said anything about this."

"I haven't talked to you for three days if you'll recall. Anyway, she just phoned this morning."

"I'm sorry about her ankle, but I assumed you'd be coming back here. I've already made arrangements to send a car to have you driven back to Wolfhaven. What about my grandmother's stories? How is she ever going to finish her book if you keep leaving?"

"I can still work with Lila via phone, and Chloe has a fax machine in the store I can use."

"You know how I feel about you being away."

"Well, you let me come to Marcie's, so going back home shouldn't make a difference."

"You can't compare LA to here. It's a hell of a difference and you know it."

"That may be, but it's where I grew up, and it's still my home."

"Damn it Pippa, don't do this. Not now. Not when I don't have the time to find out what's really going on with you. I sense something isn't right here."

"Everything's fine. I just want to go home for a while. What's so difficult to understand?"

"I thought you might consider Wolfhaven your home now."

Her fingers squeezed the phone.

"Why, Shade? Tell me why you think that?"

"Because I . . ." He stopped and said something to someone else.

"Don't let me keep you. I can hear the pilot saying he's ready to take off. Have a nice flight, Shade," she said, and hung up before he could say more.

She could only imagine how angry he must be. People probably rarely hung up on him, if ever. She called Chloe to tell her she'd be heading home via bus. She shoved her few clothes into her backpack, left a note for Marcie, locked the house, and headed for the service station in town where she knew the bus stopped.

When she told Shade to have a nice flight, Pippa meant for him to have a nice life – without her. There were too many variables involved. The wolf issue, that appeared she would never be informed of, and the seed of doubt Marcie had planted about how difficult it would be for any woman to fit in with his lifestyle.

Once again the dream of becoming part of a family turned out to be a foolish fantasy on her part. She'd been a charity case all her life.

It seemed that wasn't about to change.

Shade couldn't stop thinking about Pippa when he hadn't been dealing with the crisis that forced him to leave her in such a hurry. In all the years, and with all the women he'd known, no female had driven him to the heights of such extreme levels of emotion that she managed to do.

When she wasn't frustrating him, or worrying him to death, she was carrying him to pinnacles of pleasure whenever they made love. No other female had ever been able to touch his heart in quite the same way as Pippa.

Right now his anger was running neck and neck with his concern at this latest debacle between them. He had a feeling part of her wanting to leave Wolfhaven was his fault. He hadn't given her the attention she deserved. God knows he wanted to, but there had been so many other things demanding his time he'd been stretched to the limit.

He ached to be with Pippa, but he hadn't been able go anywhere until he'd finished his work here. That didn't mean he hadn't kept tabs on her. He continued to fume until his phone rang.

He checked the caller ID, and answered.

"Did she arrive back all right?"

"Yes, Mr. Avalon. I'm sitting in my car right across the street. I watched her go into the store myself and then to her apartment later."

"I'll be flying out of here right away. Be sure she stays put."

"Yes, sir. What would you like me to say if she does try to leave before you get here?"

"I don't care what the hell you tell her, but she'd better be there when I arrive."

Physically and emotionally exhausted, Pippa tried to sleep on the bus even as her stomach rolled every time the big lumbering vehicle swayed around another curve. She'd finally given into her fatigue when they'd gotten out of the mountains. It hadn't been a restful sleep, thanks to Shade's anger.

She wanted to go to bed as soon as she arrived. First she needed to spend time allowing Chloe to apologize for having her come home.

"The ankle's not as bad as I thought. I overreacted on the phone. I'm sorry."

"That's okay. It's time I came back anyway."

"You look so tired, honey. I can see taking care of Marcie, and helping her with the wedding wore you out. Do you still want to stay with me or are you ready to go back to your place?"

"My place. I've missed my own bed, lumpy mattress and all."

"What about you and the dark? Will you be okay?"

"It's time I stayed on my own again. I'll keep the bathroom nightlight on like I used to do."

Pippa didn't make it to her room until evening. She shrugged out of her clothes, and took a quick shower, barely managing to slip a sleeping shirt over her head before crawling into bed; yawning deeply, she fell asleep within minutes.

She stirred moments before dawn, and saw the outline of a man sitting in a nearby chair. Was she dreaming? She almost screamed, when he got up and came over to stand by the bed.

"Shade!" she gasped.

He began to undress.

"What are you doing?"

"What the hell does it look like I'm doing?" he growled, throwing his clothes on the floor and flipping back the blankets. "Why can't you get a decent size bed? Move over."

Pippa hesitated before scooting to one side of the bed trying to create as much room as possible for him.

"Didn't you go back to Wolfhaven?"

"Does it look like I went back? I'm giving you one last warning. Stop running away."

His voice matched his flinty glare.

"I didn't run away. I came home. And anyway, you can't tell me what to do."

"I just did," he said, and dragged the shirt over her head, before snatching her to him.

She pushed at him with her hands.

"Stop it. Or, I'll . . . I'll scream."

"Yes you will, but it won't be because you want me to stop."

There was no tenderness in him. She'd caused him to spend too many hours vacillating back and forth between being infuriated and worried. Torn between the need to punish her, and to take away the ache that threatened to consume him, Shade couldn't stop himself from doing both.

His words had been cold with anger, but his lips were hot with desire, as he took her mouth in a kiss that bordered on being savage. When his hands pushed her into the mattress and lifted her hips, Pippa trembled and cried out. But not to ask him leave.

Just as he had predicted.

Minutes later, they fought to breathe. Crushed by Shade's weight, Pippa lay limp as a ragdoll, too weak to protest. He rolled off of her, but kept one muscular leg atop her thighs holding her body in place. She stared at him while he scowled at her.

"I called Chloe. She said her ankle wasn't that bad. You've been away from her for weeks. You could have delayed a few more days. Why didn't you at least wait until I got back before you left?" he demanded in a voice harsh with anger, and had he but known it, torment.

"I thought it was for the best."

"That is no kind of answer at all. I repeat the question. Why didn't you wait for me?"

"If you must know, I'd begun to feel like I was irritating you. Just when I thought I might be able to be a part of your family, it felt like you were having doubts. I used to wonder why the people didn't want me when I'd be taken out of yet another foster home, especially if I liked where I was. I remembered how embarrassed I felt. So my going, was a way for me to save myself the humiliation of being asked to leave. You should be happy I didn't wait until you had to end up throwing me out."

"How could you think I'd ever do that to you?"

"You weren't the same."

"What are you talking about? How was I different?"

"When you brought me back to Wolfhaven you made me believe you wanted me there. You seemed more distracted with other things as time went on. I know you're an extremely busy man. I didn't expect you to spend every waking moment with me. But even when we were together

213

you acted like you were preoccupied. I left before you regretted taking me in like some charity case, which is how I usually felt in my foster homes."

"Surely no one ever said such a thing to you."

"No, of course not. They were always nice, but I was a kid. It just seemed like that to me."

"Well, you're not a kid now. And I've never thought of you as a charity case. But as long as you think you are, you'll keep setting yourself up to be one. Running away starts the cycle all over again. Can't you see that?"

"Look at it from my perspective. I'm used to being shuffled around. I thought I detected signs you were tired of me. I wanted to help Marcie, but I also hoped by being gone you'd miss me."

"How could I miss you, when I came to see you?"

"You barely touched me when you did. It proved my point about you needing a break."

He rolled his eyes toward the ceiling.

"Jesus God. You are one insecure woman. The place was filled with people every time I went there. What the hell did you expect me to do, tumble you in the garden? Drive to a back road and do you in my car?"

"You needn't be so crude about it."

"I'm feeling more than crude. I'm furious. I'd like to knock some sense into your head. But since you've already been hit there, perhaps that's why your reasoning is so screwed up."

"My reasoning is not screwed up. But if it is, it's only because you keep confusing me."

She pushed at his leg, shivering as the hair roughened limb rasped over her thighs.

"Get off of me."

"So you can run off again? Not on your life."

Shade pulled her more fully against him, so their bodies were touching from toe to breast.

"Stop telling me what I can and can't do."

"Someone needs to. Just for my own curiosity, did you think I wouldn't come after you?"

"Why should you? This is where I belong; not at Wolfhaven."

"Tough, because you'll be going back with me."

"There you go being bossy again. I didn't expect you to spend every waking moment with me, Shade. I know how busy you are. But complete indifference is enough to make anyone feel unwanted. Why should I go back? You'll either shut yourself up in your rooms, or get on that fancy jet of yours and take off for Washington for your emergency – or whatever it was."

"It just so happens, it was an emergency. Clearly after that sarcastic comment I have to give you the details in order to satisfy your suspicious mind. The man heading my office there had a stroke. His schedule included taking an important meeting with CEO's from several international firms. I had to fill in for him because there wasn't time to get anyone else prepared."

Pippa lowered her lashes and mumbled.

"Oh. I'm sorry."

"Yes. Oh! Satisfied now? I also wanted to spend some time with my manager. He's been with the company for a lot of years. He's become a trusted friend and colleague. I had to make arrangements for someone to take his place, while assuring him he'd have his job back, even though it's doubtful he will ever be able to work again. It wasn't an easy thing for me. So excuse me all to hell for not sticking around to nurse your wounded ego."

Pippa gnawed her lip, filled with shame at her immature behavior.

"No wonder you're so fed up. I'm really sorry about your friend. I did it again, didn't I? I caused you a lot of trouble when you obviously didn't have the time to waste on me pitying myself. I can only apologize yet again for being such a nuisance to you."

215

"It would help if you'd tell me when you're feeling unsure of a situation, instead of letting your imagination take over until you think the only answer is to run off. I can't make things right if I don't know what's bothering you. Come home with me, and we'll start fresh."

"I don't know why you'd even want me back after what I've put you through. Besides that, my coming and going at Wolfhaven has become like a revolving door for me. Even though your grandmother's affection and her stories are important, I need something more from you. Something personal, so I wouldn't feel so insecure all the time."

"Name it."

She smoothed her fingers over the hair on his chest.

"This is very awkward for me, Shade."

"Something personal. Hmm. Let's see if I can help you out with a few of the reasons why I need you at Wolfhaven. I want you there with me because I love the way you stand up to me when I start to bully you. I love the fact that a sunrise or sunset means more to you than my bank account. I love your sense of humor and your willingness to help people in need. I love the way you feel when you're lying next to me in bed and the way you call out my name when we make love."

Pippa swallowed.

"No one has ever said so many wonderful things to me."

"I'm not done."

"There's more? You've already given me a lot."

"I'm in love with you, Pippa Elizabeth Scott."

"Oh my. Your grandmother said you love me, but I wasn't so sure. I hoped, but . . . oh my."

"That's all I get from you in return for opening up, and baring my soul? I thought you loved me too. Fine blow to my self-esteem."

Pippa knew he was teasing. But any man who'd just opened his heart to the woman he loved had the right to expect something more than a couple bumbling *oh mys* in return.

"I love you. I really, really do. I think I loved you from the first moment you called me a 'scruffy late arrival.' I love your body, and the way you can make my pulse race just by lifting an eyebrow. I love you for your devotion to your grandmother. I love the way you never brag about your beautiful paintings and keep your name anonymous, while you give millions of dollars to people in need. I hope that gives you some idea about how I feel about you, Shade . . ."

"Don't stop now," he grinned.

"I was about to say all three of your names, but I don't know your middle name."

"Wolf."

"What . . . what did you say?"

"Shade Wolf Avalon. I know it's not exactly a moniker you hear every day. My mother liked unusual names, and my dad was fond of wolves."

"Is that the only reason you were named after that particular animal?"

"What other reason would there be?"

"I'm hoping you'll tell me. I'm ready to listen to anything you say. You can trust me."

"I'll keep that in mind. Right now I think it's time you let me get some sleep."

Twenty-one

Pippa and Shade lay in a tangle of arms and legs with most of her body sprawled on top of him while he took up most of the narrow bed. Not that she felt like complaining. She wouldn't mind waking up like this every morning with him. Listening to his deep, even breathing and the sound of his strong, steady heartbeat thumping against her ear sounded very reassuring.

She peered at him noting the way his thick hair fell across his forehead. He needed a shave. She thought the dark stubble made him look sexier than ever. Pippa continued to study his face, and resisted the temptation to trace a fingertip along the eyebrows that could convey so much with the slightest arch. She supposed she shouldn't be surprised that such close scrutiny would make her mind drift to how his features changed if he really did turn into a wolf.

Once again Pippa realized this persistent idea of Shade being an animal defied all rational reasoning. Every single brain cell she possessed told her such a thing simply couldn't be done. And speaking of brains, she wondered about Shade's. Did he still retain his human thoughts once he'd made the transformation? Or did the alteration become so complete he became pure wolf without any connection left to his human side at all? How could she know if he wouldn't confide in her?

He'd confessed to loving her, and she'd revealed her own feelings to him. Even after all that, he still hadn't shared his secret. How could there be love if there wasn't trust? What would happen when they returned to

Wolfhaven? Did Shade intend to go on as they had before living with her as a human during the day and prowling the woods and gardens as a wolf at night?

He talked of love, but no mention had been made of marrying her. What about children? Would that even be possible if he did have this strange mutation? She'd always wanted to have kids. Would it be possible for Shade to pass on his terrible curse to them? How long could she remain at his home, sharing his bed and his heart, without ever having him give up that most vital information about himself?

Pippa wanted so badly to come out and say it for him. Tell him what she suspected, and that she loved him despite his affliction, or whatever it was called. She'd always liked animals. Surely she'd be able to adjust, wouldn't she? She'd be like his mate. She cringed at how sick that sounded.

Why couldn't she get the creepy idea of Shade being a wolf out of her head? She closed her eyes hoping to think about something else. She opened them again to see him staring at her.

"What are you thinking so hard about?"

"I don't know what you mean. I've just been lying here waiting for you to wake up."

He shook his head.

"I could hear those wheels turning inside your head even in my sleep. Just for the record, if you were hoping I'd let you off the hook about going back to Wolfhaven with me, that is not an option."

"No, I wasn't thinking that at all. I want to go back with you. I'll have to talk to Chloe, though. I owe her that much. I'd like to have her blessing before I leave."

"You already do. She told me she didn't expect you to come back here. I have a feeling something else is troubling you. One day I hope you'll trust me enough to stop thinking you have to hide things from me. Isn't that

219

what all your running away is about? I thought we'd settled that. I can't make things right if you clam up on me."

"Does that mean it works both ways? If I tell you my secrets will you tell me yours?"

"Depends on the secrets. There are some things a man doesn't really want nor need to know about women, and I think it's safe to say the same is true in reverse."

"I wasn't referring to the mysterious workings of the female psyche."

"Thank the lord for that."

"Men's bodies are capable of doing mystifying things, too – some men more than others."

"Speaking from experience, are you?" he said with an amused grin.

"I wasn't thinking about, you know, that!"

"The mystery of sex, and how a man's equipment changes?" he teased, rubbing a hand over her bare behind.

"Stop trying to embarrass me."

"I wouldn't think of it."

Pippa swallowed, and prayed she was about to do the right thing.

"What I'm trying to say is, could it be possible that some men are capable of changing in ways that are contrary to what nature intended. Shade, do you sometimes . . . I mean, are you a . . ."

The ringing of his cell phone interrupted her. He held up his hand.

"Hold that thought. I always check my calls when I'm away from home."

Frustration made Pippa want to gnash her teeth. She couldn't help thinking some kind of jinx kept preventing her from getting Shade to talk about his incredible secret. If she didn't find out soon she was going to lose what little mind she had left.

He leaned over, snagged his slacks off the floor, and dug in a pocket.

"It's coming from the house," he told her. The conversation was brief and tense.

"I'll leave right away."

Shade shoved his phone back, and moved away, climbing out of bed. Pippa scrambled to her knees while he began grabbing his clothes.

"What's wrong? Was that about your friend? Has he had another stroke?"

"No. It's my grandmother. She's ill in bed. Enid's called the doctor. I want to get to her as soon as I can. How long will it take you to get ready?"

"Not long."

She scrambled out of bed, and hurried to the bathroom. Concern for Shade's grandmother drove all other thoughts out of her head. Lila's age and frail health meant the simplest ailment had the potential to become something serious.

Shade stayed busy on the phone making arrangements to leave. Pippa rushed to dress and gather a few things before making a quick call to Chloe, explaining the urgent situation. She'd just hung up when a car arrived to take them to the airport where he'd landed the night before.

Pippa tried to think of what she could say to Shade to express her feelings. Any words she came up with sounded trite and inadequate to her. So she simply told him how sorry she was, and hoped he understood she meant much more.

"I appreciate that. A thought just occurred to me. Did it ever enter your mind that my grandmother became ill these last two times right after you left or went missing?"

Pippa blinked in surprise.

"Why no, I honestly never thought of that."

"Maybe it's time that you did."

They remained quiet the rest of the drive to the airport. Pippa couldn't stop thinking about Shade's observation. Did her presence at Wolfhaven really mean that much to Lila?

"I'm going to sit up with the pilot. You aren't going to take that as a personal brush off and try to parachute out of the plane, are you?" he said, as soon as they boarded the aircraft.

Pippa had to admire his attempt at humor considering how worried he must be about his grandmother. She decided to go along with him to help keep the mood light.

"I don't know how to use one, and I have a feeling it'd make me look fat. You know how women hate that. I'll sit here, have my tea, and look out the window for shapes in the clouds."

"That should keep you plenty busy, knowing you and your imagination."

She gave him a sharp look wondering at a hidden meaning, but he'd already turned his back to disappear into the cockpit.

The plane made a mockery of the long hours it took Pippa's bus ride to go the same distance. Worrying about Shade's grandmother made her want to get to Wolfhaven as quickly as possible. Despite him trying not to show his concern, she knew he felt the same way.

They found Lila in her bedroom, looking very small sitting up in bed, wearing a rose colored bed jacket.

"What's this I hear about my best girl not feeling well?" Shade said strolling up to her.

"Such a fuss over a little cold. Enid shouldn't have worried you," she scolded, but let her cheek rest against Shade's shoulder with a soft sigh, when he leaned over to hug her.

He stepped back when she let him go, and made room for Pippa to offer her own embrace.

"We came as soon as we heard. We were very worried about you." She gave her a gentle hug and pressed a light kiss to the delicate skin at Lila's temple where a pulse throbbed in a narrow blue vein.

"You mustn't fret about me. Are you all right, Pippa?"

"Yes, and once again I'm very sorry if I caused you to be upset."

"It upsets me when I don't know whether or not you're safe. I want you to think of this as your home, child." She took hold of Pippa's hands. "Please try to be happy here. Tell me what Shade and I can do, so you won't think you have to keep leaving us."

Pippa looked from one to the other. Two pairs of eyes so different in color, but both so full of hope they made tears burn in her throat. To be wanted this much. To know a beautiful place like Wolfhaven was being offered as her home made her heart swell with love and gratitude. She'd been wrong to think she didn't matter to them.

Shade touched her cheek.

"Well, Pippa, will you stay with us?"

"How could I refuse?"

Shade made love to Pippa that night. Slow and thorough, his hands aroused as they stroked her soft flesh, playing her body like a musical instrument until she felt her blood sing with sheer joy. Cool eyes sliding over hot flesh. Soft murmured words of love. Promises made that came from deep within. He made room for her in his enormous bed, just as he made room for her in his heart.

When morning came she awoke still in his arms with his body ready to claim her again. Pippa knew she must work on convincing her weak self-esteem to believe she really could belong here. Shade was certainly doing his best to persuade her at this moment. She sighed, met his urgent kisses, and surrendered to him with a raging need of her own.

Lila felt well enough to join them for a late breakfast. She talked of new stories in the anthology that apparently had no end in sight. Pippa didn't mind. The stories gave her the opportunity to channel her imagination into a harmless outlet, as well as a pleasant way to help Lila and to feel needed at the same time.

Shade finished eating, and got up from the table.

"I have some work to do."

He stared at Pippa a moment.

"If you get a wild urge to take a walk in the woods, do you think you'll be able to curb the impulse until I can go with you? Or should I fit you with a tracking collar?"

"I don't plan on going anywhere, but just in case I do, you'd better keep the Search and Rescue Team's phone number handy," she replied, joining in his humor.

"I have it memorized."

He kissed Lila's forehead.

"Don't let yourself get overly tired."

"This old body of mine would never allow me to be so careless."

He turned back to Pippa, and although he didn't kiss her, she saw the desire in his eyes.

"You, I will see later . . . in private."

Lila clapped her hands with delight as soon as Shade left the room.

"I knew you would be good for him. To see my grandson being so playful is a rare thing. Few people have ever been able to manage that. You fascinate him. That's wonderful."

"I also exasperate him. I don't mean to. It happens because I feel so unsure of myself."

"Such is the way of love, and I can see he loves you more than ever. Has he told you yet?"

"Yes, and I've reciprocated with my own feelings. I really do love him very much, even though I know I haven't always handled it well. I'm a little nervous about some things, but I'm committed to staying here at Wolfhaven no matter what the future brings."

"I'm pleased to hear it. You've made him very happy. He's needed someone like you for a long time. Most of Shade's life has been quite lonely. He never had time to form personal attachments. He had to grow up much too quickly with responsibilities thrust on him at an early age. While most young boys were playing their sports and flirting with girls, my grandson was sitting in on board meetings, learning about stock market reports, mergers, and acquisitions."

"I understand how that goes. Not about the kind of responsibilities you just mentioned, of course. But I also had a lonely childhood, just for different reasons."

"I'm sure it didn't make it any less lonely."

"No it didn't."

"It's difficult for Shade to be able to trust anyone because of who he is, and what he will and will not do, with the enormous resources he has at his command. People often believe that because one has a lot of money, they will automatically have everything they need, and therefore are guaranteed happiness."

"I've never had any money, so I admit I've been guilty of thinking wealth is the answer to a lot of problems. I guess it doesn't work that way."

"No it does not. Vanessa is a perfect case in point. That young woman had everything at her fingertips, including wealth, talent, beauty, and intelligence. Sadly all that wasn't enough."

Pippa shifted uneasily in her chair. Had Shade told his grandmother about Vanessa?

She cautioned herself to be careful in her reply.

"What more would she want, with all that going for her?"

"She wanted my grandson."

"Oh. Well, that's not difficult to understand. I kind of like him myself," Pippa said hoping to infuse some humor into a conversation that had suddenly become too uncomfortable for her.

Lila reached over and touched Pippa's hand.

"You needn't worry about breaking a confidence. I know what Vanessa did, and I shall never forgive her for trying to harm you, or driving you away from Wolfhaven."

"I didn't realize Shade told you about all that."

"He didn't. He prefers to keep me protected from unpleasant things, such as a family friend's betrayal. I have my ways of finding things out when I feel the need. I just let him have the delusion of thinking I'm in the dark. I know Shade will do anything to shield me. I love him for it, so we won't spoil that and let on I found out about Vanessa."

Pippa made a motion with her fingers at her mouth like she was locking her lips with a key.

"Your secret is safe with me. I have to say I never would have pegged you as sneaky."

She grinned to let Lila know she was teasing her. Lila grinned back.

"I may be old, but sometimes I can be as sly as one of the foxes in my stories." She laughed, obviously delighted with her own humor. "Now that we're on the subject of those clever little animals, I had a wonderful idea last night for another new tale."

"What about your wolf story? We never really did write an ending for it."

"That's because there are still some things that have to happen before it can be finished."

"What things?"

"You'll know when the time comes."

Pippa frowned.

"We're still talking about a story, right?"

"You are."

"I'm afraid I'm a bit confused. I'm not sure I understand what you're trying to tell me."

"You will."

"But I . . ."

Lila held up her hand to silence Pippa.

"Don't look so worried, my dear. You mustn't trouble yourself because you don't have all the answers you seek at the moment. Please be patient. Events at Wolfhaven will unfold when the time is right."

Her cryptic words hung in the air, making Pippa's frustration level rise to new heights, despite Lila's reassurance that things would be revealed to her. She wanted to know now, but forced herself to accept Lila's cheerful attitude that all would be well.

They spent the rest of the morning outlining Lila's idea for her fox story until she pleaded fatigue. Pippa promised to have a rough draft to go over when she returned. She sat at the desk as soon as Enid wheeled Lila away, and using her notes, began writing out a copy.

As soon as she finished with Lila's tale, Pippa started working on a story idea of her own about the animal life she'd encountered in the deserted farmhouse. But no matter how hard she tried to concentrate, she couldn't stop thinking about the things Lila said about the wolf story.

What had she been alluding to? Why did everyone have to keep making her brain chase after every little hint trying to decipher their elusive clues? Why wouldn't they just come right out and tell her about Wolfhaven's mysteries? They all expected her to trust them. Shouldn't that work both ways if she ended up making this her permanent residence, as they insisted they wanted?

Did their silence mean they were too ashamed to reveal their secrets with her? Or could it be fear of what she might do if she knew the truth? Pippa thought about that. She had to admit, if her theory about Shade condoning illegal testing on the wolves here turned out to be correct, that would make him more of a beast in her eyes than if he turned out to be a wolf himself.

Being part wolf he couldn't help, but she would not accept him deliberately hurting animals for gain. She blew out an exasperated sigh. He'd shared his bed and his heart with her.

Would he ever be ready to share his soul?

Twenty-two

Pippa couldn't get her ideas together enough to put anything down on paper because thoughts of Shade kept intruding. She decided as long as mental exercise wasn't going to work, she'd have to go for the physical. She called Enid on the house phone and told her where she'd be.

She changed into her swimsuit, pinned her hair up, grabbed a towel, and headed for the pool.

Pippa saw she would have the room to herself, as she expected. She set her towel on a lounger, slipped off her shoes, and dove into the sparkling clear water. The temperature felt just right. She struck out and began to swim to the other side of the long pool.

She'd just made her turn for the third lap when a sudden disturbance in the water made her stop. She wiped water out of her eyes and watched Shade swimming toward her, his long arms making short work of the distance. He reached her and they faced each while treading water.

"What a good idea. There's nothing like an invigorating swim to clear away the cobwebs."

"I wish I could say the same for myself."

He lifted a brow.

"Problems?"

"Writer's block." She wished she could tell him the reason. "I thought a swim would help."

"Then I hope you don't mind that I joined you."

"Why would I mind? It's your pool."

"Are you in a bad mood?"

"No."

She swam to the edge and climbed out. He quickly followed.

"This is more than a case of writer's block. What happened to all that communication we talked about? Tell me what's bothering you."

"I'm not the only one around here that doesn't communicate. You're not so great yourself."

He pulled her into a light embrace.

"Ask me anything."

Pippa opened her mouth to speak, but couldn't come up with a single word when Shade began pulling the pins out of her hair. He combed his fingers through the curly tresses with slow, sinuous strokes making her feel as though she would start purring at any moment.

He touched his lips to her temple, moving down the side of her face, and over to her jaw before settling on her mouth with sudden urgency. She put her arms around his neck and gave him an answering kiss filled with her own fiery passion. Desire pulsed through her until she felt as though her nervous system was sending out enough electrical impulses to light up a small building.

Just when Pippa thought Shade would take her to the lounger and continue their lovemaking, he lifted his head and began to rock them slowly from side to side. The next thing she knew he was moving his feet in short, easy steps that she had no choice but to follow.

"What are you doing?"

"I'm giving you your first dance lesson."

"Without music?"

"It's inside my head. Just follow my lead."

Pippa let her body sway with him, as he widened his steps and added more variety.

"I thought I would be wearing a ball gown when we did this," she joked.

"Next lesson. You're doing very well."

"You make it easy. You're very good. Is there anything you can't do?"

"Any number of things."

"Name one."

"Well, let's see now. I can't nurse a baby."

"I'm serious," she said, almost choking with laughter at his surprising answer.

"So am I. That's one thing I definitely wouldn't want to do. I'd hate having to go around with my nipples killing me all day. I don't know how women manage."

Pippa smiled, enjoying his silliness. They continued dancing until the house phone rang. He waltzed her over to the wall and answered it while still swaying back and forth.

"Is everything all right? Lila?" she asked, watching his face for a clue.

"She's fine. Ross wanted to let you know my grandmother is ready to take lunch and work with you on her story."

"Oh, okay. But first I need to shower and wash my hair. The chlorine, you know."

She walked over to pick up the pins he'd scattered on the floor earlier. Shade helped her.

"We could shower together and conserve water."

A quick burst of heat made her blush. "Is bathing the only thing you had in mind?"

"Probably not." His eyes darkened for a moment. "Make that definitely not. Another time, then. What did you want to ask me earlier about communicating?"

Pippa couldn't bring herself to shatter his good mood. How often did he get a chance to let himself go? Not much according to what Lila told her. Once again she'd have to bide her time.

"Nothing important. Just some female thing."

He winced.

"Forget I asked."

"I thought you'd say that. Thank you for the dance lesson."

"You're welcome. Next time we'll try it with music."

"I'm looking forward to it. Will I see you at lunch?"

"No. I've work to do. This was me giving myself a break."

She leaned over on an impulse and brushed a quick kiss across one nipple making him suck in a breath at the unexpected gesture.

"You may not be a very good nursing mother, but I think you'd make a great father," she giggled and ran from the room.

Pippa stood in the shower wondering what Shade thought of her statement. He might be thinking she dropped a hint about them getting married and having children of their own. He must have been an adorable baby. Would there be photos of him? Probably. Chloe had filled several albums with pictures of Craig's babyhood. She would ask Lila to show her some of Shade. But not a family portrait. That would be too hard on the poor woman.

Curiosity did make her wonder what his family looked like, though. She remembered what Shade told her about his parents. His father liked wolves. Could that be because he'd been part wolf himself? Which Avalon handed down the mutant gene? How long had it been going on? Perhaps for generations. Would Shade's children inherit the same bizarre condition? Maybe having kids wouldn't be such a good idea. It'd be up to her and Shade to end the curse.

She loved him as a man and for the umpteenth time she had to ask herself whether or not she could accept him in his wolf form. And for the umpteenth time she also wondered if she had lost her mind. Pippa would never forget the night she climbed out of the window and came face to face with the wolf. She couldn't forget her reaction, either. She'd gone all girlie and fainted. Her cowardly response could be why Shade had been delaying his decision to tell her his secret.

Perhaps if she could take him in small doses, and learn not to be so nervous, she'd be able to build up their time together while he was in his four legged shape. How could she ask him? Even if she got up the nerve and he agreed, what would they do together? Have her throw a stick while he ran to fetch it? It'd be laughable if it wasn't such a depressing thought.

Maybe they could compromise, and she'd only be around him when he was in his human form? As for having kids, they could always adopt. That is if Shade would agree. As usual there were too many questions and not enough answers.

If only she could find a way to search the area and discover whether or not there was a place where the animal experimentations happened. If it even existed, of course. She couldn't go looking at night. Not just because she wanted to avoid the dark. She'd have to have some kind of light to see, which would announce her presence.

Pippa thought about going during the daytime on that same path she'd found before. But what would she do if she ran into someone or even the man who'd escorted her back to the house before?

Maybe she could go, but stay hidden among the trees while following the edge of the path.

Getting there would be tricky because it seemed to her that everyone working around the house and grounds watched her. Despite being very discreet, she knew they kept an eye on her. Obeying orders from Shade, no doubt.

Pippa supposed she couldn't blame him. She'd gotten herself lost and look what a fiasco that turned out to be. Conked on the head by a party or parties still unknown, people called out to search for her, a stay in the hospital, upsetting Lila, and worry for Shade. In short, intended or not, she'd caused a disturbing disruption for a lot of people.

Shade wanted to protect her. She got that. But it also kept her from snooping around. He wanted her to be at Wolfhaven. She understood that, too. The thing that never got mentioned was her presence here obviously had to be under his rules.

The more Pippa thought about it, the more she decided she was never going to be able to find out the truth on her own. She also knew he couldn't continue to go on like this. She would ask Shade to tell her the truth when they were in bed tonight. No more sidetracking; and unless the house was falling down around them, she wasn't going to allow anything to interrupt her.

Pippa found Lila sitting by herself when she went into the dining room with a definite aura of sadness about her. Lila explained Shade's absence with the news that his friend and manager in Washington had suffered another stroke and died.

"Oh Lila, I'm so sorry. Shade told me he was a good friend."

She meant her words of sympathy, but it didn't prevent her from feeling guilty recalling how she'd ridiculed Shade for missing Marcie's wedding to go to Washington. Sometimes she decided she really did need a key to lock her mouth shut.

Lila managed a wan smile.

"Oliver – a wonderful man. Not only capable in his work, but a good influence on everyone around him. We're all going to miss him."

"I can see you're upset." She touched Lila's hand. "Please don't feel you have to sit here to keep me company. If you'd rather take a tray in your room I'll understand."

"Thank you for being so thoughtful, but I'll be better if I stay here and have dinner with you. Your company will do me good."

Lila barely ate more than a few bites as it turned out. Seeing her distress put Pippa off her appetite as well. They both ended up retiring to their rooms early. She wanted desperately to go to Shade and offer him comfort, but she knew if he really needed her he would let her know.

She climbed into her lonely bed to lie awake until gradually the combination of the comfortable bed and the sound of the wind blowing through the trees lulled her to sleep. Time slipped by as she slept, while images, clear and unclear, danced in and out of her dreams.

The moon hanging bright and full in the sky glowed like a beacon between the opened drapes touching Pippa's face until her eyes slowly opened. She lay there listening to the creaks and groans of the old house settling itself. She thought about going to the window to close the curtains, but felt too lazy to get out of bed – until she heard her wolf.

The howling drifted into the room. Perhaps it was the sound of grieving. The family had lost a valued friend. Pippa couldn't help herself. She pushed back the blankets and scurried over to the window. She saw the wolf, or Shade if her theory turned out to be correct. He roamed the rows of flowers in his mother's garden. She watched as he threw back his head to emit another long cry that sounded almost like sorrow to her.

She couldn't stand his suffering. As long as she hadn't been able to console him as a man, she would offer him comfort as he was right now. Strangely enough Pippa realized she was no longer afraid to face him in his wolf form. Perhaps because in her heart she felt he needed her.

She dressed quickly remembering to throw on a jacket against the night chill. She let herself out of her room and crept down the stairs through a hallway that she knew led to a side door close to the garden. Pippa headed to the spot where she saw Shade from her window. He wasn't there.

She supposed he was doing his prowling. She walked down the rows of flowers softly calling to him. Perhaps he'd decided to go to the gazebo. It may make him feel closer to his mother's spirit and bring him comfort.

She thought of calling his name louder, but didn't want to take the chance that someone in the house might hear her and come out to investigate. Pippa wanted this time alone with Shade. Her mind was so involved with what she should say to Shade that she stumbled back a few steps when he suddenly emerged from behind a large bush. Just as before, she wasn't sure which one of them was the most surprised by the unexpected encounter.

If Pippa had to guess, she'd have to say it was her. Shade probably caught her scent before now. He stood there staring at her in the same way she remembered from the other times she'd seen him. It didn't take her long to realize he wasn't happy to see her.

She recognized the signs he'd given off before. The low growl in his throat, and a slight curling of his upper lip, exposed very impressive fangs. She knew wolves usually avoided people, but would stand their ground if they felt threatened.

Surely Shade knew her, although he certainly wasn't acting very friendly now. Could it be that his brain lost all human memory when he transformed into a wolf? God, she hoped not.

"Shade, if this is you then you know this is Pippa. Right?"

He answered her with a deeper, more menacing growl, and began to walk toward her in the stiff legged walk she knew meant he was getting ready to attack. Her heart hammered. Blood pounded, making a roaring sound in her ears. Pippa had no qualms about screaming and waking up the entire household now, if only fear hadn't suddenly rendered her mute.

She began to inch back. Shade bunched his muscles and made ready to lunge. Pippa knew she was going to die. Killed by the man she loved; and he didn't even know it was her. She wasn't sure which one of them would feel the most regret.

She closed her eyes, too filled with terror to watch the big animal any longer. The roaring in her ears grew louder. The surreal moment intensified. Just when she'd braced herself to feel the horrible fangs rip into her throat, Pippa heard a strong male voice call out a command.

"Hold!"

Twenty-three

Pippa's eyes flew open. Instant fear made her vision blurry. She blinked several times trying to focus. She could make out the wolf still standing there staring at her visibly quivering from his aborted leap. Another figure came out of the shadows rapidly striding toward them, walking on two legs, she was relieved to see.

She recognized Shade. Wait. How could this be? She shot a quick glance at the wolf and back to the man. Bewildered, she squeezed her eyes shut wondering if her vision had gone haywire. When she opened them again she saw him stroking the animal while talking in a low, soothing voice. She watched in amazement as the beast nuzzled his leg and began to relax his tense muscles.

Pippa wished she could say the same for herself. Her whole body felt like a tightly wound coil. Her heart still bounced against her ribcage like a tennis ball smacking into a wall. She wanted to cry out. Fighting for control, she pushed the sticky sickness of fear away and stared at Shade.

"Shade?" she asked in a shaky voice.

"Do you mind telling me why you're out here upsetting Samson like this?"

Pippa looked at the animal and back to Shade.

"Samson? You mean the wolf? He's the one upsetting me, especially since he was getting ready to do some serious chomping on my body."

"You frightened him."

"I frightened him!" she sputtered with indignation.

The chill of fear turned to blazing anger.

"What the heck do you think he did to me?" She pressed her hands to her chest. "He almost gave me a heart attack."

"Samson is my pet. We often walk together in the gardens at night. He prefers to avoid humans he doesn't know. You must have done something to make him think he had to defend his territory. I had no idea you were out here. If I did I wouldn't have let him run loose. Why aren't you in bed?"

"I knew there were wolves here," Pippa said, ignoring his question. "I kept trying to get someone to admit it, but you all made it into a big secret."

"By necessity, not by choice."

"I realized that once I figured out what was going on."

Genuine surprise left him speechless for a few seconds.

"You know? How long?"

"Almost from the beginning. I kept hoping you would confide in me, Shade."

"I wasn't at liberty to say anything. How did you find out?"

"By putting together different things that happened. So this Samson is your pet?"

"Partly, yes."

"Are there other wolves here?"

"Yes."

"Is he just a wolf, or a shape shifter like you?"

Shade's brows drew together.

"What did you call me?"

"I realize this must be very hard for you to discuss. If you're worried about me blabbing your secret to anyone else, you needn't be. I've kept quiet this long. I promise to continue keeping it to myself."

A nervous laugh escaped her.

"I mean, who would believe me, anyway?"

239

"I really don't have a clue what you're talking about. You said you knew what was going on. Now I'm beginning to think we're on two different wavelengths here."

"Okay, if that's how you want to play it. I know you're a man by day and a wolf by night."

There! She'd finally said it, and felt the relief slide through her. "But if you really wanted to keep it a secret you shouldn't have gone around howling all night long announcing your presence."

"Please tell me this is some strange twist of your humor."

"Why would I tease you about something that has to be very difficult? It'd be like making fun of someone who has a handicap. I couldn't be so cruel."

Shade stared at her, his eyes slowly filling with shock.

Pippa reached out and patted him on the shoulder. "Don't be mad at me. I didn't say it to upset you. I just thought it was time everything finally came out in the open. You expect me to live here and be a part of your household. How could I with this deception going on?"

"Sweet Mother of God, you're serious, aren't you? You really think I'm a werewolf?" he asked incredulously. "Surely you know such a thing isn't possible."

His expression made Pippa feel like she'd received a slap alongside the head waking her from a very perplexing nightmare. Faltering now, her eyes darted between Shade and Samson.

"I never thought of you as bloodthirsty. But I . . . I saw you more than once in the garden right after the wolf came prowling through there. One of those times you walked by my room in the middle of a rainy night. The wolf was wet and so were you. And . . . and you were naked."

"I got caught in the rain. I didn't want my wet clothes leaving water marks in the house."

"What about the night I hit you/him with my car and you showed up with a bruised hip?"

"All right. I can see where that would add to your confusion. You did hit Samson. After Ross came and told me I went out to find him. I had to be sure he was all right. He limped for a few days, but there wasn't any permanent damage done. I hurt myself when I slipped on a wet boulder going through the woods looking for Samson."

"Vanessa said there was something about you I didn't know. What did she mean by that if it wasn't the wolf thing?"

"I have no idea. Perhaps she was setting the stage for our fake engagement."

Pippa's composure began to crumble as realization crept in. Hadn't she told herself over and over how too much imagination could be a curse? She wanted to be happy for Shade not being a wolf and that this part of her strange fairy tale she'd created had a good ending for him. Pushing the limits of reality turned out to be the bad part for her.

She hadn't lost her mind. It just slipped off balance for a while. Now she knew the truth that Shade was all man, humiliation started to take hold of her. How could she have allowed herself to give into such an absurd fantasy, and actually stand here confronting him with her crazy idea?

He stood looking at her with a mixture of disbelief and pity in his eyes. The pity made Pippa wish she could push back time and erase this encounter. All the hush-hush at Wolfhaven had nothing to do with Shade being a wolf. Something might be going on, but certainly not that.

"I wish Ross would have leveled with me when I went blathering to him about hitting you with my car that night. He must think I'm nuts. I can see that you do."

"No."

241

She bit her lip to keep it from trembling. "I need to go back in the house now. Please make sure your pal here doesn't decide to change his mind and come after me."

Shade spoke a command to the wolf and the animal instantly bounded off.

"You've had a fright. Let me help you."

Pippa shook her head, feeling more self-conscious by the moment.

"I'd rather you didn't."

"There's a lot more I need to say to you."

"It's a little late for that. None of this would have happened if you and everyone else here hadn't carried on with your secrets. I gave you enough openings to tell me what was going on."

"We couldn't tell you."

"Couldn't? Or wouldn't? It doesn't matter now. Please leave me alone. I've never felt more foolish in my life. I kept telling myself I wasn't being rational. But every time I turned around there was more evidence to the contrary. Do you have any idea how embarrassed I feel right now?"

"I'm so sorry. I had no idea you were thinking such a thing. How could I? I knew you suspected something, but I wasn't at liberty to tell you. I have a reason for that. We'll talk about it later when you're not so upset."

"I don't want to talk about it. What good would it do me now?"

Shade raked long fingers through his hair. "I blame myself for keeping you in the dark. I could have saved you so much grief if I'd been more forthright. Forgive me."

"Well, as you've said before, there needed to be more communication between us."

"I promise you I'll be better in the future. Once I can tell you everything you'll understand."

"I needed your explanation a long time ago. I told you, it's too late for that now."

"You mustn't say that." Shade started to reach for her. Pippa took several steps back.

"I told you and Lila I would stay here. Now can't you see that's not possible for me after what just happened? I'll never be able to face any of you without recalling my idiocy."

"So you're going to run away again instead of staying to work things out?"

"I have to. I admit I spent a lot of time escaping into a fantasy world when I was growing up because it often seemed better than what was going on in my life. But I always knew the difference between real and make believe."

"The two just blurred together. Perhaps from the stories you and Gram are doing."

"It's more than that. I think I lost touch with reality the moment I entered Wolfhaven. All the things that have happened to me since I've met you made it seem as though I've been living in a dream world. There's nothing you can say that will make me forget my utter stupidity. I don't want to stay here and be reminded of what obviously has been temporary insanity on my part. The only way I'm going to be able to deal with my mortification is to get away from here."

"I should have told you about Samson."

"That would have helped a lot. Here's something else you may as well know as long as I'm spilling my guts. When I wasn't thinking you were a wolf, I thought you may be using them in some awful experiments in a lab hidden around here. I even tried to find it, but got turned back."

Shade gave her an appalled look.

"No, Pippa, no, I would never do that to any animal. God, what a mess I've made. Please don't go. Not like this. Stay and allow me to put things right."

"I can't. I just can't. If you have any feelings for me at all, you'll let me go."

"I know you're embarrassed. That will pass in time."

"There will never be enough time to make me forget. I don't see how you will, either."

"I will put it behind me because this wasn't your fault. You know I love you, Pippa."

"Then you'll let me leave, and this time you won't come after me."

Chloe looked at Pippa and frowned. "If you get any thinner a good wind is going to blow you away. Starving yourself isn't going to bring Shade back to you."

"I'm not starving myself, and must I remind you yet again that I don't want Shade back. I made it very clear we were finished. That's why I left Wolfhaven, remember?"

"If you don't want him, then why do I still hear you crying in the storeroom? Listen to me, honey. People do and say embarrassing things all the time. That makes you human. You've been back almost three months. It's time you forgive yourself and get over the awkwardness."

"Is that what you call what I did?"

Pippa covered her face with her hands for a moment.

"I actually believed the man was a wolf. I'll never get over the total ridiculousness of that. I'm sure everyone at Wolfhaven thinks I'm insane. Do you really expect me to go back there, see their pity, and know they're laughing at me behind my back? I may be an idiot, but I'm not a masochist."

"You're a storyteller. You just got caught up in your imagination. That doesn't make you an idiot. But if you keep thinking that, you're going to brainwash yourself into believing it."

"I already believe it, because it's true."

"Oh Pippa, Pippa. What am I going to do with you?"

"Put me in a pair of cement shoes and drop me in the ocean. But don't tell Shade because he'll probably try to rescue me."

"That should tell you something about his feelings. You're not going to be able to avoid him forever. When the trial for those women and . . . and Craig starts, you'll have to be here."

Pippa squeezed her hand.

"I know how hard it is for you to talk about that."

Chloe squeezed Pippa's hand back.

"I'm okay, but wouldn't it make things more comfortable for you both if you called Shade before you have to come face to face with him in court?"

"I'm not going to call him. Now please, please can we talk about something else?"

"All right, but first I have one more thing to say."

"I'm begging you to stop. It makes me ill to be reminded of my lack of common sense."

"I wanted to say, as long as you try to solve your problems by running away you never will."

Pippa blew out a long sigh.

"So much for being my understanding friend."

"If I wasn't your friend I wouldn't be bringing this up. I'm not saying anything you don't already know. You've been running away from Shade, and not just because you humiliated yourself. You're afraid to let him love you because you think he couldn't with all your flaws. I hate to break it to you, but no one is perfect – even Shade Avalon."

"He's pretty darn close," Pippa grumbled.

"Hogwash. He's a human being, isn't he?"

"Oh yes. That I can finally attest to. Although if you would have asked me a few months ago I wouldn't have been too sure, thanks to my . . ."

Chloe held up her hand and shook her head.

"Do not call yourself stupid again, Pippa."

"Okay. Maybe I am afraid to let him love me. The whole thing is a Cinderella story gone wrong. I'm a novelty to Shade. Let the poor girl in her shabby clothes rub elbows with the rich."

"Having money doesn't give a person value. It's what's in here that counts," Chloe said tapping herself on the chest.

"You sound like Lila. If I hadn't left Wolfhaven when I did, I'm sure Shade would have grown tired of me by now anyway."

"Be careful, or all that self-esteem is going to slip off the head of the pin where you're keeping it. You can either stay here, and continue to wallow in self-pity, or go to New Orleans."

"It's not self-pity, it's self-disgust. Big difference. I'm . . . wait a sec. What's this about New Orleans?"

"That's what I'm getting ready to tell you. I have a friend who lives there. She says her apartment isn't fancy and quite small. But it's in the French Quarter within walking distance to the shops and restaurants."

"So? I don't understand what that has to do with me."

"She's getting married and is going on a six weeks honeymoon. She has a little dog she doesn't want to board that long. She needs someone to stay in her place and take care of her Bonnie. She leaves next week. I told her you'd do it. The change of scenery will do you good."

Pippa jumped off her stool.

"What! Well, you can just call back and tell her I turned down the offer. I'm not taking care of anyone's dog. You know how I feel about any animal remotely related to the wolf family."

"Oh do sit down and listen. I'm not talking about a wolf, for goodness sake. Bonnie is a toy poodle and very sweet according to Eva, my friend. You used to tell me you always wanted a dog."

"That's before I started thinking people turned into four legged creatures."

Pippa slumped back down onto the stool.

"Besides, I can't afford to travel there. You know that."

"Eva will cover your airfare, and give you some extra money for other expenses."

"I won't take advantage and leave you again."

"I'm not going to let you use me as an excuse to get out of this. You've whittled yourself down to a nub. The change will do you good, and I'm kicking you out because I can't stand to see your long face around here any longer."

"Even if I went, I'd still be taking my problems with me."

"Leave them there. It's time you stop being afraid to let yourself be happy."

Pippa wrinkled her nose.

"That doesn't make sense. Why wouldn't I want to be happy?"

"That's what you're going to try and figure out."

"You told me I should stop running away. What do you call going to New Orleans?"

"Finding yourself."

Twenty-four

Pippa still wondered if she did the right thing in agreeing to Chloe's plan, as they drove to the airport. She planned to continue mulling over her decision on the plane, but the chatty woman next to her ruined that idea. She supposed she should be feeling grateful for this opportunity to see New Orleans, instead of wanting to crawl into a hole.

Get over it, her brain urged. Get on with your life, such as it is, she mentally mimicked herself. She probably would have continued silently whining had she not remembered Chloe accusing her of wallowing in self-pity. Not a pretty image in anyone's mirror.

She hadn't done much these last few months to help herself feel any better. Now that Chloe had gone to all this trouble to help her, Pippa knew the least she could do was try to put the past behind her, and take care of her friend's dog. She just wished Eva had been more of a cat lover.

On the taxi ride to Eva's apartment, Pippa used the time to try and work up some enthusiasm for her new surroundings. After paying the driver, she hefted her suitcase, and walked into the musty interior of the building with its elaborate grill work. What a surprise to see that someone had installed an elevator. Pippa hadn't expected the modern convenience in such an old structure. She pressed the up button for the third and top floor, readying herself to ride to what would be her home for the next few weeks.

Feeling a bit apprehensive, she knocked on the door next to Eva's apartment, as she'd been instructed to do.

Ben, the neighbor, opened it after a few seconds.

"Hi. You must be Pippa. I'm Ben." He stuck out a hand.

She extended her hand, while taking in the full view of the man in front of her.

He was nice looking in a surfer kind of way, complete with sun streaked blonde hair and a slender body covered in a golden tan, which he was obviously proud enough of to show off by going shirtless.

Pippa felt her muscles tense, when he continued to hold onto her hand.

"Hello," she said, slowly easing her fingers away, "I understand Eva left her key with you."

"Yup, got it right here." He waved her into his tiny entryway. "How was your flight?"

"Not bad."

"Can I get you anything to drink? Beer? Iced tea?"

"Just the key, thanks. Should I assume the dog will be wanting to go out?"

"Yeah. Walking dogs isn't my thing, but I told Eva I'd take her out this morning. She'll need to go again. Eva left you a list of instructions, including where you can walk the pooch."

"Sounds good."

"Hopefully I'll be seeing you around now that we're going to be neighbors. I'm a waiter. I work all kinds of crazy hours."

His eyes did a quick appreciative scan of her body clad in white slacks and pale pink blouse. "Maybe you'll take a rain check on that drink some time."

"Maybe."

Pippa held up the key.

"Thanks again."

"No problem."

She stepped back into the hall, over to Eva's, and let herself into the compact apartment. She'd barely had a chance to set her suitcase down, when a tumbling ball of white fur greeted her. Pippa couldn't resist such an enthusiastic welcome. She picked up the soft, wiggly animal, and hugged the tiny dog.

"Bonnie, I presume," she laughed and received a wet doggy kiss on one cheek. "You know, now that I see you, I think you may end up being a pretty good roomie, after all."

Pippa leaned her head back and let the sun warm her face, as she sat at the small wrought iron table. Tourists filled the restaurant inside and out. She liked the crowds. People watching here had turned out to be fun because most everyone looked so happy and content.

She touched the square doughnut on her plate testing to see if it was cool enough to eat without burning her mouth. The waitress warned her that the beignets were always served very hot. Pippa took a bite, licking the thick coating of powdered sugar off her fingers. She sipped the café-au-lait savoring the delicious combination of coffee and milk.

She wanted to try some of the other restaurants her budget would allow, and sample their unique delicacies. And jazz. You couldn't come to New Orleans and not spend some time listening to that toe tapping music. Even at this early hour, the melodies filled the air along with the tangy spices of Cajun cooking.

Hopefully she'd manage to visit some of the historical homes in the area via a carriage ride later on. Thanks to Bonnie she already had a routine after the third day. They'd take their morning walk, have breakfast, play, watch a little television, and take another walk. Then she'd go exploring while Bonnie napped. Still, all the busyness left too much time to think.

If Pippa thought her life had been a muddle before, it was a downright jumble of confusion now. It seemed to her ever since she went to Wolfhaven and met the Avalons, she'd undergone a personality transplant. Half the time she didn't recognize herself. She ended up being either a ranting shrew insulting Shade, or a wimpy crybaby trying to run from her mistakes.

The most appalling thing of all, had been her lunacy thinking he turned into a wolf. Even now her face burned with mortification. She also couldn't forget about Craig's betrayal. No trial date had been set yet. Pippa knew the time would have to come. She dreaded it. Thinking how upsetting it would be for Chloe sitting in a courtroom, filled her with sadness for her friend.

Pippa knew she had to make more of an effort to keep her promise to that good woman about trying to be happier, which was why she'd accepted a date with Ben tonight. He'd confessed to recently splitting with his girlfriend, and needing some cheering up himself.

He invited her to a friend's birthday party at one of the local cafes. Pippa had a feeling alcohol would no doubt be part of the celebration. She told Ben she didn't drink. He assured her that wouldn't be a problem. Somehow his words hadn't done much to calm her nervousness.

She bought a sundress covered with red hibiscus flowers hoping to put herself in a more festive mood. She twirled in front of the full length mirror that evening. The new dress, careful attention to her makeup, and a different hairdo did make her feel better – on the outside, anyway. She slipped on a pair of low heeled sandals seconds before she heard his knock.

Ben's eyes lit up with appreciation, when Pippa opened the door.

"You look terrific."

She smiled at his khaki shorts and dark brown sports shirt.

"Thanks, so do you."

"All right, then."

251

He took her by the hand and tugged her into the hall. "Let's do this."

Pippa supposed she didn't enjoy herself as much as everyone else seemed to, because she was the only stranger at the party. Not only that, they all were highly intoxicated, including her date. By the time the festivities ended in the early hours of the morning, Ben could barely walk.

She took charge, and hailed a cab. To make matters more uncomfortable for her, Ben was a sloppy, kissy drunk, and kept trying to grope her in the backseat. Pippa felt as though she'd been wrestling with an octopus by the time the driver dropped them off at their building.

He pulled Pippa down onto a wooden bench outside, and began pawing at her bodice. She slapped at his hands trying to fend him off.

"Stop it, Ben."

"Don't play hard to get. Come on, kiss me."

Pippa tried to work her leg free to knee him in the groin when Ben's weight suddenly lifted from her. A quick hit on the jaw made him go limp before he had a chance to utter a protest. She scrambled to her feet, her eyes widened in surprise, and her mouth gaped open in disbelief.

"I must be dreaming."

"More of a nightmare wouldn't you say?" Shade answered in a grim voice, nodding at Ben.

Pippa watched as he hoisted the younger man on one shoulder and walked into the building, while she hurried to follow. She noticed he pressed the correct number for her floor when they got inside the elevator. With so many emotions rolling through her right now, she didn't know which one to give into first. Having Shade witness her being pawed, added one more layer to her disgrace.

"I suppose Chloe told you where to find me. I want to make it clear I didn't ask her to."

"I'm aware of that. I had business in the city. It seemed neighborly to see how you were doing as long as I was here. And speaking of neighbors, what's with lover boy here?"

"Ben? His girlfriend just broke up with him. He was feeling depressed, so when he asked me out I didn't think I should refuse. He's been a gentleman until tonight. I bet he's going to feel terrible when he realizes what he tried to do. At least nothing happened."

"This time."

"It's the alcohol. I'm sure he didn't really mean to do anything."

Shade snorted.

"Pippa, the man was on top of you with his fly unzipped."

They got out on her floor. He felt in Ben's pockets until he found his key. Pippa stood there feeling more uncomfortable by the minute. Shade opened the door and dumped Ben on his couch.

"He's going to be out for awhile. Let's get out of here."

Shade held out his hand toward her as soon as they were in the hallway again.

She looked at his palm and frowned.

"What?"

"Give me your key."

"I'm perfectly capable of unlocking my own door."

But her hands belied her words by shaking when she tried to open her purse. Delayed reaction, she supposed from Ben's behavior. Not to mention Shade showing up so unexpectedly. He took the bag from her, plucked out the key, and opened the door himself. He led her to a chair before walking into the kitchen, only to return a few seconds later carrying a glass of water.

"I'm not thirsty."

"Drink," he insisted, holding the glass to her lips.

She drank, until he was satisfied. Bonnie waddled in, and gave Shade a sleepy yawn. Pippa reached down to pull the dog into her arms, needing the comfort of the warm little body.

"Some watchdog you have there."

"She's not a watchdog. She's a companion. Why are you really here, Shade? And don't give me that excuse about it having to do with business."

"I do have business here, as a matter of fact. But I would have come even if I didn't. I've left you alone for almost three months. That's long enough, especially for someone who collects trouble like beads on a bracelet. You're welcome for my help with Romeo, by the way."

"I was getting around to thanking you."

He lifted a brow.

"Thank you. Three months may be long enough for you, but not for me. You've done your good deed. You can leave now."

"You need someone to look after you. I've appointed myself your guardian."

"Stop thinking you have to take care of me. I can fight my own battles."

"That's debatable. Did you really think I'd let you go after I told you I'm in love with you?"

"I don't know how you can love me considering all the trouble I've caused you."

"Beats the hell out of me, but I do. Maybe I also miss your soft, comforting arms."

"Yeah, right. An old flannel shirt could do the same, and be a lot less trouble."

He chuckled.

"But not nearly as exciting."

"Personally, I've had my fill of excitement. Seeing you takes me back to the wolf issue. That's the last thing I need to be thinking about. Your being here isn't going to help me forget."

"You've milked that long enough. You didn't have to leave my home."

"That's easy for you to say. I'm the one who made an ass out of herself. I couldn't stay there knowing everyone would be staring at me like I was some kind of freak."

"Good God, Pippa, it's not as though you had acid thrown in your face. There aren't any scars you need to hide."

"The scars are inside."

"Only because you continue to let them be."

"How can I not, when I know everyone at Wolfhaven has to be laughing at me for thinking you turned yourself into a wolf. I still can't believe I could be so stupid. I bet they're all talking about the crazy redhead. I know I would be if the situation was in reverse."

"No one is laughing, and no one thinks you're crazy. Ross and I are the only ones who know what you thought. The only reason he does is because you told him it could have been me you hit with your car, the night you bumped into Samson. I'm the one who's ashamed for having everyone lie, including myself about there not being any wolves at Wolfhaven."

"You didn't think it was important enough to tell me even after all the hints I kept dropping. All I needed was one word from you, Shade. Instead you left me wondering while I nearly drove myself insane with my relentless imagination."

"I told you I couldn't say anything. I also said I'd explain why. You're the one who insisted you had to leave. You wouldn't listen when I tried to stop you. You thought you had to go because you needed to hide. I understand what happened made you feel ridiculous."

"That's putting it mildly. I felt like I'd been caught dancing naked in Times Square and had it televised on national television."

"What an intriguing vision. You were so busy beating yourself up that you never gave me a chance to clarify things from my end. How much longer were you going to shut me out?"

"Pretty much for good. At first I needed to hide from everyone at Wolfhaven. Then every time I thought about my silly juvenile fantasy, I tried to hide from myself."

"How's that working out for you?"

"Not very well. Deep down, I did want to call you. My pride wouldn't let me."

"Pride's a lonely partner in life."

"Yes it is." She rubbed her cheek against the fluffy topknot on the dog's head. "Don't you ever get tired of rescuing me?"

"It's what I live for," Shade replied in a dry tone.

"Since you were here tonight I guess that means you've been watching me. Did you set this whole dog sitting thing up? Is there really an Eva? Is this her place? Her dog? Or has it all just been an elaborate deception? We both know you're good at that."

"Eva does exist. This is her place. That ball of yarn you're holding really is her dog."

"I'm surprised. Does Chloe actually know her?"

"I introduced them via telephone. They helped me put this plan together. That idiot next door wasn't part of the agenda. I'll be dealing with him when he sobers up."

"I told you he's been very nice to me up until tonight."

"Don't bother to defend him. If he can't hold his drink any better than his behavior indicated tonight, then he needs to stay away from alcohol. My grandmother thinks you're very naïve for a woman of your age. It appears he took advantage of that."

256

"Lila thinks I'm naïve? Great. It's one more reason for me to feel self-conscious."

"She cares about you very much and wanted to be sure I understood how things are." He took the glass into the kitchen and came back. "Where does the dog sleep?"

"On my bed."

"Not tonight. Go shower the stench of that drunk off of you and get into bed."

Pippa stiffened.

"I don't want to share a bed with you, Shade."

"I'm not leaving, and I'm not sleeping on that flimsy sofa. If you're worried I'll continue what your neighbor started, I'm not that insensitive. Take your shower. I'll see to the dog."

She set Bonnie on the floor and stood up.

"How long have you been watching me?"

"A while."

"I never saw you."

"That was the idea. I'd planned to reveal myself to you tonight and take you out to dinner. Benny boy beat me to it. I'm sorry I didn't get here sooner. Are you feeling any better now?"

"I'm still a little shaky. I'm also still trying to take in the fact that you set this up."

Pippa waved her arm around the room.

"We both know why I'm here, and what you hoped the time away would accomplish. But nothing's going to change until I know about the wolves. I need to understand why everyone lied to me, even after I heard and saw so much."

"You will in the morning. I promise. You're tired. Shower and bed for you right now."

"I wish you'd stop treating me like a child."

"Then stop acting like one."

He pointed toward the bathroom.

"Go."

Pippa started to protest, but fatigue, and the shock of Ben's behavior, plus finding Shade here had robbed her of the desire to argue. Gathering what dignity she had left, she walked out of the room. She took her shower, climbed into bed, and waited for the comfort only Shade seemed to be able to give.

Pippa could pretend all she wanted trying to convince herself she didn't want him here. The truth was she did need him. Despite all her protesting, she really had missed Shade. She lay there listening as he used the shower and moved to make room for him when he climbed into bed.

He pulled her against his bare chest. The reassuring beat of his heart made her relax.

"I'm still mad that you're treating me like a baby," she said before a yawn escaped her.

"Duly noted. Now shut up, and go to sleep."

A retort died on Pippa's lips, as she closed her eyes and let herself drift until she tumbled into her first really good night's sleep since leaving Wolfhaven.

Pippa awoke to the wailing tune of a lone saxophone drifting in through the open window. Realizing she was alone in bed, she listened for sounds of Shade's presence. She called his name. No answer. Had he left her already? Disappointed, she hurried into the living room and found it empty of both man and dog.

Frowning, she wandered to the kitchen and saw a note by the coffee maker.

"Took the dog out. Coffee's made. Breakfast when I return. S."

The image of Shade holding the pink leash with the tiny little dog meandering on the other end made her smile. She drank coffee, washed, and dressed.

Pippa heard Shade come back as she finished making the bed and went to meet him.

"How'd the walk go?"

"Sociable little bugger, isn't she?"

"What can I say? She likes people, plus everyone in the neighborhood knows her."

"So I discovered."

"I bet she was a good girl. Come here, sweetie. Let me give you a great big hug."

Pippa picked up the dog to nuzzle her neck and received an excited yip in return.

"She's not the only one you should be hugging. I think I deserve a reward for various reasons," Shade said. Taking the wiggling dog, he set the little animal on the floor.

"You were going to be next. I just thought you wanted your breakfast first."

"That appetite can wait. This particular one can't."

He pulled her into his arms, and took his reward with a thorough kiss. Pippa had little doubt he would have helped himself to more if someone hadn't knocked at the door.

Shade lifted his head.

"We'll continue this later."

The heat in his eyes made her blush.

"Are you expecting someone?"

"No, but you are."

"I am not. What have you been up to now, Shade?"

"Lover boy has sobered up enough to make amends for his ungentlemanly behavior."

She raised her brows.

"How do you know?"

"Bonnie and I paid him a little visit this morning."

"Please don't tell me you hit him again. I have to live here a few more weeks, you know. "

"Which is why I set down a few ground rules."

"Did that include another punch in the face?" she repeated.

"Why don't you open the door and find out?"

Twenty-five

A disheveled looking Ben stood there leaning against the wall.

"I believe you have something to say to Pippa."

"Yeah. Um, I really am sorry about last night, Pippa. I've always had a problem holding my liquor. I'm usually more careful. I guess I got carried away and lost count of how much booze I had. I know it's no excuse for the way I behaved. I promise you it'll never happen again. Let me know what your dress cost if I did any damage and I'll reimburse you."

"That won't be necessary. I appreciate you coming here to apologize. But you know, Ben, your words would mean a lot more if you'd think seriously about giving up drinking, if last night is any indication of what too much liquor does to you."

"I can handle it okay as long as I don't overindulge. I guess I was feeling sorry for myself because my girlfriend dumped me for another guy."

He ran a shaky hand through his hair. "I hope we can still be friends," he said shooting Shade another cautious glance.

"I don't plan on us being enemies, but I don't feel comfortable being friends again, either."

"I understand."

He mumbled another apology and made a hasty retreat back to his apartment.

Pippa closed the door and looked at Shade.

"You must have hit him pretty hard to knock him out and cause his jaw to look like that."

"He's lucky that's all I did."

"Did you have to be so aggressive?"

"Would you rather I patted him on the head and made him promise to be a good boy?"

"I guess not. I just hate seeing people get hurt. I am grateful that you helped me out of a difficult situation. I realize I didn't thank you properly last night. I felt a little rattled."

"You had a rough time. My thanks is that I got to you in time before he went any further."

"I suppose I am naïve, because I try to look for the good in people."

"That's not such a bad thing. The world might be better off if we all did a bit more of that."

"Thanks, but I don't deserve any accolades. It's a defense mechanism. I look for the good in people because I want them to look for the good in me."

"Pippa, you're a wonderful person. You have a lot to offer. You need to believe in yourself more. We'll eat our breakfast now and then have that talk I promised you."

"I can only offer you cereal unless you'd like to wait while I make a run to the store. If I'd known you were coming I would have had something more substantial. Or we can go out to eat."

"Not to worry. Everything's taken care of." Shade pulled out his cell phone, said a few words, and cut the connection. "Food is on its way."

"What do you mean? This isn't a hotel. There isn't any room service here."

"There is now," he said, as another knock sounded at the door.

He opened it and stood back while two men dressed in white jackets and black slacks came into the apartment. One wheeled a cart laden with covered dishes while the other carried a small folding table under one arm and two chairs in the other.

261

Shade pointed toward the living room.

"In there will be fine, gentlemen."

Pippa watched in fascination as they laid out two place settings complete with china, crystal goblets, sterling silver, and linen napkins. Shade pulled a chair out for her. She sat down to a papaya half garnished with a wedge of lime, an omelet filled with fresh vegetables, a slab of honey cured ham, croissants, curls of butter, assorted jams, and coffee.

Shade walked the men to the door and came back to join her at the table.

"How's it look?"

"Fantastic. This sure beats cereal. How did they do all this so quickly?"

"I ordered while I was walking the dog. They were in the lobby waiting for my call."

They ate, made small talk, and enjoyed each other's company, even though they both knew the promise that he would tell her about the wolves hovered between them. Pippa put her fork down for the last time, wiped her mouth, and put her napkin on the table by her plate.

"Thank you for the delicious breakfast."

"I'm glad you enjoyed it." He picked up the coffee carafe. "Would you like more coffee?"

"What I would like is to hear about the wolves now. Or are you stalling for time?"

"Not at all. I'm just as anxious as you are to have everything out in the open."

Pippa drummed her fingers on the table, as she watched him fill his own cup, take a sip, and return it to the saucer. He reached over and touched her, stilling her restless hand.

"I'm sorry, Shade. It's just that I've waited so long for this."

"I know, and it's been way overdue in coming." He sat back in his chair. "I think it would be best if I went all

262

the way back to the beginning, to my great-great-grandfather's time."

"The one who built Wolfhaven?"

"Yes. He loved the mountains and the wildlife, especially the wolves. That was why he chose to make his home there. He did his best to protect them. Unfortunately in those days too many others in the area wanted to eradicate them by wiping them out completely."

"Because they thought they were too dangerous?"

"Mostly they felt the wolves killed off too much of the game animals. My great-great-grandfather never encouraged his guests to hunt like some of the other lumber barons did."

"So they could have their trophy heads stuffed and mounted in their dens back home," she sniffed in disgust.

"Pretty much. Everything stayed fairly even between the different species until my grandfather Warren came along. He didn't care for wolves or any of the other animals living near Wolfhaven. In fact, he hated the house, the woods, and the wildlife. He didn't care if they were all hunted to extinction. My father loved wolves and did everything he could to preserve the species."

"Let me see if I have your family straight. Was Warren Lila's son?"

Shade nodded. "That's right."

"So Lila is your great-grandmother, then?"

"Yes. Leaving off the great makes it easier. My actual grandmother died in childbirth."

"How sad. I had no idea. Lila told me the wolves have been gone for years."

"Running freely as packs in the woods, yes. My father managed to save some, and breed them in secret by keeping the pack very small. He couldn't keep them here, so he sent them to other areas when they matured. He believed in conservation of animals and the environment.

Samson is a direct descendant of the alpha male of the original group."

"I thought he was going to kill me that night in the garden."

Shade linked his fingers with hers on the table.

"He's used to being around people he knows and normally avoids strangers. He may have been curious. Or he thought you were invading his territory. He went with instinct to protect what he feels is his."

"And you. He was protecting you."

"That, too."

"I had a feeling he'd be the top dog. He seemed to have a certain bearing about him."

"He does. My father saw that I had an interest in helping him in his efforts. He had to be very careful who he could trust because of my grandfather's attitude." He played with her fingers for a moment. "I'm sorry to say they did not have a good relationship."

"Because your father was happier planting a tree or saving animals from annihilation, than chairing a board meeting," Pippa said remembering what Vanessa had told her.

"That about sums it up."

"Vanessa told me he deliberately crashed their plane to be free of his father."

Instant fury flared in Shade's eyes, and for a moment his fingers tightened on her hand hard enough to make Pippa wince.

"She's a liar. My father did not deliberately crash. They had engine trouble. He couldn't have done anything differently. The investigation bore that out."

"I'm sorry. I shouldn't have mentioned that knowing the kind of person she is. Did you want to keep Samson a secret from me because you were afraid I'd tell someone?"

"Yes. I've been working with the proper authorities for the last few years to finally reintroduce a wolf pack into the forest around Wolfhaven. Part of gaining their cooperation involved keeping the project a secret. We're not ready to go public yet. That's why I haven't announced our plans. It's going to be hard for me knowing I won't be able to protect them when they wander off my land. But I knew that when I took this on. I've already let Samson roam as you know."

"That must be how I saw him my first night. You said he's your pet."

"He is, as the other alphas before him. They bonded with me. But my goal has always been to allow them to run free."

"Weren't you worried about me hearing the wolves before you hired me?"

"I had to take that chance. The doctors said Lila needed some kind of diversion when her health began to fail. I knew she wanted to write her stories. We both assumed being a city girl you'd accept our explanations."

"I can't believe I would be the only one who heard Samson's howling. Surely someone else in the area must have said something to you or your dad."

"Some people have. We told them we'd prefer if they turned a deaf ear. We also let it be known we would appreciate their discretion when they did their trapping."

Pippa raised her eyebrows.

"You have that much power to assure such support?"

"It's not so much power as a willingness to respect our wishes. The Avalon family has done a great deal for the surrounding communities over the years. People tend to remember that."

"Don't bite the hand that feeds you kind of thing."

"Something like that."

"What about a woman named Nona? I overheard Ross firing her. She threatened him, saying she could cause trouble. Did she mean the wolves?"

Shade shook his head.

"No. Ross told me about the incident. She worked at the house helping with the cleaning. He caught her trying to steal some of my grandmother's jewelry. Her threats were a way to try and keep her job. He didn't report her because he knows her family."

"Well, that clears up another mystery. Where do you keep the wolves?"

"They have their own area hidden away. You were right about that part."

"Is the man I saw on the path that day involved in the program? He carried a leash."

"Jim. Yes, he's one of the handlers. He told me about running into you."

"That puppy I thought I heard the night I got lost. Did I imagine that, or was it from there?"

"You didn't imagine it. One of Delilah's pups somehow got out; and unfortunately you heard it and tried to save him. I'm very sorry about what happened to you because of it."

"Did you ever find out who hit me, or how I ended up at Sam's hospital?"

Shade's mouth thinned into a tight line.

"No."

"What about the puppy? Were you able to locate the poor little thing?"

"Yes, and he certainly fared better than you did that night."

"Its mother's name is Delilah? You mean as in Samson and Delilah?"

He nodded.

"My father's idea. I kept the names out of respect for him. I add numbers to distinguish each generation."

"Aren't you afraid Samson will leave and not come back when you let him out?"

"No. Besides being my pet, he won't leave Delilah. She's his mate. Wolves mate for life."

"Lila and the Hendersons know about all this, of course."

"Yes they do."

"I kept trying to get them to tell me, mostly because I thought you were a wolf."

She huffed out a breath.

"Lila's right, I am naïve."

"All part of your charm."

She rolled her eyes.

"Some charm. I'm surprised you didn't offer to send me to a shrink."

"Why do you insist on using yourself as a whipping girl?"

"Because I'm so used to it. I've always tried to put up a good front, but underneath all that I'm insecure. You have to understand that every rejection, every betrayal is like a punch in the stomach to me. You get mighty sensitive after awhile."

"It could help if you'd stop dwelling on that."

Her laugh was short and bitter, as she pulled her hand away from his.

"My mother threw me away at birth. I ended up having to leave every home I ever lived in growing up. A man I thought of as a brother betrayed me for money, and you didn't trust me when I practically begged you to tell me about the wolves."

Pippa held up her hand, when Shade started to reply.

"You don't have to keep feeling responsible for me. I know it doesn't seem like it, but I think I've grown up a lot since I left Wolfhaven. I'm working on becoming a realist. No more wishing for a life I can't have, or indulging in ridiculous fantasies."

"I'd hate to see you give up all your fantasies just because you thought I turned into a wolf. I'm sorry if I sounded unsympathetic. Forgive me."

"It's okay. But if you thought you were going to insult me into growing more confident, you're too late. Chloe already tried that. I told you before I don't want to be an embarrassment to you, and I certainly don't want us to end up in some kind of sick codependent relationship."

Shade snatched his napkin off his lap and tossed it onto the table.

"Now you listen to me, damn it! There's nothing wrong with being codependent when two people care about each other. It's called mutual support. You think you're the only one who's vulnerable? Well, think again. I can be hurt."

"But you always seem so strong."

"Only because I've had to be. You are, too. I lost my family, and you never had a permanent one. It is sad that your mother threw you away at birth, but you don't know what her circumstances were at the time. She could have had an abortion, instead she gave you life. We've both had it rough in our own way, but we didn't give up."

"What do you call me running away all the time, if that's not giving up?"

"Repositioning while you get your bearings. You've had glitches in your life, so you kept moving on trying to find something better. And now you have."

She frowned.

"I have? What?"

Shade gave her a big grin.

"That would be me."

"Oh. I still can't understand how you could want someone like me."

"How about this, then? You're an amazing woman with an incredible capacity to give of yourself even though you grew up without anyone really giving you much in return. You were doing okay with that until I came along and screwed things up by offering you more than anyone has ever offered you before. It wasn't your fault you were left at birth. You need to learn how to believe that you have a right to be loved."

"It's difficult when you've felt unwanted most of your life. But you make me feel special."

"That's because you are special. You're just not used to people telling you." He watched as different emotions played across her expressive face.

"Come back to Wolfhaven with me when you're done here. We've all missed you very much."

"I miss everyone, too. How is Lila doing?"

"Longing to see you, and angry with me."

Pippa's eyes widened.

"Why is she mad at you? I'm the one who's caused all the trouble."

"She thinks I should have told you about the wolf project sooner."

"I had the feeling toward the end that she was leading up to it herself. I meant it when I said you could trust me, Shade. I wouldn't have revealed your secret to anyone. No matter what it was."

"I realize that now. Can you forgive me?"

"You've given me a lot to think about."

"Here's more. Why did you put yourself at risk and come to help me when you thought I was in danger after that fake message from Craig?"

"I didn't want you to get hurt."

"Is that the only reason?"

She shook her head.

"I think you know by now I did it because I love you."

"And I've said I love you. I've also tried to show my feelings with my body. Obviously those things haven't been enough to convince you to stay with me. If I asked you to choose a place where you'd like to spend a honeymoon, would that help?"

Pippa's mouth gaped opened.

"Are you asking me to . . . to marry you?"

"Sounds like it."

"I don't know how you could possibly want me as your wife after all the trouble I've put you through. I insulted you. I ran away. I blamed you for getting myself lost. I accused you of having an affair, and the worse thing of all was thinking you were a wolf."

"My answer to all that is, no one can say life around you is dull."

"You are a glutton for punishment."

He shrugged.

"I like a good challenge."

"Speaking of a challenge, I'm thinking of one of those puzzles where you have to make all the little steel balls fit into their holes. It looks like I've finally managed to do that thanks to you. I guess you were all I needed to help me win."

He tugged her into his arms.

"That's what I've been trying to tell you. What do you say?"

"I love you so much it's unbearable to think of life without you. I've given you every reason I can think of to reject me, but you keep coming back. So, I won't be running away anymore. You'll be stuck with me for good. How's that for an answer?"

Shade scooped her up, and carried her to the bedroom.

"It sounds like you just accepted my proposal."

Twenty-six

Shade's ringing cell phone disturbed the room's quiet sometime later that morning. He groaned, and rolled onto his back taking Pippa with him until he could see who was calling.

"It's my grandmother. I have a feeling she'll want to talk to you."

"Does she know you came here to propose?"

He handed her the phone.

"Only one way to find out."

Pippa took the phone from him, feeling a little embarrassed to be lying naked with Shade while talking to his grandmother.

"Hello. It's good to hear your voice, too. I'm fine, thank you."

She swatted at Shade's hand when he fondled her breast. He gave her a wicked grin, and moved to the other creamy globe earning a warning glare.

"How are you? Oh, good. Yes, he did ask me to marry him, and I accepted. I'm so glad you're happy. I'm very excited, too. What? Yes, he did tell me about the wolves. No, it doesn't bother me at all. I've always liked animals. Okay, we'll talk later. Here's Shade."

He said a few more words and cut the connection.

"You've made her very happy."

"I'm still trying to accept that this isn't a dream and I'm going to wake up any moment to find out your proposal was nothing more than wishful thinking on my part."

He pinched her on one bare buttock.

"Ouch! Why did you do that?"

"Just wanted you to know you weren't dreaming. May I suggest you brace yourself, because between my grandmother, Chloe, and Marcie you are going to be in for one hell of a shindig the day we wed."

"Oh, but wouldn't you prefer a quiet little ceremony at Wolfhaven?"

"Yes, and I did suggest keeping it simple when I told Gram I was going to propose. She immediately got on the phone to the other ladies. They want you to have the dress and flowers and whatever else goes along with being a bride. Think you can handle all that?"

"I guess so. But will you manage?"

"I don't care how or where we get married, as long as I get my ring on your finger."

She kissed him on the end of his nose.

"You're so brave."

"Just a guy in love."

Pippa felt so happy a little imp inside her couldn't resist teasing him.

"Marcie had Sam wear a white tux with a pink bowtie and matching cummerbund when they got married."

"I'm not that brave. I'd rather stand there naked."

"All the ladies would love that, but I like the way you look in black."

"Bless you."

"I should be saying that to you. Knowing I'll never be alone again is a gift that means more to me than you can ever know."

"Oh, my little love," he said, his voice thick with emotion. "Every breath you take brings me to a level of happiness I never thought I'd ever feel."

He drew her face down to take her lips in a slow, gentle kiss, when his phone rang again. Pippa pulled back making Shade groan in disappointment.

"Leave it," he said against her mouth.

"It might be important. Lila could be calling you back."

Holding her on top of him with one hand, he picked up the phone with the other.

"I should have turned the damn thing off. It's Chloe. She probably wants to talk about the wedding. Any chance I can convince you to call her back later?"

"I'd really like to talk to her. Do you mind terribly?"

Shade reluctantly handed Pippa the phone, knowing her mind would no longer be on making love once she started talking to her friend. She wiggled away from him, and sat up in the middle of the bed immediately drawing his eyes to her lovely breasts.

Shaking his head with regret, he swung his legs over the edge of the bed, tortured himself with one last look, and headed for the bathroom just as he heard her burst of excited laughter.

Eva's small apartment wasn't conducive for Shade to do business, so he rented office space in a nearby building. Work sometimes didn't allow him to have dinner with Pippa, but nothing could keep him from sleeping with her every night, which also meant they breakfasted together.

She received several phone calls every day with the three important women in her life going over wedding plans. Shade shuddered to think how involved those plans were becoming, but he wanted everything to be perfect for Pippa. God knows she deserved the best considering she'd been forced to live with so few material things all her life, plus depending on people for whatever handouts they chose to give her.

They were into their third week. Shade kept in daily contact with home. He couldn't help smiling every time he talked to Lila, knowing how much she enjoyed being a part of the wedding plans. Enid verified that Lila was all but blooming with excitement.

He also checked with Ross for daily reports on how things were going in the wolf compound, and was pleased to learn that Delilah was expecting another litter of pups. Shade didn't like being away from his wolves so long, especially Samson, even though he knew they were all being well cared for. He looked forward to taking Pippa to the secret lair, and giving her a proper introduction to Samson along with the rest of the pack.

Shade felt rich in more ways than having money. He would soon be married to the woman he loved. He'd finally shared his secret wolf project with Pippa. His grandmother's health had improved and all was well at home. He couldn't ask for things to be any better than that.

Jerry paced back and forth over the planked floor of the small cabin before he stopped and stood there literally quivering with excitement.

"I'm tellin' you Harv, I saw a whole pack of wolves."

"What are you goin' on about? You know there ain't been no wolves around these woods for years and years. You been at the hooch again?"

Jerry pulled a chair out from the table and sat across from his friend.

"No, I ain't drunk. You know darn well we both heard the sound of howling and always said it must be the wind. Well, they're real all right. I saw them with my own eyes. They're bein' kept all nice and tidy behind a fence. You know, like they was prized pets."

"A fence? That's means they belong to someone. Did you go back on Avalon land again?"

A deep flush reddened Jerry's neck and face.

"I was just lookin' around."

"I thought we agreed you weren't goin' there no more after you found that girl."

"I ain't been back until today. I been real good about that, so you don't have any cause to get so riled at me. I didn't think it'd hurt to look."

"Okay, so you looked. That means you can stop goin' on about it now."

"I don't know, Harv. It seems like we oughta report this, or something' There ain't supposed to be wolves around here. Don't it make you wonder what those uppity Avalons are doin'?"

"I don't care what they're up to, and you shouldn't either. Stay out of their business."

"Don't seem right I got to keep my nose clean while they do stuff like keepin' wolves."

"Yeah well, if a person has enough money, he can do pretty much anything he wants."

"You think they're goin' to sell them wolves, and make themselves more money?"

Harv shrugged his bony shoulders.

"How should I know? Why do you care anyhow?"

"I'm curious. A man's got a right to be curious. I bet that's what they're doin'. Yep, probably raising those animals in secret and selling them to zoos or something. I saw a big healthy looking male walking around all lordly like he was king of the world. An animal that fine could bring in a lot of cash."

"Well, it ain't gonna be money in your pocket. It's Avalon business on Avalon property. I don't want you goin' back there no more, so just stop talkin' about them wolves. I mean it."

"You're getting to sound like an old woman, Harv. Those folks already got themselves barrels of money. It don't seem right they get to have more, and not share it with the rest of us who live around here."

Jerry wagged his head back and forth.

"No sir, it just don't seem right."

"It don't matter if it's right or not. Them wolves don't have nothin' to do with us."

"They got a lot of 'em. What would it hurt if one was to go missin'?"

Harv slammed his fist on the table causing a bottle sitting there to wobble.

"You listen to me now. Poachin' rabbits is one thing, but don't you go thinkin' you can steal no wolf. There's probably all kinds of high tech security around that compound, and people watchin'. You're just askin' to go back to jail. Is that what you want?"

"Course not. But they can't be watchin' the place all the time, especially if their attention was pulled somewhere else. You know, like if something was to happen that made them forget about them wolves for a spell."

"What could happen? What are you talkin' about?"

"Nothin'. I was just joshing. Relax. I ain't about to go up against no Avalon." He stood up.

Harv narrowed his eyes. "Where you goin'?"

"You are an old woman. I'm just goin' check my snares."

Shade sat only half listening to one of the trio of men talking. He'd agreed to meet them out for breakfast, even though he'd much rather be back at the apartment with Pippa. He was about to lie and say he had an urgent phone call, when he felt his cell phone vibrate.

"Excuse me, gentlemen."

He pulled the phone out, and saw a message from Ross.

"Urgent! Call home."

Sheer strength of will kept Shade's voice level.

"I'm sorry, but it appears I have an emergency," he said and held up his phone.

They nodded and he left the table to hurry outside.

Ross answered immediately.

"Oh Mister Shade, thank God it's you."

"What's happened?"

Shade gripped his phone.

"Is my grandmother all right?"

"She's fine. We've had a fire here at the house."

Fear leaped inside Shade's chest.

"Was anyone hurt?"

"No. I called Dr. Arnold. He and his wife have taken Mrs. Avalon and Enid to their home."

"How bad is the fire?"

"Pretty bad. The whole house would have gone up in flames if we didn't have the indoor sprinkling system. Most of the damage seems to be confined to the ground floor. I called in every available man working on the property to come and help. The county fire trucks are here now."

"I appreciate your quick action. Do you have any idea what caused the fire?"

Ross cleared his throat.

"It's a little early to be sure yet, but there's talk of arson."

"What the hell! All right, stay available in case I need to call you back. I'll leave here now."

He called for his plane. He contacted Pippa next and wasted little time telling her what had happened. He cut through her horrified gasps to let her know he was on his way to the airport.

"Arson? Oh dear God. What about Lila and the Hendersons. Are they all right?"

"Yes. They all escaped unharmed. Ross sent the women to Sam and Marcie's."

"Thank the lord. Do you want me to go with you? I'll ask Ben to watch Bonnie. I doubt he'll refuse. It won't take me long to get ready."

"I would like to have you, but there's no time."

"I still wish I could be there for you. I can't get over all these awful things that have happened. Me getting lost, that business with Vanessa, Marcie's accident, your friend dying, and now this."

"Events in life do seem to come in waves. Sometimes they lift you up, and other times they have you crashing down."

"Oh Shade, your beautiful house. I can't bear to think of it being damaged. I'm so very sorry. Who would do such a thing?"

"I don't know. But save your pity for the person who started the fire, because when I'm through with them they will regret the day they ever learned to strike a match."

Twenty-seven

Harv lifted the tarp covering Samson's still body before he dared an anxious glance toward Jerry. "He's a real handsome one, ain't he?"

"God Almighty boy, what have you done now? Is he dead?"

"Course not. He ain't no good to us dead."

Jerry clenched his jaw.

"You took the Avalon wolf after you promised you wouldn't."

"I didn't really promise. I just told you I was joshin' when I really wasn't. Besides, I only took this one. They got lots more; pups and everything. It ain't like I left them with nothin."

"How'd you get this one?"

"Tranquilizer gun. I hid behind a bush, and popped him when he came out."

"You said they were behind a fence. Someone musta seen you."

"Nah. Everyone was too busy tryin' to put out the fire."

"Fire? What fire? You ain't makin' no sense, boy."

"I threw oily rags in a few spots around that fancy house of theirs and tossed a match."

Harv's sunken cheeks paled.

"Oh my God. You've really gone and done it now. They're goin' put you in jail for sure. And this time you're goin' to be locked up for a long time."

"How they goin' catch me? No one knows I was there. But listen. I got good news. I made some calls. I told ya there'd be people lookin' for these animals. I got a fellow who wants this wolf real bad, and he's goin' give me a big wad of money. He'll meet us halfway with his van. It'll be a good five hour drive for us, so we'd best get started."

Harv shook his head.

"I ain't goin' with you. You crossed way over the line on this one, and I ain't aimin' to be locked up when they catch you. And they will."

"What kind of talk is that about you not comin'? I did this for you, too, Harv. I done told you I'm gettin' real good money. I'll split it with you."

"I don't care about no money. I just want you to go and take that animal with you."

Jerry covered Samson with the tarp again, and climbed into the Jeep.

"Okay. I'll go make the delivery and be back with your share of the money. Then we'll have a doozy of a celebration."

"No, Jerry. I don't want you back. I don't want no part of this, includin' the money."

Hurt clouded the younger man's eyes.

"You can't mean that. We're a team."

"We ain't no team in this. People live in that house, Jerry. I heard tell old Mrs. Avalon is in a wheelchair. Did you think about that when you torched their place?"

"You don't have to worry about that none. I seen them all come outside. The old lady, too,"

"Well, thank the good lord for that. You better go on now before that beast wakes up."

"You gotta let me come back. I don't got nowhere else to go. You know that. I promise this'll be the last time I go on Avalon property. I mean it, Harv."

He held out his hands in a gesture of entreaty, his voice almost whining now.

"You already promised you wouldn't go there again. But you did anyways. You shoulda thought about how I'd feel before you started this crazy stunt. Go on now, I'm done with you."

He pointed to the lane leading away from the cabin before going inside.

Jerry stared at the closed door and shouted.

"I know you're real sore at me right now, so I'll leave you here to simmer down. I'll be back. I know you didn't really mean for me to stay away."

Jerry waited several seconds. When the door didn't open he started the engine and drove off, looking over his shoulder until he could no longer see the cabin. He couldn't believe his old friend didn't want him back.

All he'd been able to think about was getting his hands on the money. Not just for himself. Harv was his friend and the closest thing to a father he'd ever known. They took care of each other. He knew Harv was getting older. He wanted to have the money to do something nice for him, like buy him a new mattress to replace the one he had now that sagged in the middle. He'd buy the old man some new bedding while he was at it. Those blankets were looking pretty thin. And he'd get him some new boots. Yeah, that would make Harv happy. He'd buy all those things, and add a couple bottles of some real fine drinking whiskey. Harv was bound to forgive him and be his friend again.

Satisfied that his plan would get him back in his friend's good graces, Jerry settled in for the drive ahead of him. He'd pulled off his skimpy track onto another road, not much wider, but one that he knew would take him directly to the main highway he needed. Fifteen minutes later he came out of the woods and turned onto the road.

Jerry knew all the sharp curves. The fact that the steep drop to the canyon was on one side of the road actually made this highway more dangerous than the rough dirt lanes he'd just driven on. He turned right, and had only gone a few miles when he cursed in frustration at the sight of the pickup truck pulling the travel trailer driving in front of him.

"Darn tourists have no business being up here in the mountains with their rigs the way most of 'em drive," he grumbled.

He pressed his foot down harder on the gas pedal making ready to pass. But just as he'd cleared the other vehicles a deer jumped out in front of him. He instinctively swerved to miss the large animal. That proved to be a mistake, and the last one he would ever make. The Jeep skidded, veered off the highway straight over the edge plunging down toward the canyon, expelling both man and beast, as it bounced and rolled to the bottom.

Pippa held the phone to her ear with one hand, and stroked Bonnie with the other, seeking comfort. She knew she wasn't the only one feeling edgy. Shade's voice sounded tight with tension. She couldn't blame him. The house belonging to his family for generations had suffered serious damage in the fire. To make the situation even more upsetting it could have cost Lila and the Hendersons their lives.

"Where are you staying right now?"

"We're all bunking at Sam and Marcie's."

"How is Lila handling having her home almost burn down? She must be terribly upset."

"She's doing better than I dared hoped, although the shock of the fire and damage to the house did shake her up initially. Sam gave her a light sedative. Enid and Marcie put her to bed."

"Thank goodness for those two good ladies."

"I couldn't agree more."

"I'm almost afraid to ask. Will Wolfhaven ever be livable again?"

"Eventually. The ground floor is going to need some major renovation. We'll be able to duplicate most of the wood that was destroyed. We lost some of the gardens closest to the house, but most of the rest is intact."

"I'm glad of that. What about the second floor? Were any of your paintings damaged?"

"They're all out on exhibit. The fire didn't reach there. The studio did suffer smoke and water damage. The place is a mess, but in time it'll be as good as new again."

"Hold onto to that thought, Shade. It'll help in the days ahead."

"I know."

"Will you continue to stay at the Arnolds?"

"No. They did offer. I turned them down. It's too much of an imposition with so many of us. I know my grandmother would be happy to have more privacy, as would I. Marcie has a line on a big enough house here that I can rent furnished until Wolfhaven is ready. I don't want to move my grandmother any further from her home than necessary. She's already gone through enough."

He sounded so tired and dispirited that Pippa wished she could be there to offer him more tangible comfort. "I know you have a very full plate right now. I want you to know I'll understand if you need to postpone our wedding until the restoration to the house is completed."

"Thank you, but I don't want to delay that. It's the one thing that will keep all of our spirits up around here. My grandmother needs to have something positive to focus on right now."

"I understand. Shade, I've been thinking about the wedding. I've changed my mind."

The sound of him sucking in a breath broke through his stunned silence.

"About marrying me? My God, Pippa. Are you trying to rip my heart out?"

"No! What I meant was I don't want a big church wedding. I got caught up in the idea when the ladies started talking about it. But the more they said the less I realized I wanted to go through with all of that pomp. What's really important to me is marrying you, and being surrounded by the people I consider my family."

Now the breath Shade released came as a relief.

"Jesus, you had me going there for a minute. What did you have in mind, then?"

"I think the perfect spot would be your mother's gazebo. Please, please tell me it wasn't destroyed in the fire."

She gripped the phone waiting for his answer. His voice wasn't quite steady when he spoke.

"My mother's gazebo is still intact, as is most of the garden immediate surrounding it. How like you to come up with something that would mean so much to me. That you would think of it makes me love you more than ever. Thank you my dear, sweet girl."

"It'll make me happy to do it this way, too. Oh how I wish I could be there with you now."

"You're going to be sooner than you think. That's another reason I called. I told Eva about the situation here. Apparently she planned to call us. She's homesick and misses her dog. She'll be in touch as soon as she has all the travel arrangements in order. I'll see about getting you back when that's settled."

"I'm so glad. I can't wait to see you. I'm ready to come home, too, even though I've enjoyed being here and I'll miss Bonnie. She's such a sweet little thing."

"It's easy to get attached to an animal once you bond with them."

"I understand that now. I'm looking forward to having a proper introduction to Samson."

Shade paused a moment.

"I'm afraid that won't be happening."

"But you said you wanted me to get to know him better. Why have you changed your mind?"

"I haven't changed my mind. Remember how we talked about the different waves in life?"

"Yes. What's happened?"

He's gone, Pippa."

"You mean he ran away? I thought you said he wouldn't do that."

"He didn't run. Someone took him."

She heard the strain in his voice.

"How? I thought the compound is well guarded."

"It is. But everyone ran up to the house to help fight the fire. My guess is whoever set the fire is probably also responsible for taking Samson."

"Oh, Shade, I'm so sorry. I hope they didn't hurt him."

"We didn't find any signs of blood or a struggle and he wouldn't go without a fight. He may have been tranquilized."

"Why would someone do these awful things?"

"Any number of reasons. Sometimes having money makes you a target, especially with people who are envious."

"But you do good things with your money."

"Not everyone knows what I do. Even if they did it's not possible for me to please everyone. Someone out there obviously wanted to hurt me, and they knew how to do it."

"Okay, that makes sense in taking Samson, but not in trying to burn your house down."

"It does if you consider they can't have it, so why should I? I'm not even sure if I believe Wolfhaven is the main issue here. Samson could have been the real target. The house fire may have been a diversion to get everyone away from the wolves."

"You said the compound is well hidden. How could they find it?"

"You know you're not the only person who heard Samson's howls. It had to be someone familiar with the area. I'm looking into that possibility right now. I have a feeling it was someone who's been dipping their poaching hands into my property. They must have stumbled across Samson and the others, and decided to take their poaching to a new level."

"I imagine a beautiful animal like that would be worth a lot. I bet whoever took him will probably try to sell him. Don't you think?"

"I hope to God that's all they wanted him for, and not his pelt. If he's still alive, that means I have a chance to get him back."

"I pray that you do."

They said their goodbyes. Pippa hung up, and hugged Bonnie to her, while sadness for Shade's loss made unshed tears burn at the back of her eyes. She may have feared the wolf, but now she knew what the animal meant to him. Samson wasn't just a pet. His very existence came from a legacy left from Shade's father; just as the gardens were from his mother.

Shade stood at the bedroom window in Marcie's house staring into the darkness thinking about Samson. He rubbed a hand over the dark stubble covering his face. He'd been so close to finishing his project. All the years of secret breeding and working with the government had finally reached the point of completion. The first of the wolves were scheduled for release into the wild.

He wouldn't be doing that, until he found Samson. He refused to believe his alpha wolf could be gone for good. Shade couldn't bear the thought of failing his father. He touched the cold glass as if he could somehow reach through the barrier and communicate with his special pet.

Shade didn't know how long he'd stood there, or when he laid down fully clothed on the single bed in the small bedroom. He awoke to the sun coming in through the window, surprised that he'd actually slept, considering all the stress going on in his life at the moment.

He lay there staring at the ceiling while the shadows of yesterday's events crowded inside his head blending with what he planned to do to put things right. He swung his legs over the side of the bed, and headed for the bathroom. A shower, shave, and a change of clothes had to be his first priority. He still hadn't quite got used to the novelty of sharing such a small house with people that weren't family, or longtime live-ins like the Hendersons.

Shade smiled, when he thought how interesting life was going to be once he and Pippa were married and they started living together. Of course, she would be officially family, by then. The thought of that made his smile widen, and a warm, tender feeling flow through him.

He found his grandmother sitting in the kitchen, while Enid stood at the stove preparing breakfast. He bid them good morning, and bent to kiss his grandmother on one cheek.

"How's my best girl doing this morning?"

She smiled at him.

"Second best I'm happy to say, now that you have Pippa."

He gave her shoulder a gentle squeeze and looked around.

"Am I late? Where is everyone?"

"Sam is on duty at the hospital, and Marcie had another meeting with the realtor about that house she mentioned for us. I had the impression she thinks we'll be moving in soon."

"That'll be good."

He looked at Enid.

"Where's Ross?"

"He went to check on the wolves and said he'd call you."

Shade just finished his breakfast when his phone rang.

"This is Ross now. How do things look?" He listened for a few moments. "I'm on my way."

"I hope that was good news, Mister Shade."

"Yes it was. Don't wait lunch. I'm not sure when I'll be back."

"Dear boy, I'm going to wonder myself into a tizzy if you don't tell me what Ross said."

Shade leaned down and gave Lila a light hug.

"I'll ask you to wait a bit. But I will say this. I'm a sucker for a good story, especially if it has a happy ending. So get your pen and pad ready because I have a feeling this particular tale is going to be my favorite."

He gave them a two finger wave and rushed out the door to his car.

Enid smiled at Lila.

"I have a feeling Samson's been found."

Lila smiled back.

"I have a feeling you're right."

Twenty-eight

Shade couldn't contain the anticipation coursing through him, as he sped along the highway. His heart thumped with eagerness like a child getting ready to open a longed for gift. He felt as lightheaded as a young boy by the time he turned down the road that had at one time only been known to him, and a few trusted employees.

He pulled his vehicle to a stop, jumped out, and jogged down the incline where several flat roofed buildings stood in a large fenced area cleverly hidden among the trees. Ross opened a heavy steel gate, and stood back, as Shade hurried inside.

"Where is he?"

"In the infirmary. He's banged up a bit, but Doc says he'll heal just fine."

Shade marched into one of the long cement buildings painted to blend in with the surrounding forest. He stepped inside feeling a rush of gratitude when he found himself being greeted by a familiar soft woof. He walked over to stroke the dark head.

"Hello, boy. Welcome home."

Shade listened to the compound's veterinarian telling him about Samson's condition.

"His prognosis for recovery is good, but I still have some lab work I want to do on him to settle something in my own mind."

"What do you expect to discover?"

"I'm sure I'll find evidence of some drug in his system, which I assumed had to be given to Samson before his abduction."

"The coward, or cowards, wouldn't have been able to take him otherwise. What about his injuries? Ross said he was banged up."

"He's either had a fall or was thrown with some force to the ground. Thankfully I haven't found evidence of any internal injuries. My guess is whoever took him wouldn't want to carry him for very long. They must have put him in a vehicle. Perhaps he jumped out once the drug wore off enough. The good news is he found his way back here."

"He knows where he belongs. Don't you, boy?"

Shade continued stroking and talking to Samson, letting him become aware of his presence, while the animal drifted in and out of sleep. He reluctantly pulled himself away after a couple of hours and left to drive the short distance to Wolfhaven, knowing his pet would be well looked after.

Shade's nostrils flared while his eyes stung from the odor of burnt wood. Workers wearing masks and protective clothing swarmed about methodically sifting through and removing rubble. He hadn't exaggerated when he told Pippa the house was a mess.

Tension tightened his chest and restricted his breathing for a few seconds, until he reminded himself to focus on the future. The house would be made right again, and Samson would recover.

Now he had to concentrate on finding the culprit, who had caused such havoc.

Shade drove back to Marcie's. She greeted him with the good news that the house she'd told him about was ready for his inspection. Although he wished it wasn't necessary to move into another place, it had to be done. He didn't want the people he was responsible for being underfoot at Marcie's, despite the invitation for them all to stay. Even with hiring so many people to expedite the restoration, he knew Wolfhaven wouldn't be livable for several weeks.

"Thank you, Marcie. I appreciate your help. I'll run by after lunch and settle everything. I just need to talk to my grandmother about a few things first."

"You don't have to leave. You know you're all welcome to stay here, especially if you think Lila's health will suffer with so much moving about."

"You're very kind to offer, but I think we both know this is for the best."

"I suppose you're right. I'm going to miss having you in my house. I hope I'll have visitation rights when you all leave."

"I'm sure I speak for the rest of my group, when I say you're welcome to come as often as you like."

"How about Pippa? Will she be coming back soon?"

"Soon, but not soon enough, if you get my meaning."

Marcie patted his shoulder.

"You two have certainly had your share of being apart. But you know the old saying about absence making the heart grow fonder."

"Well, my heart's going to bust out of my shirt if it grows any fonder than it already has."

Two days later Shade had everyone settled into their temporary home. He'd just finished making arrangements to have Pippa fly back, when he received a call from the sheriff with news about the fire. He felt his insides constrict with fury, as soon as he walked into the office and saw the thin gray haired man sitting there, giving him a wary look.

Could this elderly man be responsible for so much grief? Despite his frailness, Shade still had a strong desire to yank him out of the chair and shake him senseless. But the sheriff quickly explained the guilty party had died when his Jeep went off the road, and ended up in the canyon. The man here had come to identify his friend's body.

"I'm sorry about your friend, but I want to know what the hell he hoped to accomplish."

Harv proceeded to tell them everything that had happened while he fought back tears.

"What's the name of the person who was going to buy my wolf?" Shade demanded.

"I don't know. I told Jerry I didn't want to know nothin'. He thought it'd be okay to take the animal. Told me you had others."

Shade and the sheriff exchanged a knowing look over the old man's head.

"The wolf your friend took is my pet. He was wrong about there being others."

"It ain't so much dying that's hard on a man, it's livin'. Jerry wasn't very good at it. He wasn't mean. Not really. He just got things mixed up sometimes. Didn't always think stuff through. I tried to steer him straight. We didn't share no blood, but he was like family to me. I was real mad at him for what he did. Told him this time he went too far and . . . and not to come back."

"Did he ever come on my land before?"

"Yes sir, he did. He mostly only took small game like rabbits and squirrels, and such. I should have been more strict about him not doin' that, I guess. But we needed the meat, you see."

"Is that all he took? "Shade snapped, not bothering to hide his anger. "Did your friend kidnap a young woman lost in the woods one night?"

Harv's eyes filled with shock.

"Oh, no, no, Jerry didn't kidnap her. He'd never do that. He feared she might of seen him, so he brought her to my place."

"Well, that solves the mystery of who took Ms. Scott," the sheriff said to Shade. "How did she end up getting hurt?"

"He didn't mean to hit her so hard. Jerry sometime didn't know how strong he was. He felt real sorry about 'bout that. We weren't sure if she came from your house or not, Mr. Avalon. That's why we took her to the hospital."

"And dumped her," the sheriff said, scowling at him.

"We wrapped her in a blanket, and laid her down real gentle."

"Why didn't you notify me, or someone in the hospital?"

"We was afraid we'd end up in jail if we showed ourselves. I hope the lady's okay."

"You'd better count your blessings that she is," Shade said, still glaring at Harv.

"I'm real glad to hear that. You tell her we meant no harm." Fresh tears welled up in his faded eyes. He wiped them on the sleeve of his worn flannel shirt. "I'm sure sorry for what Jerry did to you, Mr. Avalon. But he won't be hurting you no more now."

"It's too bad he didn't listen to you."

"You know how it is with young folks. They think they have all the answers."

Shade's anger slowly eased away at the sight of the old man sitting slumped in the chair.

"Was that Jeep your only vehicle?"

Harv nodded.

"Yes sir."

"What about food? Will you have enough to eat now that you won't have your friend hunting for you?"

"I'll get by. I don't need much."

Shade motioned for the sheriff to follow him outside.

"See that he's taken care of. I'll reimburse you."

"That's very generous of you considering the circumstances."

"I'm not about to let the old fellow starve to death. He's skinny enough already, and his clothes are practically rags. Does he have a place around here?"

"He lives in a one room shack he built himself using scrap materials. It doesn't have any utilities, and he's quite a few miles from here. Apparently he walked to the main road and hitched a ride, when his friend didn't return. Now with that Jeep gone, he doesn't have any way to get around. I'll see about moving him into town. It looks like his misguided friend's death may end up being a lucky thing for the old guy after all."

"Sometimes we make our own luck, and sometimes someone else does it for us."

"Yeah. Your pet going to be okay after all he's gone through?"

"Eventually. I'll be in touch."

The sheriff nodded, and walked back inside leaving Shade standing on the sidewalk.

Shade wasn't happy that he'd been unable to personally punish the culprit, but the man had suffered the ultimate penalty with his death.

Three months later on a lovely sunny afternoon, Shade and Pippa stood in his mother's gazebo. They took their wedding vows surrounded by Cara's beloved flowers and the people who mattered the most to them.

That night, as they lay in bed wrapped in each other's arms they heard Samson's howl, and somehow Pippa thought it didn't sound quite so melancholy. Although the very special animal would always have ties to Shade, technically he was running completely free now.

Perhaps his howl seemed sad to Pippa before, because of her own unhappiness at the time.

Whatever the reason, she knew her nights would no longer be lonely, and her days would be filled with the joy of finally having a place where she felt she truly belonged.

She'd always felt naked inside with so many things missing that most people took for granted – a blank background lacking in family traditions, or memories to share; her empty heart yearning to love and be loved, and a soul that cried out to be fulfilled – to belong. Just to belong. That's all she ever wanted.

Samson found contentment by being able to leave behind the limitations imposed on his life, while Pippa found her happiness by embracing them. For her, boundaries didn't mean being boxed in. Thanks to Shade, they gave her the security she'd been looking for all her life.

She and Lila finally finished the story of Wolfhaven's illusive wolf. Of course, nothing was mentioned about Pippa thinking Shade had been a shape shifter.

Some deceptions, real or imagined, were best not talked about.

Other Select Books Published by Fireside Publications

Available at: www.firesidepubs.com or Kindle / Nook
http://kadinbooks.com and Amazon.com

The Crystal Angel	Olivia Claire High
Rose Cottage and	Olivia Claire High
Dreams: Shadows of the Night	Olivia Claire High
A Stranger's Eyes	Olivia Claire High

Essays: On Living with Alzheimer's Disease:	
The First Twelve Months	Lois Wilmoth-Bennett
The Furax Connection	Stephen L. Kanne
The Find	James J. Valko
Above Honor: Rachel's Story	Donald Himelstein
Beyond Forever	Taylor Shaye
The Cleansing	B.F. Eller
The Long Night Moon	Elizabeth Towles
18 Days in September	Allen N.Hunt, Ph.D
Independence Day Plague	Carla Lee Suson
Odds & Ends ~Bits & Pieces	Joye O'Keefe
The Serpent Sea	Linda Lehmann Masek
Where Danger Lurks	Judith Groudine Finkel
Texas Justice	Judith Groudine Finkel
Ice Rose	Alison Neuman
Searching for Normal: A Memoir	Alison Neuman
Raven April	Nelson Trout
Amanda's Voice	Eileen Bennett
Silver Strands	Eileen Bennett